MORTAL MEMORIES

BETWEEN REALMS
BOOK ONE

F. A. EDEN

CONTENT GUIDE

This book contains depictions of grief (one of the main characters is grieving his late fiancée).

One of the main characters also has pretty severe amnesia.

Lastly, one of the main characters is a sex worker and one side character does take issue with this. It is resolved swiftly and thoroughly.

If you come across any other content that you feel should contain a warning, please do feel free to let me know! I can be reached at faedenbooks@gmail.com.

CHAPTER ONE

$\mathcal{R}$ain pooled on the cobblestone streets, and the reflection of the streetlamps wavered in the water. A woman slipped from one shadow to the next, clinging to the darkness, desperate not to be seen.

Unsure of where she was, she stumbled down the streets. Her feet ached, the world seemed to spin around her, and the only thing she was certain of was that she wasn't allowed to be here.

She turned a corner, looking for a landmark she might recognize. But she couldn't orient herself, and when a shout rose from behind her, followed by quick, heavy footsteps, she cursed and broke into a run. No good could come of being discovered. If only she could remember what turns to take to leave the Quarters…

"You! Stop!"

She didn't. Faster and faster she ran, until her foot landed on a slick leaf and twisted with an awful snap. She tumbled to the wet ground, gathering bruises on her palms, her knees, and her right cheek. She tried to stand, but the pain in her ankle radiated up her leg, sharp and all-consuming, and she feared it might be broken. It would not bear her weight.

She slumped to the ground, defeated.

Seconds later, the person who'd been chasing her caught up and hauled her to her feet. Her ankle protested the motion, and she cried out, shifting to keep as much weight off the injury as possible, but the large man beside her paid her no heed.

"A human in the Quarters, alone. State your business clearly. Quickly."

But she couldn't. She couldn't remember why she'd come.

She couldn't even remember her name.

All she knew was that she was in trouble and that her life would be over soon.

"I—" Her words froze in her throat. "I—"

"She is with me." An arm wrapped around her waist, solid and sturdy, and lifted her enough to fully take the weight off her broken ankle. She sobbed in relief as the pain eased, then turned her head to get a better look at her savior, but he was too close, and his face was shrouded with a heavy black hood.

"She was alone," the guard said.

"And now we are together. I was just down the street." His voice rumbled, low and rich, and the sound of it soothed her.

"The punishment for a mortal alone in the Quarters is—"

"There is no need," the stranger said, his interruption low and cold. "She is no mere mortal. This woman will be my wife, come dawn."

"Your wife?" The guard's voice shifted, tinged with incredulity. "But she is human."

"Yes. You may check the official records in the morning."

A long silence stretched between them as the woman leaned into her savior's side. If the guard was to believe they were engaged, then she would have to do her part to sell the lie. Her life depended on it.

The arm around her side tightened, and the stranger's lips press against her hairline. It was only for a second, a ghost of a kiss, but her skin warmed where his lips had touched it.

"Now, if you will excuse me, I need to get her home so I may attend to her ankle. Mortals are so fragile." He said it with affection, as though he truly cared about her.

Maybe he did, she realized with a jolt. Maybe he wasn't a stranger at all. Maybe his story wasn't a lie but her own life that she'd forgotten. She couldn't remember her own name or why she was in the Quarters; it was possible she had forgotten this man by her side, who claimed to be her fiancé.

She almost hoped that was not the case—forgetting the man she loved was almost as bad as forgetting herself.

"I will have to report this," the guard said, taking a step closer. "Mortals cannot be in this part of the Quarters unaccompanied. For *any* reason." His voice dropped deadly low. "I will have to take her in. Perhaps my superior will be lenient."

"I apologize," the stranger at her side murmured against her hairline. He gently placed her back on the ground in a seated position, and though her ankle twinged sharply at the movement, she was able to stretch it before her in a way that left it almost free of pain. "Wait for me there," he said, before closing the distance between where he'd placed her and where the guard still stood.

His voice dropped so low she couldn't hear what he said, but she watched as the guard shook his head in response. After a short back and forth, the stranger lowered his hood, revealing thick black hair that fell in loose waves to just below his shoulders. From where she sat she could just make out the slight point at the top of his left ear. It should not have come as a surprise, being that she was in the Quarters, but she sucked in a sharp breath all the same, and her heart raced at the sight of it.

The guard stumbled back and gaped at the sight of her savior's face, then slowly shook his head again. This time there was a hint of hesitation in the motion.

"Very well," her savior said, his voice cold. Detached in a way that sent fear skittering through her.

She braced, steeling herself for the possibility that he might come back and tell her that he could not save her. That he did not care enough to fight on her behalf. A panicked tear slipped free, and she angrily wiped it away. She could not afford to get hysterical now.

Because she knew the punishment for a mortal alone in the Quarters.

Death.

But the stranger didn't return to her side, nor did he walk away entirely. Instead, he took a single, imposing step toward the guard.

For a moment, nothing happened.

Then the guard fell, and the audible impact of his knees against the cobblestone street made her own knees tingle with a sympathetic pain. The man who had saved her knelt beside the guard and whispered something in his ear, then took a step back, watching him with one hand still flexed toward him. The guard's face grew red, and he gasped for air.

He was choking. Asphyxiating.

The stranger cocked his head, still looking down at the guard at his feet.

"Care to reconsider?" he asked, his voice carrying easily across the street. He wanted her to hear this part, she realized. "Perhaps she was never out of my sight."

He released whatever hold he had on the guard, who gulped three deep breaths before the stranger toed at him with a highly polished shoe.

"Yes. Yes, I saw you with her. She was—she could have been with you the whole time," the guard rasped.

The man returned to her side, his hood now firmly back in place, and knelt beside her without sparing the guard another glance. She flinched away. She'd seen what he'd done to the guard, how he'd stolen his breath so easily. She didn't want him anywhere near her.

"You have nothing to fear." His silver eyes glinted beneath his hood, though there was little light for them to reflect. Overall, the effect was eerie and only served to remind her that, here, she was prey. "No harm will come to you by my hand."

She glanced at his hand dubiously. He hadn't needed it to hurt the guard. She knew the tricks that hid between the words uttered in this part of the world, where sentences were cleverly crafted so they could escape the lips of the liars.

"I will not harm you," he amended, correctly guessing the source of her consternation. "I swear it." Heat flared in her chest, and she pressed a hand to the physical manifestation of his vow. Behind him, the guard struggled to his feet and gave them one long searching look before he turned and disappeared into the fog.

"Come. We must get you to safety," the stranger said, offering her a hand.

Some part of her mind screamed not to take it. But if she refused his help, someone else might find her in this section of the Quarters, and his saving her would have been for nothing. With a broken ankle, she couldn't move quickly and would be unlikely to get far before another guard finished what the first had started.

She fought her fear and put her hand in his.

The stranger lifted her into his arms. She couldn't remember the last time someone had done that, but she felt safe tucked against his broad chest, and his light footsteps lulled her to sleep.

She awoke to a bright light around her and the sound of a heavy door falling closed. Lights flared to life around them. It appeared they were in the foyer of a large, very grand house. Hers, his, or someone else's—she had no idea, and fear crawled its way up her spine. But she had no energy to fight or even to ask where they were.

He had saved her; she had to hope that indicated he would not immediately lead her into danger.

"Welcome to my home," he said, striding across a massive

entryway and up a broad staircase. He shifted her weight in his arms, then opened a door and carried her across a large room, before finally depositing her on a plush bed. The room was dark, his shape nothing more than a shadow, and she squinted, trying to make out his form.

He murmured something she couldn't quite hear, and gentle light infused the room. "We have much to discuss, but first, allow me to tend to your ankle." He waited for her response with his strange silvery eyes pinned on hers, and she simply nodded weakly. Between her fatigue and the sharp pain lancing up her leg, she couldn't think clearly. Her ankle needed attention now. Any discussion could come later.

His fingers gently cradled her ankle, cold against the fiery heat of inflammation, and she hissed at the touch. His eyes flickered up to hers before he turned his attention back to the injury. He murmured something under his breath, and warmth engulfed her ankle. She closed her eyes, bracing for him to set it, but instead, the pain ebbed, softening to a bearable level almost immediately.

Within seconds, every lingering trace of the pain was gone.

"Thank you," she whispered, rolling her ankle, amazed at how quickly he had healed it.

"Do not thank me," he countered, his voice suddenly sharp. "You should know better than to do that here."

She opened her eyes, suddenly much more alert at the tone of his voice.

"I—"

"Do you know where you are? Do you know where you were when I found you?"

Of course she knew where she was; he had only had to save her because humans were not allowed in the Quarters alone.

Her blood ran cold, and she sat up abruptly. Her head protested the movement with a sharp jab just above her right temple—it seemed no part of her had made it through the night unscathed.

The stranger stretched out a hand, and she flinched away, but all he did was lay it on her forehead. Seconds later the pain in her head was gone. Her blood ran cold as the gravity of her own words hit her. She wanted to take them back. But she couldn't.

"What do I owe you?" she asked, glancing around nervously. Nothing came free in the Quarters.

"You owe me nothing. You are my responsibility—my guest—for now, so the healing is free. I also made a decision tonight that will alter the course of your life. For that, I am sorry."

His words hung between them. Like *thank you*, this was a phrase you didn't hear often in the Quarters. He'd held her gaze while he said it, and she knew it was deliberate: a way for him to even the score between them. The accompanying warmth in her chest made her want him to say it again.

Seconds later, she recalled the rest of what he had said, about the choice he had made, and her stomach dropped.

"You said that we're getting married. Was that the choice? You want to hold me to the words that you said? Because *you* said it, not me."

He stiffened. "I *swore* it. To save your life."

"I don't want to get married. Not at all, and certainly not to a complete stranger."

"Then you will die for being caught unaccompanied where you were."

She flinched.

"I am not threatening you; it is a simple statement of fact. You will not die by my hand, but if you do not marry me, you will die by the hand of another. Marriage to me would garner you enough grace to ensure your survival. Your alternative—to flee—would set the guards on your trail."

Her stomach roiled as she contemplated the choice before her: to marry this stranger, with all the rules and secrets that came with the Quarters…or to die. Maybe if she could remember why she was in Quarters in the first place she could begin to make sense of things. Maybe somewhere in her buried memories was a path to survival that didn't hinge on getting married to a stranger.

A *fae* stranger.

"Tell me your name," she demanded from the bed he'd placed her in.

"Straid. And yours?"

"I—I don't know," she mumbled, glancing down at her lap through tear-blurred eyes as her mind raced, trying desperately to remember a name that she simply could not recall no matter how hard she tried.

Suddenly, the gravity of the situation overwhelmed her. She wanted to go home…but she didn't even remember where home was. "I don't remember my name."

"Then choose a name to use until you remember."

"Wouldn't we need my real name for the wedding?" She wasn't considering it, not seriously, but the conversation bought her time to think, and to assess the fae who had saved her.

"For a mortal wedding, perhaps. Fae weddings work through soul bonds; a name is immaterial." His voice grew distant as he spoke. Cold.

She turned her head away, fighting her rising tears as a pit formed in her stomach.

A soul bond sounded way more binding than a human wedding. Not something to enter lightly, especially when neither participant seemed wholly willing.

"I don't know what name to choose." The task of naming herself, though daunting, was the less painful problem to focus on. She didn't even know anything about herself; how could she choose something as monumental as a name?

"This is not me agreeing to the wedding," she hastily stated. "But you saved me, and I'll hear you out. So tell me: why should I marry you?"

"Before I explain, know this: I will do what I can to keep you safe, no matter the path you choose. If you run, the guards will likely succeed in hunting and killing you, but I would try my best to avoid that outcome. I swear to do what I can to ensure your safety."

Her chest grew hot for a brief moment before it faded back to normal. She might not know him, but she did know that fae were bound to honor anything they swore; he could not break his promise even if he wanted to.

"Marrying me provides the only guarantee of your safety. According to the laws brokered between our people under Queen Efestre's reign, you may not return to your mortal world for one year after the wedding. You would have full access to the house, save for my private rooms, and would be free to explore the grounds as you wish. There are certain parts of the Quarters you would have full access to, as well. Of course, certain areas would still require that you be accompanied by a fae escort, but one could easily be arranged—me, or someone else, if you would prefer. At the end of the year, you would be free to return home, provided you returned to the Quarters at least one night per month, as per the law. In the meantime, you would not be a prisoner, but an honored guest, and I would treat you as such."

"But we'd be… married."

"On paper only," he assured her, his face stony. As though he, too, dreaded the thought. "I would expect no true marital relationship, not when you had no choice in the matter. We would coexist in the same house and, hopefully, one day be friends. I neither expect, nor offer, anything more."

She heard the implication in his words: he wouldn't love her, and there would be no sex. Not that she would mind sex with someone who looked the way he did, with his sharp cheekbones and silver eyes that glinted in the room's low light, but it was reassuring, nonetheless, to hear him say that he wouldn't expect it. And, because Straid was fae, she knew that he meant what he said.

"What's the catch?"

"Nothing beyond the bounds of the law. You would not be

allowed to marry again unless I died, and neither would I, until the end of your natural life."

"So I couldn't ever be with anyone else?" It wasn't the most important consideration, but the idea of committing to lifelong monogamy with someone she had met mere minutes ago wasn't exactly an enticing one.

"Not in marriage. However, if you chose to take a lover—carnally or romantically—I would not object. Your life would be yours to live as you wish."

"Where's the loophole?"

"There is no loophole," he told her, his voice serious and his eyes steady on hers.

"You would marry me and then expect nothing else from me? Nothing at all?" She scoffed. "I don't believe that."

"I swear it."

There it was again, that heat in the center of her chest. She savored it for a moment, grateful that this fae in front of her was willing to take such drastic measures to set her at ease. Although she only needed his vows because he had forced her into a marriage that she had never wanted. She would do well to remember that.

"Why?

His eyes dimmed, the silver fading to gray before he looked away from her. "I have my reasons."

"That's not good enough."

"Mortal lives may be short, but they are worth saving whenever possible," Straid said quietly.

There was an entire story in those words, in the tone of his voice. A story she frankly had no interest in hearing, at least not tonight. The last thing she wanted to feel was sympathy—or pity—for the person who held her life in his hands.

"And if I choose the other option?"

A shadow crossed his face. "The guards will check for proof of our nuptials in the morning. If you run, it needs to be now. I will do what I can to help you escape, but I told the guard we will marry. I spoke in haste and was careless in my wording. There is only so much I can do." His voice had fallen to a raspy whisper, and she could swear there was genuine regret in his eyes. But only for a moment. "The plan carries many risks, and even with my help, I cannot promise you safety. I cannot guarantee the guards will not hunt you down." He paused. "Or, that I will not assist them in an honor-bound attempt to rectify my falsehood. I have sworn that I will not harm you, but I cannot guarantee, in this case, that I will not be forced to deliver you to someone who would."

"So I either live here for free and get to go home, wherever that is, in a year, or I leave behind everything I know and still might die?"

"Those are the two options, yes."

There wasn't much of a choice. Her shoulders slumped as she accepted her fate. "Okay, I'll stay."

"Good." He tapped her ankle. If she hadn't felt the pain earlier, she never would have known it was broken mere minutes before. "Rest now while you can. I will collect you just before dawn for the marriage ceremony. The bathing chamber is through there." He pointed to the door that led to the private chamber. "You may wear any clothing from the wardrobe. What name will you be using?"

"Anna." It was the first name that came to mind. She was fairly certain the name wasn't hers, but it was one she could live with. Right now, that was all that mattered.

CHAPTER TWO

Straid did not want to marry. He had not wanted to since—

He would not let himself think about it.

Fifty years later it still pained him, and it felt like a betrayal—to both himself, and to *her*—to offer marriage so freely. And to another mortal, no less. But something about her had felt almost familiar, and he had hoped that saving her would lessen the guilt that still plagued him after all these years.

He already regretted it. The promise of marriage, yes, but also what he had done to the guard, a step away from taking a life without a second thought. It had felt too easy, almost good.

He pushed the idea from his mind.

He had done what was necessary.

He had saved a life. He was not a monster, he told himself, straightening his tie.

Not anymore.

A chime sounded, a light tinkle in his inner ear to alert him of a presence on the doorstep. The chime the wards made for his dearest friend.

He steeled himself. Corlan might be a friend, but he was also one of the few who would be honest with him, who would tell him the plain truth without using words and loopholes to obscure his opinion. His arrival signaled the beginning of a conversation Straid would rather not have. Still, it would be easier to explain to Corlan than to anyone else. And if he had to marry, he wanted his closest friend at his side, no matter the circumstances.

"What is so urgent you needed me to come in the middle of the night?" Corlan dropped into a chair the moment the door to Straid's study closed behind him, fully relaxed in a way few people were around Straid.

His hair had grown longer in the months—years?—since Straid had seen him, and a piece had escaped its binding to fall across his face in a shock of gold. "The days of you calling me on a whim or with any sort of urgency are long over." He peered at Straid. "Are you alright?"

Straid bristled at the comment, but there was truth to it: he had mostly kept to himself these fifty years, and spontaneity was purely a thing of his past. And, if he were being honest, he was not, as Corlan had put it, alright.

"I need a favor."

"Perfect. I do, too." Corlan grinned. "Go ahead, tell me what's so important that the great—"

"I need you to marry me."

Corlan spluttered.

"I will be married at dawn," Straid clarified, "and I need for you to perform the ceremony."

"That's somehow worse. Who is she? Do you even know anyone anymore? How could you possibly be getting married?"

Straid launched into an explanation, though it fell flat, even to his ears. Anna, as she had chosen to be called for now, had made her own choices, and he could have left her to face the consequences. Under scrutiny, his decision to take such drastic measures to save her fell apart.

By the end of Straid's explanation, Corlan sat upright with his mouth hanging open. "You don't know this woman. This *mortal* woman. You have no way of knowing why she was in the Quarters. For all you know, it could have been a deliberate attempt to get close to you, and now you've brought her into your home. Give it some thought, Straid."

"I have. If we are not wed by dawn, she will die."

"Why does that matter?" It was a fair question. Straid had left many people, mortals and fae alike, to their fates. He had carried out a few of those fates himself.

"I had the opportunity to save her. A mortal, close to death in the Quarters, at this time of year. How could I leave her there?" He attempted to remain stoic, detached, but he could hear the slight wavering in his voice, and evidently so could Corlan. Because the truth was that there was no logical reason for what he had done; the decision had been purely emotional. A reminder, however slight, of the worst thing he had lived through.

His friend studied him with his eyebrows raised, and then finally sighed.

"I think it's a bad idea, for the record. But okay. Okay. I'll marry you," Corlan said with a disbelieving grin. "But I need a favor in return."

"Of course."

"Kexxia is missing. She left a week ago to visit her sister—to meet the new baby and bestow the traditional gift upon her. She never arrived. Which, of course, leaves the baby vulnerable. Everyone's attention is on the child, to keep her safe. But Kexxia was excited about the gift. She wouldn't have changed her mind. Something is wrong, and I need your help finding her."

Straid had only met Kexxia once, at a party Corlan had convinced him to attend some years back. He had taken refuge in the garden, a respite from the noise and the *happiness* inside, only to have someone sit on the other end of the bench he occupied. He had bristled, angry at losing his solitude, but Kexxia had barely acknowledged him. By the time Corlan stumbled outside, drunk on too much moss wine, Straid and Kexxia had formed a fragile friendship forged in near silence.

"I will help you find her," Straid agreed.

"Then let's get you married."

Unable to avoid the moment any longer, Straid stood outside Anna's door, strangely nervous to knock. She was a guest in his home, in a few minutes she would be his wife, and yet he found himself unsure of how to approach her. He had left her to rest and to dress herself, and only now did it occur to him that he should rehire servants if he was planning on hosting a guest for the next year. True, most humans did not have them, but there was a certain level of decorum that would be expected of him, and making this woman—Anna—dress herself and cook her own food would be deemed unacceptable, especially for a fae of his status. Besides, he had no interest in having to cook for her whenever she was hungry.

He raised his hand again to knock, but before he could, the door swung open.

Anna stood before him in a rich red dress that hugged her ample curves and picked up the red undertones in her smooth brown skin. Before, he had been too focused on saving her to notice her beauty, but now that the immediate threat had passed, and she was clean and outfitted in a silk dress that fit as though it had been made for her, it was impossible to ignore.

"Are you ready?" he asked, his voice quiet so she wouldn't hear the desire in it. This relationship had no room for that.

"As ready as I'll ever be."

"There is still time to change your mind, if you would rather flee." A part of him hoped she would accept the offer: that she would make the foolish choice, and he would not have to go through with this wedding.

"I'm going to marry you," she said quietly.

He steeled his heart against the memory of another voice

saying those words and held out his arm for her to take. Together, they walked down the stairs and out the door into the sprawling gardens.

If he had planned the wedding, he would have done it in early spring, when the garden bloomed its hundreds of colors, and the fragrances of the flowers created a heady atmosphere. As it stood right now, everything was past its peak: flowers withering and leaves curling in reaction to the heat that radiated, even now in the height of night. The garden was still beautiful this time of year, but not fit for a wedding.

It relieved him that the garden looked so different than it had in its prime—than it would have for that other wedding.

For he had planned one, once, when he was young and naive, when love had so consumed him that he had dedicated entire weeks to ensuring the gardens would be perfect for the ceremony.

He glanced at his soon-to-be bride, wondering how deep her disappointment ran at the state of the venue. Even after all these years, he knew the kinds of things a woman, even a mortal one, would want for a wedding: perfectly cultivated landscaping, a working fountain untouched by algae, and fragrant blooms that rivaled her own beauty. It was a shame he could not make these things happen for her, but there was nothing to be done for it now. If he had had even a day to prepare, he could have enlisted the help needed to make this wedding spectacular.

He wondered if she would have wanted that, given the circumstances. Even if everything had looked perfect, it could not be the wedding she may have dreamed of. Not with a stranger for a groom.

They came to a stop in front of the fountain and stood before Corlan with their hands clasped. Her hands were so small in his. Delicate, in a way he was glad for: they were different from the hands he had grown accustomed to all those years ago. Different from the hands that had smoothed his brow and traced secret words on his chest.

Anna's breath left her in small white clouds that hung between them, and her skin was dotted with bumps from the cold. A part of him felt compelled to step closer and pull her against his chest to warm her. But he stayed where he was.

Corlan looked at him reproachfully and Straid relented, sending a gentle warm breeze Anna's way. It was not enough to warm her entirely—he did not wish to have a conversation about his gift tonight—but her shivering subsided, and the tip of her nose faded from red to pink.

"I will keep this short so your bride may return to the warmth of your home." Corlan's voice rose above the dying plants and Straid nodded his thanks, even though he could hear the myriad emotions in his friend's voice: the disapproval over Straid's sudden marriage—to a mortal, no less—and the worry that still lurked over his friend's fate.

The vows passed quickly, and Straid barely paid them any attention as he swore to protect her as best he could. He tamped down all thoughts. All feelings.

This was not the wedding he had planned.

This was not the bride he wanted.

If he allowed himself one moment to feel, the grief would consume him.

So he simply went through the motions. He repeated the words he was told to say and looked at his bride without truly seeing her.

He felt Anna's hesitation as she swore to uphold her end of the bargain, even though she agreed to nothing more than staying in the Quarters for the allotted year and returning monthly once she was free. His chest flared cold as she swore her vows, and he allowed a small smile to grace his lips at the feeling of it.

It had been years since he had felt the chill of a mortal's promise; the warmth of a fae's oath paled in comparison. Perhaps he felt that way because he had always loved the cold.

"Now that you've sworn your vows to one another, you may

seal this marriage with a mingling of the souls." Corlan's mouth twisted in displeasure, and Straid turned quickly from his friend.

Straid bent his head to his bride's, pressing his forehead against hers, shocked to find it icy; in his grief, he had ceased the flow of warm air.

"Take my hands," he murmured, threading his fingers through hers. "Now we will breathe together, and our souls will join. If you would prefer to run, this is your final chance."

Her eyes fell closed, and she leaned into him. "No. I'm ready, let's just get this over this."

"Then breathe with me." He watched her chest rise as she inhaled slowly, and he matched his breath to hers.

Then, together, they exhaled.

His next breath fortified him. It tasted of honey and orange, of stone and silver and the deep dark of sleep. He shuddered, holding the air in his lungs for as long as he was able; when he released it, he would lose the taste of her soul.

"That was…" Her voice shook.

He nodded against her forehead and fought to urge to ask after the flavor of his own soul.

Corlan slipped away, leaving the two of them in the garden. Straid wanted to prolong the moment; the marriage might be nothing more than a convenience, but the fullness in his chest demanded more.

Perhaps it was the piece of her soul that now clung to his that made him draw their entwined hands to his chest.

"Anna."

"Yes?"

She shivered so violently that he feared she would break. "You are cold."

He gathered Anna against him and carried her back to her room, taking slow, measured steps to prolong the feeling of holding her in his arms.

She deserved better than this sham of a wedding. She deserved a husband who would have noticed the cold seeping into her skin. She deserved many things he was incapable of providing.

"Wait here a moment. I have a gift before I leave you for the night." The words left his mouth before he had a chance to truly consider them.

"A gift from a fae?" That was fear lacing her words and worrying her lip.

"Not as dangerous as mortals would have you believe." He crossed the hall and grabbed the item from his study, where it had lain for five decades tucked in the drawer of his desk. He brushed a thumb across the gold filigree encircling the mirror. His bride deserved better than a gift purchased for someone else, but it was what he had to offer. He hoped her reflection would aid in reclaiming her identity.

"It's beautiful," she whispered, taking it from him with reverence. "What do I owe you?"

"Gifts do not incur debts; it is yours."

"Tha—that's kind of you." She flushed at the near misstep, and he retreated a step. She turned to place the mirror on the hearth, exposing the buttons along the back of her dress. The uppermost one hung open, as though she had attempted to undo them in his absence.

He imagined her frozen fingers fumbling with the closures, the image quickly shifting to his own hands on the garment, his fingers skimming her spine. He ached to see the contrast of his tan fingers against her brown skin and feel her heat beneath his touch.

Straid mentally chided himself. The woman was beautiful, with her heart-shaped face, honey-brown eyes, curls that exploded in every direction, and curves that would consume him if he let them—but her beauty was immaterial. She was someone he had saved, nothing more.

He would do well to remember that.

In the morning, he would hire servants, including a lady's maid for Anna. She needed someone by her side so her cold fingers would not have to fumble with the closings on the dress. Someone who could tend to her every need.

That person could not be him.

He could not undress her or help her into a bath. He could not gently brush her hair from her shoulder or wrap a towel around her when she was done.

He could never be that person for someone again.

"Goodnight, Anna."

"That's it? You're just…leaving?"

"You need rest. I will see you in the morning."

Straid stalked across the hall to his study, shifting his thoughts away from the woman in the other room—his new wife —to the work he had promised Corlan he would do. Now that he looked at the papers his friend had left neatly stacked on his desk, he found himself cursedly glad for the distraction. He had promised Anna she would not have to interact with him much, and this would be an excuse to stay away from her.

As he began to read, his brow furrowed. According to Corlan's papers, there had been trouble in town for years, something Straid had been oblivious to—save for his hooded walks to clear his mind late at night, he rarely left his home. He wondered if Kexxia's disappearance was the result of the unease, or if it was more targeted.

He had ignored it, attributing it to the fact that the Ousilie's comet would appear this year. Each passing of the comet strengthened the fae's powers, which then waned slowly over the course of the century until it returned once more.

Kexxia possessed the ability to bestow gifts on whomever she pleased, a rare power that had faded even from her ancient family's bloodline. Perhaps her disappearance was someone's misguided attempt to regain a sliver of their power without having to wait for the comet's return.

If that was the case, they could not assume Kexxia's disappearance to be an isolated incident; the Quarters would not be safe until the comet's arrival this winter. He would have to amend his deal with Anna and tell her she could not leave the house without an escort.

A sharp pang in his chest had him gasping for air, and he cursed himself when he could finally breathe again. The fact that he had sworn to uphold his promises in a *wedding* vow had only sealed them further. There would be no amending the terms.

He would have to show her the evidence and hope she came to the same conclusions he did. He could convince her. He was sure of it. And if not, he would simply have to find a way to keep her safe, whatever it took.

CHAPTER THREE

*A*nna awoke in a plush bed with soft sheets and a blanket that felt like heaven. The air was clearer here, each breath more fortifying than she was used to. She felt a smile stretch across her face and allowed herself to lay in bed for a few minutes, slowly welcoming the day.

There was no sign of her injuries from last night: her ankle moved perfectly without so much as a twinge, and her head didn't ache in the slightest.

In fact…if she concentrated hard, she could almost remember things. She still didn't know what she'd been doing in the Quarters, but she remembered running from someone—or something—that had scared her. That was when she'd come across the guard and Straid…her new husband. She still couldn't remember what, exactly, she'd been scared of, but the fear was a clue in itself. And based on how confidently she had moved through the streets, she was fairly certain she had been there enough times to be familiar with the town.

She was a consistent rule breaker, then. She must have had a good reason for doing so.

A knock at the door shook her from her musings, and she threw on a dressing gown from the wardrobe before opening the door a crack and peering out. Straid stood in the hallway wearing an emerald green suit and a slightly stern expression.

"Good morning. I hope you slept well."

The sight of him brought memories of last night flooding back: the way his impossibly soft fingers had felt between hers; the feel of his forehead against her own; the taste of velvet and rosemary, of snow and silk and something ancient beyond her comprehension.

Between the darkness and her pain, fear, and exhaustion, she had barely registered the way he looked, but in the light of morning, she was speechless in the face of his beauty. Silver eyes regarded her from beneath thick, dark brows, and his hair tumbled down his shoulders in sleek black waves that curled more tightly at his temples. His sharp nose led to soft, full lips, and his tawny olive skin was free of even the faintest stubble.

The sight of him arrested her, and she had to fight to remember the question he had asked.

"I did, tha—" the word was halfway out of her mouth before she slammed her mouth shut. Her new husband was fae; she couldn't say things like *thank you* or *sorry* to him.

"Breakfast is waiting downstairs. And then I hoped you would help me in interviewing staff today. I have lived by myself for a long while, but you deserve the full comfort expected of a fae home. I endeavor to make sure the staff I hire are to your liking, especially the lady's maid, as you will be interacting with her closely over the next year."

"Oh, I don't need a lady's maid, or any staff at all for that matter," Anna said. She thought she might be used to cooking and cleaning for herself. And if not, she would learn.

"Nonsense," Straid said, his voice dropping low. "You are here out of necessity, not true choice, and as such you will have every comfort available to you: someone to cook your every whim, someone to clean your rooms, and someone who can help you out of a dress when your fingers are too cold to do so on your own."

He had a point. After the wedding, her fingers had fumbled with the closures on the back of her dress, and she'd finally given up and stuck her hands in the hot bathwater until they'd warmed enough to be able to handle the buttons. She hadn't even attempted to unclasp the necklace that hung around her neck; she'd worn it in the bath, hoping the water wouldn't ruin it. It had been the only possession of her own she'd worn as they exchanged their vows, a delicate gold chain with a flower dangling from it.

"You could have helped." She didn't mean to accuse, but her voice came out harsher than she meant it to. It would have taken him mere seconds to help her out of her dress and would have made her night a whole lot easier.

"I would not undress you after promising that I expect no marital relations between us," Straid said, lifting his head and keeping his eyes trained on hers. "I would not risk unsettling you or making you wonder if I meant the words I had said."

"You swore them," she whispered, her heart racing under Straid's intense gaze.

"And you are used to mortals who may go back on their promises, and perhaps fae who use their words cleverly to seem as though they are making a promise that they are, in fact, not binding themselves to. I would not have you think I was attempting to find a loophole. I want you to be comfortable here, Anna, and safe. I would not jeopardize that."

His words rang true. Somewhere in her mind, there were memories locked away of promises that had been broken, of times she had thought she could trust somebody and been proven bitterly wrong. She blinked, surprised to feel lingering traces of anger simmering beneath her skin from some long-ago memory lost in the depths of her mind.

"I appreciate that. I...understand your actions." It was a clumsy way of saying thank you without using words that would create a debt between them, but she knew that he understood her meaning. "But I needed help, and you could have at least let me ask for it."

"Yet you deny the need for staff. What will you do the next time I decline to remove your clothing?"

When phrased like that, she didn't have a response.

"I would be happy to escort you to breakfast, if you are ready?"

She looked down at her dressing gown and the surprisingly sturdy, yet delicately beautiful, nightgown beneath it, then raised a brow at his. "Do I look ready?"

"You may dine in your nightclothes if you so wish. This is, after all, your home for the next year, and I understand mortals are used to dining in casual dress. If, however, you would rather change, I will wait here and walk you down when you are ready. The house is large, and I would not want you to lose your way."

"I'll change as quickly as I can."

It proved harder to do than she'd expected, with so many clothing options in the wardrobe. Though none of them fit as well as the dress she had chosen last night, most fit her well enough for now.

She finally settled on a simple brown dress that gleamed when the light hit it just right, and she left her hair down, her curls tumbling past her shoulders.

Together, they walked down the hallway toward the grand, sweeping staircase, and Straid told her what lay behind each of the doors that they passed.

"Guest rooms," he said, pointing to both sides of the hallway. "Through there is the library. Please let me know if there are specific books you would like for me to acquire, and I will." He paused, turning back to face the direction they had come from. "Across from your room is my study. It is one of two rooms off limits to you without express permission, just as your room will now be off limits to me without express permission."

"What's the other room I can't go in?"

"My bedroom." He said nothing else, just swept her down

the stairs and into the dining room, where a beautifully-laid table was waiting for them.

"The presentation is disgraceful," Straid said apologetically. "Once we have hired staff you will have proper breakfasts befitting a guest. Befitting my wife," he corrected, blanching. It comforted her to know that he was as uneasy about this marriage as she was.

She couldn't help but laugh. "This is perfect. I'm pretty sure this is a hell of a lot nicer than what I'm used to."

"Pretty sure? You are not certain?"

"No." She took the seat that Straid pulled out for her.

"How much of your memory is missing?"

She stared at the table, willing herself not to cry as the enormity of her memory loss threatened to overwhelm her.

"All of it," she whispered around the lump in her throat.

"You remember nothing?"

"Something scared me last night, that's why I was running. And I knew where to turn, so I know that I'd been there before. Maybe a lot of times. But that's it. I don't remember anything before last night."

"I will endeavor to help you remember," Straid said, his voice gentle. "For now, please eat." He gestured to the food on the table between them.

She reached out to take some fruit but paused with her hand in the air. "It is...safe?"

"Of course. You should not believe everything you hear about the fae. The food is perfectly safe for your consumption. Your fear stems from nothing more than a story mortal parents tell their children so they will not dine with the fae. A meal creates many opportunities for words to be uttered that would create debts, as well as other situations humans should not find themselves in. But the food itself is not the issue, barring poisoning, of course, but that exists in the mortal realm, as well. Our poisons are typically harmless to humans, and most would not go through the effort of acquiring ones that would work on a mortal guest. There are…easier ways to accomplish that goal, if one is trying."

She swallowed hard, suddenly nervous—and she wondered if Straid was, as well. So far, he struck her as a fae of few words, but here he had given her a longer answer. One that only increased her nerves.

"I have scared you," Straid said regretfully, "when all I intended was to set your mind at ease. Eat, and be assured that I will never intentionally harm you or stand by while another does. I swore it, and I will again."

Her chest bloomed warm, and she rubbed it absentmindedly.

"I knew about fae vows being binding, and that you need to be careful what you say to the fae," Anna said, piling her plate high with fruit and pastries. "I don't know how I knew that, but I did. I think I have had…dealings…with the fae before."

"Good. We will discuss it later, to make sure you are aware of exactly what you can and cannot say; a year is a long time and leaves many opportunities for missteps. I would not want you to be caught unaware. Furthermore, I would appreciate you only speaking to me directly to me while interviewing staff today, so you do not risk saying something that may get you in trouble."

"I want to go over the rules now, so that I can speak to them directly," she countered, bristling at his suggestion even though she believed he was only trying to protect her. "If I'm going to be part of the interviews, then I'm going to *actually* be part of them. I am not someone who's willing to sit back and defer to my husband, especially if that husband is someone I didn't even know until last night."

His silver eyes pierced her over the platters of fruit and bread. "If I am confident you will be able to get through the interviews without undue promises or favors, then I see no reason why you could not be more active of a participant."

Breakfast passed quickly, with Straid quizzing her on the fae rules and customs she might encounter during the interview process.

She knew not to say please or thank you, but when pressed, she remembered subtler things, as well: to always give a compliment in return when she received one; never to ask a fae's age; and to treat her personal information as though it were valuable —because many fae treated secrets as a form of currency.

Once he was satisfied she knew the rules, they moved on to a practice conversation. At times she paused for too long while working out her answer, but Straid assured her that would not be seen as a social slight worthy of retaliation. Not today, at least, when she would be the one of higher standing.

By the time a group of fae had gathered in the foyer to be interviewed, Anna felt ready. And she felt like maybe a year here, with Straid, might be okay. Enjoyable, even. They'd gotten along fine at breakfast, even if he was a bit stoic for her tastes, and he'd shown enough concern for her wellbeing that she truly felt safe under his care.

As safe as she could feel as a human in the Quarters, anyway.

By the third interview, she'd let him mostly take the lead, only chiming in with the occasional question. By lunchtime, he had hired two maids and a butler.

Lunch itself was an interview, with each hopeful chef preparing a selection of foods for Anna and Straid to try.

At Anna's insistence, each of the chefs joined them during their meal. She gathered from their reactions, and Straid's, that this was uncommon, but if she was going to have servants, she wanted to get to know them. She wanted them to actively be a part of the household that they would be running.

Besides, what better way to conduct an interview than over a delicious meal?

Brey's pastries had started them off strong: a mixture of sweet and savory, with flavors like strawberry lemon, orange-marinated beef with thyme, and something floral Anna had never tasted before that left a pleasant buzz in her mouth.

Though all the food they sampled was good, none of the fare from any of the other contenders stood out—until

Elesina, a tall, willowy fae woman with pale green skin and pink hair with rose blossoms threaded through it, served them roast duck with candied rosemary. Everything Anna had ever eaten paled in comparison, and Straid seemed to agree. They sat in silence for the first few minutes, wholly focused on their food.

"This is absolutely incredible," Anna finally said, breaking the silence. "Where did you learn to cook like this?"

"My grandmother." The chef's voice was quiet, and Anna recognized the tinge of grief threaded through it. She had also learned to cook in her grandmother's kitchen. She smiled to herself, savoring the hazy memory of an old woman's hands guiding her own as they kneaded a loaf of bread together. She couldn't remember her grandmother's face, or anyone else's from her past, but she didn't care; the beauty of this memory was enough for now.

"She taught you well," she told the green fae woman. "This is the best food I've ever eaten."

Elesina gave a bland smile in response to Anna's heartfelt words. "I appreciate the flattery."

"It is not flattery," Straid countered. "It is also the best food I have ever eaten. The position is yours."

Elesina stilled, tears coming to her eyes. "Truly?"

Anna watched the interaction, confused at Elesina's differing responses, before she realized why their words might produce such different responses: as a human, Anna was capable of lying. As a fae, Straid was not.

The rest of the meal passed quickly, until Anna found herself alone at the table with Straid, her stomach full.

"I will hire Elesina and Brey, if you are amenable."

"I am more than amenable."

The corner of his mouth tipped up ever so slightly. "Good. That is settled."

After lunch, all that was left was the lady's maid. She was tempted to let Straid take the lead again, but he deferred to her, and she supposed it made sense: the person who filled this position would be working closely with Anna, after all.

But she was out of her depth, completely unsure how to pick a good lady's maid. Everyone they interviewed seemed like they would do a good job, and she found herself growing more and more restless as the afternoon progressed. Eventually she told Straid that she trusted his judgment to decide, and she retreated to her room.

She sank into a bath and let the steaming water relax her. Based on the fact that she had been surprised that the water was already hot when it poured from the tap, she assumed that was not a luxury she had at home. That didn't tell her much; *most* humans had to boil water for their baths. If she was one of the few who didn't need to, she likely would not have balked at the thought of having servants.

She sank down until her head was fully submerged, and only rose once her lungs began to protest.

A memory surfaced of a woman smiling at her, and fingers running through her wet hair. The resulting fluttering in her belly made her wonder if the woman was a lover from her past. It didn't matter now; even if they had been together, Anna wouldn't see her for at least another year. Besides, Anna was married now.

Straid's words rang in her ear, reminding her that she was free to take a lover if she wanted. So she had a new goal, then: remember who this woman was, so she'd know whether to seek her out when she returned home in a year.

CHAPTER FOUR

Anna had only been here two days, and Straid had yet to find security for her or explain his worries, yet she was already asking to leave the house. He had made a promise he was bound to keep, so if he could not convince her to stay indoors, he would simply have to accompany her himself.

He contemplated whether he had ever had to worry about someone refusing to obey his wishes but could not think of a single time—none where it truly mattered, at the least.

Straid watched Anna over the table, his steepled fingers pressed against his chin. He wondered, briefly, what her real name was; he wondered if she would tell him once she remembered. Perhaps she already *had* remembered and held the name close to her chest like a fiercely guarded secret.

She would be wise to keep her secrets here.

She had begun to relax around him: her eyes had lost a little bit of their challenge, and her posture had lost much of its rigidity. And when she told him that she planned to go into town, there was no trace of fear or hesitation in her voice.

"I must speak to you about an important matter before you go, and I would request that you accept an escort, whether it be me or somebody else."

"Can't I go on my own, now that we're married?"

"You will be allowed unaccompanied in certain parts of the Quarters you previously would have needed an escort in, yes. Others will still be off-limits to you, as a mortal. However, there is something I must explain to you before you leave, and I would hope that you might understand my security concerns and accept my company."

"You didn't mention any security concerns earlier." Her eyes narrowed at him across the table, and he was struck by how beautiful they were: golden, like the honey he used to collect from the bees in the garden, back when the garden had been his sanctuary, and he had been young and naïve enough to believe that he might actually be *happy*.

"New matters have come to my attention. Come, I will show you."

They abandoned their empty dishes, and it struck him how quickly he had become accustomed to having servants again— two days, and he had already fallen into the habits he had lost over the past fifty years.

He led her to his study and paused outside the door. Inviting her in would give her access for the rest of the day, something he was not particularly keen to do. But he needed her to listen, and to trust him, and inviting her into his study would certainly help with that.

"You may enter, this once. What I need to show you is behind this door." He stepped aside to let her precede him into the room.

Anna hesitated at the doorway and turned back to him. "Is it safe?"

"Always."

Chills ran down his spine as she stepped across the threshold, the house's way of alerting him that the wards had been crossed by one given the requisite permission.

He closed the door behind him with a soft click and gestured to the chair beside his desk. "Sit."

Straid waited for her to comply, fighting a shiver at the sight. He was not used to anyone being in this room—even Corlan's presence a few nights prior had been unusual—and he did not think he enjoyed it.

Once she was settled, Straid sat behind the desk. He gripped the arms of his chair, soothed by the comforting feel of leather beneath his fingers. Her presence had thrown him, but the sturdy chair that had been in his family for countless generations was a reminder that some things remained the same.

He retrieved the paper from the top of the stack before him— the one on which he'd written Kexxia's name. In the days since the wedding, he had done a cursory search into her disappearance. He had not found any useful information about her, but he had found others whose families and friends were also searching for them, to no avail.

Along with Kexxia's, there were nine other names. Most were fae, but three were human: mortals who had last been seen in the Quarters. He presumed the number of mortals on his list would rise if he were to ask about disappearances in the human town— a place he would not be welcomed.

He did not yet understand the connection between the missing people—if there was a connection at all, aside from the brewing unrest in response to fae power being at its lowest in the hundred-year cycle. He had been born thirty years after the last Ousilie's comet, so he had no frame of reference for how bad he should expect things to be. Corlan would not know either, but Straid made a note to have him ask one of his many friends.

He handed the paper to Anna, then sat back in his chair, studying her over the desk. She took it and read the names, then raised a single eyebrow.

"What's this?"

"The names of people, both fae and mortal, who have disappeared in the past few months. They have been reported missing and, in some cases, the best trackers have been employed to ascertain their whereabouts, but to no avail. There has been no trace left behind in any of these cases, and none of the missing have been recovered."

"The best trackers were employed? For all of them? Even for the humans?"

He heard the skepticism in her voice and winced, though it was valid. Perhaps he winced *because* it was valid.

"For at least two of the three humans, yes. One was dearly missed by the fae that employed her, and the other's mortal kin spent quite a bit of money in an attempt to recover her. The third worked for a household that declined to discuss their efforts to retrieve her."

"What does this have to do with me?"

"Until we know more about the disappearances, I would be more comfortable if you stayed close to home, and only left with an escort. I would be happy to hire a personal security detail so you may leave whenever it suits your fancy, but I would not risk losing you."

"What if I refuse?" she asked, the challenge in her voice dark and dangerous. A part of him thrilled at her temerity.

"I would strongly advise against it."

"But if I went out on my own anyway?"

Images of her alone, unprotected, ran through his mind. Another disappearance. Another person under his protection whom he failed. He fought the urge to forbid it. The vow he had sworn ensured the words would be meaningless even if he somehow managed to force them to cross his lips.

"For today, I would follow you to ensure your safety."

"But you'd let me leave." Her voice had softened some, a bit of the fiery edge sapped from it, but it was still ripe with suspicion.

"I swore it. I cannot force you to stay inside my home, nor would I want to. But I ask that you accept some level of protection, for your own safety and to set my mind at ease."

She stared at him for long seconds that seemed to drag on forever, her honeyed eyes stormy. Finally, she dropped her gaze to the page. As she reread the names, her brow furrowed. He longed to reach out a finger to smooth the crease, then quickly chastised himself for the impulse.

"I know this name," she murmured. She laid the page on his desk and pressed a finger to the second name. "Ichold Burtaign Cravellia Plots. I know him."

That was impossible. Ichold notoriously rarely left his home, and humans rarely had occasion to do business with him there. She must have heard his name somewhere, but she could not know him personally. Straid told her as much. "Maybe someone you know had dealings with a member of his household," he suggested, but Anna shook her head.

"No. Ichold. Ich. Ichy, but only if…" she trailed off, and unease roiled in his gut. He had heard someone say the same, a long time ago. Isabella's voice rang in his mind, a ghost from a long-ago time. *He likes to be called Ich,* she had said. *Ichy, too, but only once he's known you carnally. You can never repeat what I've said,* Isabella had said with a laugh. *Swear it.* And he had.

The bond of the vow had died along with his cousin, but he would not betray her confidence, even after all these years.

"How do you know he sometimes uses the name Ichy?" he asked, forcing his voice to remain steady even as he contemplated the impossible.

"I told you. I know him." The freshness of the revelation was evident on her face, as well as a wonderment he presumed must be from remembering a part of her life from before two days ago.

"Carnally." It wasn't a question; he knew it to be true.

"I—Why do you assume that? It's a nickname; plenty of people use those." Her words were steady, and if he had only been listening to her, he would have believed what she was saying. But her eyes and her pulse betrayed her: her pupils widened ever so slightly, and he could see her heartbeat racing in the side of her neck.

He decided to let the matter drop for now, though curiosity

burned beneath his skin. He should let her keep her secrets; he had enough of his own.

"I will be investigating these disappearances. If you remember anything about Ichold that may be relevant, please let me know. In the meantime, I would be happy to accompany you into town today, if you are amenable."

She nodded, her eyes still on the paper on the desk between them. "I just need to change, and then I'll be ready," she said, sweeping out of the room.

He was left to stare after her, with a paper full of names and a head full of questions he could only hope he had the answers to soon.

CHAPTER FIVE

*a*nna closed the bedroom door behind her and leaned against it to take a deep, steadying breath. When she'd seen that name, Ichold Burtaign Cravellia Plots, a memory had come rushing back.

He was one of the first fae she had ever met. She'd stood in the entryway of his home wearing borrowed slippers—he made everyone take their shoes off just inside the doorway and provided slippers for humans to wear so their feet weren't too cold on the white marble floor. It was a thoughtful gesture that had caught her off guard, so different from what she'd been told to expect of the fae.

She remembered hoping, as she'd nervously watched him approach, that he liked what he saw, that he would decide to hire her after this meeting. She'd never been with a fae before, and knew their tastes were often more exacting than humans'. But he'd simply looked at her, smiled, and offered a hand, which she'd taken.

"I'm Ichold," he'd said, once they were settled in a cozy room lit only by low, flickering candlelight. It had been cozy, intimate, but not too much so. She remembered looking at his face: pale grey, and slightly weathered, but kind, with deep black eyes that she almost felt she was swimming in. "Please, tell me about yourself," he had said. She'd been used to clients who started by telling her about their desires. But he had made her comfortable and listened to her for long minutes before turning the conversation to business, and although she couldn't remember what she'd told him then, she knew she had felt…safe. Wanted, in a way that felt different than she was used to.

Now, Anna pressed a hand to her mouth to keep from gasping, then took a few steadying breaths. She couldn't say for sure, but she was beginning to suspect that Straid's assumption was correct. If the look in Ichold's eyes and the intimacy of the room had been any indication, there was very little doubt in her mind that she did, in fact, know the fae businessman carnally.

She tried her best to ignore the realization while her lady's maid straightened the clothes in the wardrobe. Straid had chosen Niana, one of the first women they'd interviewed for the position, and though she was both kind and attentive, Anna still bristled at the idea of someone else choosing her clothes for her.

"I don't know your tastes yet, so I've brought you some options. As I learn what you do and don't like, I'll adjust the offerings." Niana gestured to the wardrobe and the dozens of dresses hanging inside it, each one more beautiful than the last.

Anna rang her hands along the many options, delighted at the range of textures beneath her fingers: silk and brocade, cotton and wool, velvet—and some fabric unknown to her that felt somehow reedy and soft at the same time.

"These are all perfect," she murmured, drinking in the array of colors before her. "I'd be happy to wear any of them."

She pulled a dress from the wardrobe, admiring the gold threads at the ends of the deep green velvet sleeves.

"Would you like to wear that one today?"

She shook her head. "It's too grand."

"Nothing is too grand for a woman of your status."

"And what is that status, exactly?"

Niana ignored her, pulling a simple yellow dress from its hanger and holding it out to Anna. "This one would do nicely, if you're looking for something a little plainer."

Anna wanted to ask the question again, but something in Niana's posture stopped her—she knew she would not get a real answer no matter how hard she pushed. Though she was curious, she decided to let it go for now. Today's focus was rediscovering her memories; anything else could wait.

She slipped the dress over her head, then stood in front of the mirror as Niana fussed with the ties at the back. Its simplicity did nothing to take away from its beauty; the soft silk hugged her curves, and the bright yellow contrasted nicely with the brown of her skin. The neckline dipped just low enough to highlight her ample breasts and to show off the necklace she still had not removed.

Anna could not take her eyes off her reflection. The dress had been beautiful on the hanger, but on her it looked fit for a princess.

"Where do the dresses come from?"

"Straid sourced them himself. I don't recognize the craftsmanship of this one—many dressmakers have their tells, but I don't think I've seen any work from this one before."

Anna slipped her feet into the shoes Niana had placed before her, sturdy slippers that felt like walking on air.

"Your husband is waiting for you downstairs," her lady's maid said with a mischievous smile. "He'll be speechless when he sees you."

The dress swirled around her ankles as she descended the stairs, and Straid's eyes flared as he watched her.

"You look stunning," he said thickly.

"It's the dress. Isn't it beautiful?" She twirled, laughing as she spun, then came to a sudden stop as she remembered spinning in a shabby ballroom, in a dress much plainer than this. In the memory, dust motes floated through a shaft of sunlight, and she sneezed. A hand had taken hers shortly after, calloused fingers tugging her from the room with a heightened urgency.

"Oh," she breathed.

"What troubles you?"

"Nothing." She wanted to keep the memory for herself; something about it felt private. Precious.

"The dress suits you."

"It's perfect." She smoothed her hands down the front and fought the urge to ask for more. It must have been expensive; the dye alone would have cost a fortune, and she was certain she had never felt a fabric so fine in her life.

"Nearly." He traced a finger along a seam that ran down the side of her bodice. "The seam is puckered here. The next dress will be perfect."

"The next one?"

He dipped his head, his eyes still studying the dress. "You will have as many creations from this dressmaker as you desire."

He looked up, his face mere inches from hers, and the focus in his gaze sent heat flooding between her legs. She stumbled backward, then glanced away, embarrassed.

"Where would you like to go?" Straid held out his arm and she took it, still flustered.

"There's a shop I want to visit. I can't remember the name, but I was hoping you could help me? The exterior is white, with vines clinging to the walls. The vines have colorful flowers all over them—orange, pink, and yellow. I think there's an awning that's covered in trailing moss? That can't be right."

Images of the storefront had popped into her mind multiple times over the past two days, and she was certain that she had been there often. Perhaps visiting the shop would give her some clue as to who she was—or trigger another memory that might.

Waiting for his response felt like agony but, as she was beginning to expect, he took his time.

"I know the place. The moss—you remembered correctly." Was she imagining the strain in his voice? "Would you like me to

Travel you, or would you prefer to walk? It is perhaps two miles from here."

"Travel? What—" She gasped, gripped by a memory of the world compressing around her as she moved miles away in a single step, here one moment and there the next.

"Let's walk," she said, not eager to experience the unpleasant sensation again.

The walk passed quickly, though the conversation was sparse. She spent the time examining her surroundings, hoping for some clue that she had walked these streets before—some clue that might spark a memory—but none came.

Finally, they reached the shop, and she nearly wept at its familiarity. The outside was a stark white, which must have been magically maintained to stay so pristine. Vines trailed up the side of the building, covered in colorful blossoms. Plants crowded the windows, so thick she could not see what lay beyond them. The storefront was beautiful, and she held her breath as she opened the door. Her memory only included the outside; she did not know what she would find when she crossed the threshold.

The interior was open and airy, with plants lining the walls and intricately carved wooden dressers with ornate handles throughout the space.

"I will wait for you out here," Straid said, turning his back to her before she had a chance to respond.

Moments later her eyes fell on a display tucked into the corner just inside the entrance, and the reason for Straid's reluctance to join her became clear; a wooden mannequin wearing gorgeous stark white lingerie welcomed customers as they walked through the door. Lace dripped from the mannequin's body, delicate and playful. Anna's eyes lingered on the lace, wondering how much it cost.

She shook her head. She had no occasion to wear it, not now that she was married to a fae who had made it very clear their marriage would be devoid of sex.

A tiny, flying fae about the size of her hand approached her, hovering about two feet from her face. *Faerie,* a voice in the back of her mind supplied.

"Welcome to The Meadow," the faerie said. She had mossy green skin, with paper-thin cerulean wings that trailed a fine dusting of glitter behind her. "I'm Sky. How may I help you today?"

"I'm honestly not sure," Anna murmured. "I think I've been here before, but I can't remember."

Sky hummed disapprovingly. "Our store is not forgettable, and neither are our pieces," she huffed.

"Oh, I—I didn't mean to offend," Anna said, catching the apology just before it slipped from her lips. "I didn't mean to imply that they were. I'm missing some of my memories, and your gorgeous storefront is one of the few things I remember. I quite agree that this place is not forgettable."

She peered at the displays nearest her, marveling at the pieces. Most hid behind plants unless viewed from just the right angle, and the effect was stunning: delicate lingerie that blended in so perfectly with the nature around it that it almost felt as though they were one.

"Not many mortals have been in here," Sky said, settling on the counter as Anna drew near. "Would you have been purchasing items for an employer, perhaps? Or—" she glanced outside, to Straid's imposing figure just on the other side of the window, barely visible through the thick foliage.

"I wasn't here with him," Anna hurried to clarify, though she wasn't sure why she felt the need to. He was now her husband, after all. "But I think someone else might have brought me. Would you mind if I looked around? Maybe if I see something I bought, it'll jog my memory."

"Our pieces are one of a kind," Sky said, bristling again. "You won't find a duplicate of anything you've previously purchased. But you may look if you must."

Anna wandered the store, growing more and more in awe as

she discovered new sets of lingerie tucked into hidden displays in the plants, as though each piece were a coveted secret belonging to the vine, bush, or tree that housed it.

If she'd found the storefront beautiful, it was nothing compared to what lay inside.

Finally, after she had closely examined every item in the store, she had to admit that Sky was right: nothing here looked familiar enough to jog her memory. She slunk out the door, feeling frustrated with herself—and guilty at the shopkeeper's angry muttering about Anna leaving empty-handed.

"Did you find anything to your tastes?"

Anna startled at the sound of Straid's voice. She'd been so preoccupied by her musings that she hadn't noticed him leaning against the store's façade.

"Did you know that it was a lingerie store?" she demanded.

"I did."

"Why didn't you tell me?"

"You were very specific in wanting to visit this store; I assumed you had been here before."

"I think I have," she said with a sigh. "But I can't remember. You could have come in, by the way. I'm not shy about that stuff. It's just sex. Not even that; it's just *clothes*. I wouldn't have minded."

"You might have been uncomfortable in my presence," he said with a maddeningly stoic face. She appreciated his dedication to making her feel comfortable, but what woman wouldn't want a gorgeous fae man to lust after her some?

Just as she opened her mouth to suggest going home, movement caught her eye: a man waving at her from across the street. The gesture was small, subtle, as though he was trying to be discreet, and Anna was struck with the sudden feeling that she knew him.

"Excuse me for a moment," she said. Straid made to follow her, but she shook her head.

"It is not safe, Anna."

"I'll be right across the street. You can keep an eye on me if you want, but I need to talk to him. And I don't need you at my side to do it."

Straid clenched his jaw but gave her a tight nod, and she could feel his eyes tracking her as she crossed the cobblestoned street. The man she approached was shorter than Straid, though still slightly taller than her, with corded muscles that rippled under his dusky orange skin. He smiled at her as she approached, but she caught the way his eyes slid over her shoulder, landing on Straid briefly before darting away.

"Carra," he murmured as she drew level with him. "I had heard Straid had taken a wife. I did not realize that wife was you."

She glanced behind herself, where Straid was leaning against the wall. His eyes bore into her, so intense she could swear she felt the temperature rise.

"You know me?" She hadn't meant to ask that question; she hadn't wanted to give any hint about her memory issues. Not until she knew who he was and why he looked so familiar, anyway.

"Of course I do." He leaned closer, peering at her questioningly. "Carra? Have I done something to upset you? Or is this your way of saying that you cannot see me anymore, now that you're married?"

"Carra..." she repeated the name, and it felt right in her mouth, like she'd said it before, many times. Like it *belonged* to her. And the way it sounded on his lips...

She had a sudden memory of him below her, moaning her name as she rocked on top of him. His voice was low in the memory, his eyes shuttered, and she remembered feeling powerful over the fact that she, a mere human, had reduced this fae lord to such a mess beneath her.

She gasped and staggered back, and within seconds Straid was at her side.

"Is there a problem?" he asked, his eyes only on her.

"No. There's no problem. We were just...getting reacquainted. Excuse my strange behavior," she said to the stranger with the orange skin that seemed to glow in the sunlight. "I'm missing some memories, and you looked familiar. I'd hoped you could help me remember how I know you."

"You're missing a lot of memories, then?"

"I am," she whispered, her throat tight.

"I am Lord Astrea," he murmured, concern coloring his eyes. "And I will do whatever I can to help."

"Will you come over later?" she asked him, then hesitated and turned to Straid. "Would that be okay?"

Straid gave her a tightlipped smile, then turned to the other fae. "You would be most welcome any time today."

"After my shopping, then."

They parted ways, and Anna—Carra—let Straid whisk her back home, nervous and excited in equal measure for the conversation that awaited her.

CHAPTER SIX

She paced, nervously awaiting Lord Astrea's arrival. She remembered flashes of him—his mouth on hers, and a ring on his left pinky finger. The emerald had been absent today, but she was sure the hand she remembered was his.

She remembered more, as well: things that could not be possible, false memories that made her all the more glad she'd asked him to come.

"Before he enters my home—*our* home—he will need to agree to discretion," Straid said from the bottom of the staircase, where he stood, watching her cross the foyer in an increasingly frantic rhythm.

"What does that mean, exactly?"

"I will speak with him and swear him to secrecy in order to protect us. He will not be able to discuss the contents of the home or particulars of sensitive discussions with others. He likewise will be unable to disclose the nature of his relationship to you with anyone who might ask."

"That seems extreme."

"I value my privacy." Straid's eyes smoldered, and Anna's breath hitched as she held his gaze, her feet stilling.

"Yet you invited me into your home."

"There were extenuating circumstances. I could not sit idly by while you died for the crime of being human."

"I knew what I was doing." She remembered glancing over her shoulder and peering around corners before rounding them —and the fear, once she realized she'd been sighted. She had known the cost of her presence and chosen to enter the Quarters regardless.

"At the time, perhaps. But the person who committed the crime and the person who would have been punished for it were two different people entirely. Without your memories, you are not... you."

"I—"

"Lord Astrea has arrived." Straid stepped back, and she realized that sometime during their brief discussion they had drawn close to each other. She cleared her throat.

"So what now?" She asked, as Straid reached the door. Moments later, Lord Astrea knocked, the heavy, booming sound echoing through the foyer. Straid opened the door and ushered the other fae inside. Lord Astrea's eyes widened at the sight of him, then slid to her.

"Give us a moment, Anna." Straid requested.

She shook her head. "He's here for me, and I want to be a part of whatever conversation you're about to have."

Straid's clenched his jaw, his eyes smoldering. "Very well. Astrea, I presume you are familiar with the expectations of a guest in my home?"

The fact that he had dropped the title made Carra take note. She couldn't remember the nuances of fae conventions, but in the human world, it would take equal status to allow someone to do so, and she assumed the same would be true here. She filed the information away for later—if Straid was a lord, that would make her a lady.

"My identity and the nature of my relationship with my wife shall not be discussed with anybody, under any circumstance. You will not so much as hint it through any method of communication. Do I make myself clear?"

"Yes, y—"

"Enough." The two men locked eyes, tension thrumming between them. Carra glanced from one to the other, taken aback by the sudden shift.

She almost wondered if this was jealous, some sort of competition between the men over her, but no; this was something beyond her comprehension entirely.

After a few fraught seconds, Lord Astrea dipped slightly at the waist, an acquiescence that veered closer to being a shallow bow than the situation warranted. He stood on ceremony often, she remembered now, treating things with more reverence than they required.

"I will leave you to your discussion," Straid said, turning to her. "I will be in my study should you need me."

Carra watched him sweep up the stairs before she gestured toward the small room off the foyer that Straid had prepared for the meeting. She hadn't noticed it at first; the door blended into the wall behind it, but the interior was surprisingly roomy, with more than enough space for her and Lord Astrea.

"Sor—I appreciate you putting up with that. It turns out he's protective of me." A small part of her that she steadfastly refused to acknowledge thrilled at the revelation.

"As he should be. You are worth protecting."

She smiled, though she found herself suddenly uneasy. This fae lord clearly knew her well, but she knew nothing about him —save for the sounds he made while inside her, and the fact that he trusted her enough to thank her freely.

"What do you remember?" He asked gently, seeming to recognize that she needed help getting started.

"Not much. You and I...have been intimate."

He laughed. "Yes. That's the whole nature of our relationship."

"The *whole* nature?" She breathed a sigh of relief, even through her surprise. She had worried he might be a romantic partner, an entanglement she would have to navigate carefully now that she was married.

"You are a consummate professional."

It took a moment for his words to sink in, but when they did, memories flooded her mind: Lord Astrea paying her a handful of gold coins; Lord Astrea setting up a bank account for her so he and other clients could deposit the money directly; another fae, his skin shimmering in the low light, lowering himself above her.

"Oh."

She didn't feel much about it—yet. Though if she had a lord for a client, she must be very good at what she did, she mused.

"What can you tell me? Anything at all."

"I don't know who your other clients are, of course; if you shared that information, you would lose many, if not all, of us. But you are *very* good at your job, for what it's worth. You *were*, at any rate; I assume your recent marriage means those days are behind you."

"I—" She paused to consider. "Honestly, I hadn't thought about it. I see no reason I'd have to stop working just because I'm married."

"Respectfully, this is not just any job. And your husband is *Straid*."

"What does my husband's identity have to do with anything?"

"He's—" Lord Astrea froze, his mouth hanging open for a second or two before he slammed it shut. "He values his privacy. He will never agree to it."

"Well, it's my life. He'll just have to." She resolved to discuss her work with him after Lord Astrea left, and to make it clear that Straid had no say in whether she continued working or not. She had never believed that women should give up their careers or hobbies—or anything else, for that matter—for marriage; the fact that their marriage was nothing more than a desperate ploy to save her life only strengthened her resolve to have the deci-sion be purely on her own terms.

"My lack of memory might be a problem, but my marriage will not be."

"I may be able to help with that—the memories, I mean," he hastily explained. He reached into a pocket and drew out a small vial filled with a shimmering blue liquid.

The liquid seemed to swirl in time with her pulse, and she fought the urge to reach for it.

"Take it; it's yours."

"What is it?" She breathed. "And how much to I owe you?" She paused, her fingers inches from the glass.

"Our next session for free. That's the price."

"And if I decide not to work?"

"Then we'll still meet, once, and keep things strictly friend-ly." He frowned. "One hour with you, to spend as you see fit."

"In exchange for what, exactly? What does this do?"

"Restore your memories. You'll need to trigger each memory with a familiar marker: a person or place should do it. It might not restore everything, but you'll remember a lot."

"So I drink this and just… remember?"

"No!" he yelled, pulling his hand back slightly. Her heart beat faster, and the potion swirled more quickly in time with it. "Don't drink it. Never drink it. Wear it like a perfume: a dab on the wrists or behind the ear. So long as it's still on your skin, it will help you remember."

"And all I have to do is spend an hour with you? No sex required?"

"Correct."

"Why?"

"Because," he said airily, "I'm hoping that you'll choose to add sex to the equation once you've recovered your memories. But if not…" his voice dropped, low and grave. "If not, then I would not force you into it. I am under no illusion as to the nature of our relationship, but I would not want it if I thought you weren't there by choice."

He held her gaze, his eyes bolstering the truth in his words.

Slowly, she reached for the vial.

She removed the stopper, breathing deeply as the smell pervaded the air—so strong for such a small amount: she could likely hold all the liquid cupped in her hand.

With a shaky hand, she tapped the end of the tapered stopper to her left wrist.

Immediately, she remembered.

Memories flooded her all at once, and she gasped at the force of it. One after another, so quickly she could not parse them.

When the deluge ebbed, the memories felt solid, familiar, as though she had never lost them in the first place—nothing like the other memories that had felt novel and exotic. No; these were *hers*, through and through.

She clamped her mouth shut, knowing that if she spoke, she would thank him—profusely, incurring many more debts than she could afford.

"You can say it, if it would help. I will close the bonds immediately."

"Thank you," she whispered, because she knew it to be true: he was free with his words, the two of them trading *pleases* and *thank yous* as part of their arrangement, and closing every bond, settling every debt, before the bedroom door reopened. "I'll never be able to thank you enough. I—thank you," she sobbed.

He rose from his chair and kneeled before her, wiping the tears from her cheeks. "You're welcome. You're welcome. You are more than welcome, Carra."

Once her tears subsided, Lord Astrea took his seat again.

"I was with you that night." It didn't feel like a revelation; it was simply knowledge she had.

"What night?"

"The night I lost my memories. Leaving your house is the last thing I remember—until I was running from the guard late that night. Near midnight, I think."

"You're missing hours, then. You left my home at dusk. The light from the setting sun—"

"Turned my eyes into gold," she murmured. He had made the comment, then pressed a quick kiss to her lips and retreated into his house, watching from the window as she turned away. She remembered walking to the end of the street...and then nothing, until the guard.

"What do you know about me? What have I told you over the years?" She remembered very few personal conversations about her life—was that because they hadn't had many, or were these gaps in the perfume's ability to restore her memories?

"I'm not sure what I know," he said, settling back in the chair.

"What does that mean?"

"It means, Carra, that you are human, and thus able to lie. I know the things you have told me, but I have taken you at your word and, thus, did not verify the truthfulness of any of it. You said your name is Carra; I have seen no proof. You said you were 27 years old—this was two years ago now, but I do not know enough of mortals to gauge the accuracy of that statement. You never spoke much of home, but I gathered you're from the nearest human town, though that would be a far way to come for our visits."

"I was coming from the village, I think." Her home was modest, and she remembered shying away from the stone walls when the temperatures dropped. The town had been built in the last hundred years, the old stone structures of the villages abandoned in favor of wood, easier to insulate against the cold of winter. "What about my family?"

"You never spoke of them. Due to the nature of our encounters, I could hardly blame you."

"I can see how that would detract from what we're doing together, yes." She laughed, but somewhere in her mind, she heard an echo—a laugh similar to hers but freer, unencumbered, and pitched ever so slightly lower. Her mother's laugh, perhaps, or a sister's?

He told her what he could remember, and her own memories verified much of it: the clothes she wore on her visits to his home; the name of the bank where he sent her payments; the things she had been most drawn to in his home. She had told him little about her life, but he shared that information with her, as well: that she grew lavender in her windowsill, and that she was a terrible cook. Neither of them knew if these tidbits were true, but she clung to them anyway, desperate to piece them back into herself.

An hour later she saw him to the door with a promise that they would meet again.

"I'll see you soon," she told him, wrapping him in a quick hug, awed by the muscles she felt through his jacket. "I'd like to resume our regular meetings, if you still want that."

She had expected an enthusiastic agreement—after all, he had been open about wanting sex—but he hesitated, his eyes flicking to the staircase. "Do you think that's wise?"

"I'll talk to him. But our marriage…" she shook her head, mindful that it had saved her life; she didn't want to jeopardize that by disclosing the haste with which they entered it. "I will let you know what he says."

He pressed a kiss to her cheek, and she sank into the touch, closing her eyes against the onslaught of emotion that rose at the feeling of comfort given so freely. "Good luck, Carra. I hope you continue to remember."

CHAPTER SEVEN

Straid sat in his study, willing his mind to focus on the task at hand, but the traitorous thing kept straying to the woman down the hall. To the conversation she had told him she wanted to have in private. And he had agreed. Of course he had agreed. But he longed to be in the library with them. His curiosity, long dormant, had been piqued, and all he could think about was satisfying it.

He wished, not for the first time, that he had the sensitive hearing mortals assumed all fae were blessed with. But as it was, his hearing was barely better than Anna's: not good enough to hear a conversation happening two heavy doors away on a different floor.

He forced his attention back to the letter in front of him, which had arrived that morning: a list of missing names, going back further than he or Corlan had thought to look. The disappearances had grown steadily, beginning around two decades back. The first to disappear had been humans, though little attention had been paid to them; they were not employed by any fae, and only rumored to have been in the Quarters. Other mortals could not enter the Quarters alone to search for them, and few fae cared enough to help—that there was even a record of the disappearances was nothing short of a miracle.

Over the years, more had gone missing, but the first few fae were unlikely to be missed; reports had been filed weeks or months after they had last been seen. Only in the past year or so had higher-profile fae gone missing.

Straid studied the list, taking care to examine the names of every single person who had gone missing in or near the Quarters in the past decade, attempting to find any possible connection between them. But there was none. The names on the list consisted of fae and mortals alike, spread out all over the Quarters. They had different occupations, different social statuses, different jobs, and different circles of friends. They were different ages, different species, and had different abilities. He truly could find no link between them.

A knock on the door jolted him from his work. He had not realized how engrossed he had become, and he rolled his neck to release some of the tension that had built there.

"You may enter," he called. The wards would allow her into the room until midnight regardless.

She eased the door open, then peeked her head through.

"He's gone," she said, most of her body still hidden behind the door.

"Come in—if you would like."

She did and shut the door behind her before taking the same seat she had occupied earlier.

"I appreciate you letting me invite him over."

"This house is yours now, as well, Anna. You do not need my permission to entertain guests."

"It's not my house, though. Not really."

His chest tightened at her words. He had expected her to feel as though she were a guest in the home. He had *wanted* as much. So why did it bother him to hear her say it?

"Was Lord Astrea able to help?" he asked, straightening the papers before him.

"He was," she said, her eyes shining. Only now did he notice the redness to them.

She had been crying.

Something fierce and angry rose in his chest.

"He upset you." He drank in every little detail: the swelling around her eyes, the pinkening of her nose.

"No." A wondrous smile crept across her face. "He helped, and it overwhelmed me. My tears were happy ones."

Anna hesitated, then drew what appeared to be a perfume bottle from the pocket of her dress. "He gave me this."

She placed the bottle on the desk between them. As he examined it, the shimmering blue liquid inside swirled faster and faster.

"Perfume?"

"It helps with memory recovery."

"I would ask that you wait to use it until I can examine it further."

"Too late."

He glanced up sharply to find her grinning. The sight softened his ire—and his worry.

"I remembered him," she said. "Not everything; there are still some gaps. But I remembered that I was with him the night we met. I left his house with my memories intact. I remember most of my encounters with him."

"Your memory is restored, then?"

"Not entirely," she said, her smile dimming. He missed it instantly.

"He said I'll need to encounter something else to trigger the memories. Being in his presence made me remember *him*—but I still don't know about my life outside the Quarters, or any of my other..." her eyes met his for a second before darting away. "But I know my occupation. And my name."

"Your name?" He stilled, watching her closely, but she did not say anything further. "You do not wish to tell me," he guessed, fighting to keep any emotion from his voice. His strange curiosity was his alone to deal with.

"I—" she glanced at him, guilt written plainly on her face.

"You are under no obligation to disclose it," he said, though it pained him to say. "Your name is your own to do with as you please."

She nodded. Then slowly, deliberately, she spoke. "Thank you."

He reeled at the words, at the intention behind her thanking him, a fae. He scowled at her, even as he relished the cold flaring deep in chest. "You should not have said those words to me."

"I meant them, though. It means a lot that you would let me keep my name from you. I mean, your own wife…"

"As I have said, marrying you was a way to save your life; nothing more. You are not my wife in any way that matters."

She flinched, and he clenched his jaw to keep from retracting the words.

To keep from apologizing.

"Maybe you should know why I was in the Quarters that night," she said, meeting his gaze again and holding it this time. "I was with Lord Astrea," she said, in a tone that made it clear exactly what *how* she was with him. Straid willed his gaze to stay blank.

"I see."

"I think you were right when you implied I knew Ichold carnally. Professionally."

"You are a prostitute." His words were low, measured, a desperate attempt to quell the images running through his mind. Of Anna with Lord Astrea, with Ichold. Of Anna in the bath that first night, so close by and angry that he had not undressed her.

This could mean…

No.

He would not ask. He would not cross that line. Not when she had had no true choice in marrying him. Especially now. He would not use her profession as a weapon against her.

"Yes. I am." She tipped her chin up toward him. "Is that going to be a problem?"

"I am not a jealous man," he said, holding her gaze, though the resulting jolt of desire threatened to consume him. "I do not expect you to change who you are, or what you do, simply because you are now my wife."

Anna stilled. "I—you would let your wife..."

Let. A word that had no place in a marriage. He had watched the games his mother played with her paramours: dangling permissions just past their reach until she controlled every aspect of their lives. She claimed it necessary and perhaps on some level, in her case, it had been. But Straid had left that world behind and had no desire to remove any further freedoms from his wife.

"I understand the position I put you in. It was necessary to save your life, but you did not make the choice. I would never punish you for the choice I made in order to keep you alive. When I told you this marriage would be in name only, that you could take a lover, I meant it. This is no different. Vows of discretion would be necessary from each of your dalliances, but so long as they agreed, you could work as you see fit."

"You'd really have no problem with me meeting with clients?" She sounded as though she had expected a fight. Perhaps she had anticipated jealousy or anger, or perhaps some other even less excusable response. He felt none of those. She was not his lover, and even if she were, he would never expect a paramour to abandon her livelihood for his sake.

"I have no problem with it, so long as you meet them here or allow me to provide you with an escort as a safety precaution. I cannot have you go missing." He mentally cursed himself at the softness in his voice, but Anna did not seem to hear it. She grinned at him from across the table, and he allowed himself a small smile in return.

"You're the best husband I've ever had," she said, rising from her chair.

"As far as you are aware," he countered. He did his best to ignore the warmth that bloomed in his chest at the sound of her laughter as she left his study, but it was futile. Her charm wormed its way through the walls he had built around himself these past five decades, thawing him to the point that he might almost consider her a friend. That it had taken her less than a week only served to prove the depths of her charisma.

He contemplated what it would be like having her across the hall, entertaining clients. He had not lied when he had said he was not a jealous person. And yet, the thought of her so close, with other men…the idea that he might hear her with them…

Straid abandoned the papers on his desk and stalked down the hallway, to the wing of the house he rarely used. He had meant to purchase a different house, sometime in the past few years, one that carried no memories. A smaller one, better suited to his solitude. But now, surveying the suite that had once housed the lord and lady of the house, he found himself grateful that he had never managed to convince himself to leave.

He opened the windows in both rooms of the adjoining suite, then dusted the surfaces, polished the furniture, and changed the silk sheets on the bed. He replaced the candles in the sconces and tucked the old ones, worn with use, into the trick bottom of the desk's main drawer. He could not part with the candles entirely, not after everything they had seen.

Straid glanced at the clock by the bedside and cursed. He had not noticed the room growing darker around him, and when he glanced outside, the sun was nowhere to be found.

Anna would be waiting for him, ready for dinner. Or she would have given up, perhaps assuming he had intentionally avoided her after their earlier conversation.

He cursed again and ran a hand hurriedly through his hair. He was covered in sweat and dust and furniture polish—not presentable for a meal—but there was no time for a proper bath.

Anna was halfway through her dinner by the time he made it downstairs, and she smiled at him tentatively as he sat.

"I didn't know the protocol for dinner, but I was hungry…"

"I am glad you did not wait on my behalf," he said, reaching for the nearest dish and piling food on his plate, paying it no real mind. "I was caught up in a project. I would like to show you what I was working on after dinner, if you will permit me."

"What was the project?"

"You will have to wait and see." He poured mosswine in her goblet, then took a sip of his own.

"Can I guess what it was?"

"No."

"My question was rhetorical."

"My answer was not." He lifted the goblet to his lips, hiding his smile behind its rim.

Anna ate quickly, then watched him mulishly. He ate slowly, savoring every bite—and her growing impatience. The moment he placed the final bite of food in his mouth, she rose. "Well?"

He stood, suddenly nervous: what if she disliked the work he had done—or the very idea of it? She reached for his arm, and he stepped away deftly. "I am covered in filth. You would not want to touch me."

"I don't mind," she said softly, but he shook his head.

"Come. I would like to show you—I hope it is to your satisfaction." He winced, hoping she had not noticed him stumble over his words. He hoped she would like it. He feared she might not. The anxiety was new and unwelcome.

He led her up the stairs and down the hallway, following the twists and turns that would take them to the distant suite.

"You didn't show me this on the tour of the house," she mused from half a step behind him. He was acutely aware of her proximity, and sped up to put another step between them, feeling the loss of her warmth.

"This portion of the house is disused. It was disused," he corrected. "I hope you will find it to your liking."

He stopped outside the first entrance to the rooms: the heavy wooden door with ornate carvings of holly and wheat that marked the bedroom.

"After you." He gestured for her to open the door, and she stepped into the pool of candlelight he had left burning.

"A bedroom?" She wrinkled her nose in confusion. "Are you moving me here?"

"I thought you might want a dedicated place to meet with your clients. Entertaining them here would allow you to maintain the privacy of your own boudoir."

"Oh." She said nothing else, and that single word lanced through him. He had miscalculated. She was displeased. And, for some unfathomable reason, her disappointment pained him more than anything he had experienced in recent years.

She turned slowly, and he held his breath.

Anna took a step toward him. Then another.

And then she wrapped her arms around him, and her face pressed into his chest, right above the pain, and eased it.

"That was very thoughtful. I appreciate it."

He relaxed into the hug for the briefest moment before springing back and pushing her away.

"You will ruin your clothes—your face—"

It was too late: a smear of furniture polish marred her cheek, and the shoulder of her dress bore a stain larger than he would have thought possible.

She straightened, her smile slipping, and he wanted to chase it, to coax it back out of her. "Shit. I'll replace the dress."

"There is no need." He had used a simple pattern, and it did not fit her quite as well as he had hoped—and that puckered seam had only passed muster because filling her wardrobe had bene an urgent task. She deserved better, and the ruination of this dress gave him the opportunity to provide her with it.

"I will leave you to explore the space. There is an adjoining receiving room, and the washroom is through there." He pointed to the door at the far side of the room. "I will be in my study if you need me."

CHAPTER EIGHT

In the morning, Carra gazed at her reflection in the mirror Straid had gifted her the night they met. The weight of it in her hand was comforting, and shivers raced up her spine; something about her reflection surrounded by the curling gold accents felt almost magical. *Maybe it is*, she mused. It was a fae mirror, after all; who knew what sort of magic it may have been imbued with.

Wide eyes stared at her, framed with thick, dark lashes. Her eyes held no trace of the turmoil in her mind; she didn't look like a woman desperate to remember any little detail about herself.

She frowned, ready to set the mirror aside, when a memory halted her hand in midair.

"I hate when you're upset, but it gives me the opportunity to kiss that frown away." She remembered the words, and the voice that had uttered them: soft and distinctly feminine. And then a gentle press of lips against her own.

Perhaps the woman who had run her fingers through Carra's wet hair *was* a lover. Was she waiting for her back home? Would the other woman be devastated to discover that Carra had married a fae?

She angled the mirror back at her mouth and frowned again,

hoping the memory would solidify further. When it failed to, she manipulated her mouth every way she could think of: frowning at the mirror again, then smiling, then forcing her mouth into a semblance of a laugh. She sniffed at her wrist. The perfume still lingered, a light, crisp scent that reminded her of dawn.

She opened the diary she'd found in the drawer her first day here and added these new memories to it.

When she'd found it, she'd run her fingers along the cream cover, then furtively opened it, unsure what she might find inside: sordid secrets, or accounts of the previous owner's dreams, or something as mundane as a grocery list. But it had been empty; pages and pages of blank paper greeted her. So she had claimed it as her own and written down everything she remembered, including a sketch of the flower pendant that hung around her neck. It elicited no memories, but she had been wearing it that night, so it must hold some clues to who she was.

Even the perfume hadn't brought forward any new memories of it.

Looking over her clumsy sketch of the necklace, she added another piece of information below it: *clearly, I am not an artist.*

She flipped back through the diary, tracing her name with a reverent finger, recalling how it had felt to hear Lord Astrea use it and feel certain the name belonged to her. She stopped on the first page, where she'd written a list of the rules she remembered about the fae:

1. Never say please or thank you—nothing that implies you owe them anything
2. Never dine with the fae
3. They can't lie, but that doesn't mean they always tell the truth
4. Don't wander the Quarters alone

She had filled four pages with memories so far. She didn't add the memories that had returned with Lord Astrea; those felt solid, permanent, unlike the ones that had come before, which felt as though they could slip through her fingers at any moment.

"I want to go to the village," she announced at breakfast, staring Straid down across the table. "It seems like a good place to start. Someone there might know who I am—and being there should trigger more of my memories."

"Anna." He sounded pained. "You cannot leave the Quarters for the first year of our marriage."

"What?" She reeled.

"I told you this before we wed. A fae-mortal wedding binds the mortal to our world for a year following the nuptials."

"And what consequences do the fae face?" She vaguely remembered him informing her of the fact, but the night was a blur of pain and confusion.

"There is a fair amount of social stigma that comes with marrying a mortal. We also must watch our spouse die."

"Yeah, well, that one doesn't really apply to you, does it? You don't love me. You barely know me. Watching me die won't have much of an effect on you."

"I may not love you, but no part of me relishes the thought of watching you die." His voice had softened with something like… regret? Grief?

"Then you'll have to go for me."

"You want me to go to the village?"

"I'm not going to sit and wait around for the next year, just hoping my memories come back. Even with the perfume, there's only so much I'll be able to learn about myself here. If I can't go to the village, someone else needs to. And if that doesn't turn anything up, someone needs to go into town. Surely someone is looking for me; it should be pretty easy to find them."

"What good would it do? You could not return until a year has passed."

"Going back isn't my only goal. It's not even my main goal. I want to know who I am. I *need* to know who I am. I can't do that without my memories of my life outside the Quarters."

He slid a carafe of juice toward her, and only then did Carra realize she hadn't eaten anything yet. She filled her glass, then grabbed a pastry from the nearest tray.

"I will visit the village when I can," Straid conceded. "I make no promises that I can find answers, but I will try."

"That's all I ask."

His agreement settled around her shoulders—not the physical feeling of a fae vow, but an almost-tangible relief.

"I have an ask of my own," he said.

"An ask, or a demand?"

He dipped his head, the ghost of a smile playing on his lips. "The latter."

"What?" Apprehension roiled deep in her belly.

"I need to meet with any clients you intend on bringing to the house. There are certain safety measures I must insist on."

"Is that it?" She'd expected something much more drastic based on the gravity in his voice.

"You would agree to that so readily?"

"As long as you don't do anything to get in the way, sure. You met with Lord Astrea, and that went well. You prepared a whole suite for me to work from. You clearly understand how much my work means to me, and I will never turn down a reasonable safety measure."

"You would trust me with your safety?"

She shrugged, ignoring the tendril of unease that had never fully gone away around him. It quieted, occasionally, but it was always there. "You promised you wouldn't hurt me. If I can't trust you, I can at least trust the fae magic that'll hold you to your promise."

"*Do* you trust me?"

She took a sip of her juice, buying precious seconds to think. "I'd like to think I can."

His eyes burned. "Spoken like a fae."

"That's how I'll survive this next year, isn't it? Careful, clever words that don't speak to the whole truth? I'll be surrounded by slippery words; I might as well use a few of my own."

"Careful. You might learn to fit in." The words felt like a compliment coming from him, yet she fought a shudder at the implication. The last thing she wanted was to lose her humanity while living with the fae.

CHAPTER NINE

Straid had never seen someone who looked so at home among the roses. Anna had asked to see the gardens this morning, and now she walked at his side, admiring the cultivated flowers and the weeds alike.

"I love these roses. The way the red fades to white at the tips of the petals is stunning." The flower was past its prime, the edges curling with age, but she admired it as though it were still at the peak of its beauty.

She bent to smell it, inhaling deeply, and when she pulled away her face had softened. She moved to the next bush, trailing a finger along a fading rose, then jumped back with a sharp cry.

"Oh! I'm fine, the snake just startled me." She pointed to a small green creature slithering underneath the foliage. "Oh," Anna repeated quietly. A blush spread across her cheeks as her eyes darted to him and then quickly away.

"There is nothing to be ashamed of. Fear of snakes is fairly common."

"I'm not scared. I...I remembered something. A client."

"The snake reminded you of a client."

Anna nodded.

Had the client owned a snake? Or was one of her clients

offaedia? The offaedia, like all high fae, shared a common ancestor with humans—but they shared one with snakes, as well. As a result they looked much the same as Straid—save for their scaled skin, recessed ears, and long, retractable tongues.

Straid dismissed the possibility; he could not imagine a human, with their delicate sensibilities, having relations with an offaedia.

However, another look at Anna suggested he may be wrong. The blush staining her cheeks had deepened, and the look on her face was not purely one of discomfort; if he was not mistaken, that was arousal that hooded her eyes.

"Tell me about this client."

"He—" She stopped and furrowed her brow at him, gaping for a moment before shaking her head. "I can't. There's something stopping me from talking about him."

"He would have bound you to secrecy."

"So I can't tell you who he is?"

"He will have ensured you cannot."

"I wanted to ask you to help me find him. How can I do that if I can't tell you anything about him?"

Straid picked a rose, one of the few that summer's heat had not yet marred. He tucked the flower behind her ear, letting his hand linger in her curls. "You are a clever woman, Anna," he murmured. "You will find a way."

She swallowed thickly, and he watched her throat bob, captivated as she pulled away. His reaction was nothing remarkable, he reasoned with himself; merely the presence of a beautiful woman after so many years locked away in this house on his own.

He turned down the pathway that led to the silk spiders—at least, to where their home had been the last time he had visited. He supposed that after so many generations, they may have migrated to elsewhere in the gardens—or outside of them entirely. The thought saddened him.

"The gardens are beautiful."

"The gardens are in disrepair," he refuted. "However, I can arrange for them to be made beautiful for you again, if you desire."

"No. The wildness is perfect. A lot of care was clearly put into the gardens, but nature has started reclaiming them. It's poetic."

He scoffed. "Poetic."

"No matter how much we manipulate the world around us, it will always prevail, given time. Nature comes for us all, in the end."

"Nature's reclamation is not always so beautiful."

"You've lost someone." She breathed the words, and he pretended not to hear as he quickened his stride. He could not have that discussion here, surrounded by the flowers he had had installed in the garden for *her*.

They finished the walk in silence and, lost in his swirling emotions, he almost failed to notice the silk-spider nests as he passed them, exactly where he had lovingly placed them all those years ago.

"I have a question for you," Anna asked over a dinner of roasted flower blossoms drizzled with a lime dressing. He made a note to increase Elesina's wages; her fare was better than the lavish feasts he had been raised on.

"Go ahead."

"Do you know Retyiao?"

"You remembered something." During his years of solitude, Straid had forgotten the happiness he could feel for others, but it warmed him now. He fought the smile threatening to betray his pleasure.

"I did. Earlier." She widened her eyes, then touched the rose that still perched behind her ear. His happiness instantly vanished at the implication of the gesture. Unease settled low in his belly in its stead.

"I see."

"Do you know him?" she pressed.

"I am not acquainted with him personally. However, I could easily make arrangements for him to meet you here, if it would please you."

"I would appreciate it."

Straid sent the inquiry, along with a sealed letter from his wife, and Retyiao responded immediately. Within hours, the elusive offaedia was at the front door.

"You may enter." Straid stepped aside and gestured for the snake-like fae to follow him to the receiving room just off the foyer. "My wife will join us shortly."

"Your wife." Retyiao's mouth twisted, the scales around his lips shimmering as the motion made them catch the light, the color shifting from green to yellow. "She informed me she had married. I was... surprised, to say the least."

His cadence was melodic, the fricative sounds elongated ever so slightly into a hiss.

"I trust you understand why I requested a meeting?"

Retyiao dipped his head, the movement fluid. Serpentine. "I would have done the same in your place. You want to ensure... Anna's...safety, and the safety of your home in general. I do not begrudge you this. However, I find myself uncomfortable with the idea."

"You do not wish to meet with her in her husband's home."

"Or while she knows so little of herself. It would feel improper."

"She knows enough—"

"*She* is here, and really wishes the two of you wouldn't have started this discussion without her, considering she is the focus of it."

"Of course." Retyiao rose to greet her. A moment later Straid did, as well, chastising himself for the delay.

"As Straid was saying," she said, taking the empty chair

beside Retyiao's, "I know enough. I'm comfortable working—in fact, I think it would help me remember more."

Anna peered at Retyiao, her brow furrowing. She lifted a hand to scratch at her cheek, discreetly sniffing the inside of her wrist, and he surmised that the perfume had failed to induce her memories of the other fae.

"I wish you well on your journey of discovery," Retyiao said, his voice distant, "but I have no desire for our current arrangement to play a role in that. You deserve better, and so do I. Furthermore, I was under the impression that the nature of our relationship would not be divulged."

"I didn't mean to. I needed to find a way to contact you, and Straid managed to piece things together. I'll be more careful in the future."

"I wish you had been more careful now. Amnesia is a tricky beast, and I am willing to overlook this singular transgression. However, that is as far as my generosity extends. If anyone else learns what he has, or if he learns any more about it, I will put an end to our meetings."

"Does that mean you'll keep seeing me?"

"I will not meet with you under his roof, or at all until I am certain you have more than a basic understanding of who you are. Using your true name would be a good place to start. Resuming our appointments before those conditions have been met would feel too much like taking advantage, and that is a line I have no intention of crossing—for either of our sakes."

"I appreciate that."

Staid did as well, though he watched the proceedings silently. Retyiao acted with honor, and Straid found himself impressed— though not entirely at ease just yet.

"Send me a letter when you are ready, and I will gladly welcome you back into my home." Retyiao pressed a kiss to Anna's knuckles. "Until then, I wish you the best."

Anna seemed to deflate the moment the door closed behind him. "Well, that could have gone better."

"It could have gone worse." Straid had expected it to.

"You're right, it could have. I hoped it would be as easy as it was with Lord Astrea. I thought he'd want to help. I guess just because he's a client doesn't mean he's a friend."

"I could order him to help you." He would do it, for her.

"No. He's right; he doesn't owe me that. We have a clear relationship with very explicitly drawn expectations. He's under no obligation to help me. Doing so might feel like it's blurring the lines too much for him. I could see how it would ruin the novelty."

Straid wanted to argue. Getting to know Anna only made him want to learn more; he could not fathom additional knowledge doing anything but increase one's desire toward her. Instead, he nodded to her wrist.

"You did not remember."

"No. It worked so well last time. But I didn't remember anything new."

"Perhaps his pheromones reduce the efficacy of the perfume."

"His pheromones?" She wrinkled her nose in the way he had begun to associate with confusion.

"The offaedia—the high fae with snake attributes—possess powerful pheromones, some of which are ever-present, while others they are able to release at their disposal."

"Do you think he knew I was wearing the perfume and intentionally blocked it? Why would he do that?"

"It may have been a natural, unintended effect of the pheromones. Or perhaps he has something to hide."

"Either way, I didn't learn much."

"You will, in time."

Straid rose early the next morning, determined to find some of the answers Anna so desperately sought. The walk to the village passed quickly, and once there, memories of his own flooded him: of human festivals on long summer days and Lyenna's vibrant smile. He tamped them down; getting lost in the past would hinder his ability to complete the task at hand.

The village was quieter than he remembered, and many of the houses looked long abandoned. The first three doors he knocked on offered no response, but the fourth opened slowly, and a young child peered up at him, her body tucked behind the wood.

"Are you here to take me away?" She asked, her eyes wide with fear.

He scoffed. "I have no interest in human children. I seek information for a friend. Are you acquainted with a young woman named—"

He faltered. Without her true name, this excursion would likely prove futile. "I suppose, in truth, I may be searching for Anna." The name had to have come from somewhere, after all.

The child shook her head. "I don't know Anna. I don't know anyone anymore. They all left."

"Where did they go?"

"Town."

"How many people live in the village presently?"

"Only us and my gramma. And Mr. Tomas. Your friend probably went to live in town, too. That way the fae can't get her."

He bid her farewell and began the long walk into town. He would have to Travel home after, something he avoided whenever possible; he disliked the way the world warped around him when he did so, and it often left him dizzy. But he would not leave Anna to dine alone.

The child's assertion about mortals being safe from the fae in town proved true: upon his arrival at the town's edge, he found it walled with wrought iron. He walked the perimeter of the town, gauging the thickness of the wall and the distance to the center—perhaps there he would be far enough from the iron to avoid its ill effects.

However, reaching the center of town would be a feat on its

own. There were only two entrances to the town: large archways on opposite ends that would force him to walk directly under a portion of the wall. Straid was one of the few who likely could have managed it—if not for the iron inlaid into the road ahead.

If absolutely necessary, he might be able to cross the border after days of careful planning. Even then, he would need to stay in the heart of the town, and he would have an hour—two at the most—before needing to flee from the iron's effects.

A lesser fae could die if they attempted it.

He wondered at how drastically the town had changed since his last visit; fifty years prior there had been no wall. Fae had not been entirely welcome, but Lyenna had brought him before she fell ill, and had only encountered iron in one small neighborhood.

What had happened in the decades since to make the people so fearful?

The sun began its descent, and Straid Traveled home, shuddering at the sensation of the world disappearing around him. He stepped out of the void and into his gardens. His mother had built the house with its back to the street, and he appreciated the decision as he surveyed the house before him, the door framed by trees that bloomed year-round.

If I have to have a home in town, his mother had said, *I will do it my way. I will not hide the beauty of the gardens as though they are a shameful secret. If someone must come to my door, they can walk around the house to do so.*

As he walked through the gardens now, he had to admit there had been some merit to Anna's words: the wildness did hold a certain beauty.

He had arrived home later than intended, and Anna descended the steps as he closed the door behind him. A roasted duck glistened on the table, and his mouth watered at the smell of it. He carved a piece for Anna, then one for himself, then poured them both mosswine.

"I visited the village today. I had hoped to find some

answers, but it seems most of its inhabitants have moved to town."

A smile crept across her face, soft yet brilliant. "I appreciate that. Will you go to town for me?"

"I attempted to today. There is an iron wall around it; I cannot enter. Careful planning and extreme caution might get me past the gates, but I would be highly limited in my search."

"But you could do it?"

"Perhaps. With great difficulty."

"I need you to try." Her eyes shone with unshed tears. "Do you understand how important this is to me?"

"I do. However, your people are mistrustful of the fae; even were I to enter the town—at great risk to myself—I would be unlikely to find someone willing to speak with me. I would be jeopardizing my own life."

Across from him, Anna sagged. He had grown accustomed to her fire; already her dejection alarmed him.

"I will endeavor to do what I can to help you remember who you are," he said, the softness in his voice foreign to his own ears. "We have not yet exhausted every avenue. We will uncover the key to your identity yet."

CHAPTER TEN

Carra opened the front door and smiled at Lord Astrea as he swept into the foyer. She'd dabbed a small amount of the perfume on her wrists as she dressed, in the hopes that the rest of her memories with him would return.

"I appreciate you coming to me," she said with a smile that betrayed none of her nerves. She had done this before: she actually *remembered* multiple of their encounters thanks to him, and what she remembered…quite frankly, it was very, very good. Lord Astrea glanced around him the room, and she figured he had the same hesitation as she'd had—something she'd planned around.

"Straid is out for the afternoon." She took him by the hand and led him to the suite Straid had prepared for this purpose. Lord Astrea followed her through the many twists and turns to reach the faraway rooms, staying right at her side the entire time.

"I still have trouble believing that Straid married. And that he would allow this." Though he sounded dubious, he happily followed Carra without hesitation.

She clenched her jaw at Lord Astrea's phrasing, though she had used similar words herself when speaking with Straid. Still, hearing another man speak of what her husband would or would not allow her to do soured her stomach, and it took great effort to turn her mind to the seduction that lay before her.

"Let's not speak of him anymore," she purred, coming to a stop outside the bedroom door. "Today is about me and you. Come in." She tugged him into the room, past the wards that Straid had set to keep anyone but her out—anyone but her and those she'd invited. He had enchanted the wards so that he could open the door, and if she were in danger he could enter, a measure she appreciated, though one she hoped to never need.

"I must confess, I had hoped to see you again soon," Lord Astrea murmured, taking a step closer to her. "I couldn't stop thinking about you, this past week. I fear I'm getting greedy, my dear."

"I don't mind greedy," Carra promised, pressing her lips against his. "In fact, greedy is perfect. I want you to take your fill." She allowed her robe to slip off her shoulder and watched his gaze follow it. "Show me how much you missed me," she commanded, though she kept her voice gentle. Lord Astrea would never admit to giving up control, but as long as she phrased her demands like pleas he would do what she wanted and beg for more.

Lord Astrea pulled at the tie of her robe, his pupils widening as the silk slowly parted to reveal lacy lingerie in a dusky orange she'd chosen specifically to match the color of his skin. He groaned at the sight of it and ran his fingers reverently along the edges of the lace hugging her left breast.

"Do you wish this was you wrapped around my body?" she asked, and he nodded frantically, his breath coming in sharp, ragged bursts.

He trailed his fingers down the swell of her stomach, then along the top of her panties, and she let out a shiver at the sensation.

"Cold?" he asked with a wicked grin. "Allow me to warm you up." He removed his hand for a brief moment, and when he pressed it against her skin again it radiated a gentle warmth. He walked her backward until she sat on the edge of the bed, all the while running his hand over her hip.

His other hand snaked behind her, settling low on her back as he knelt before her, his face pressed against her knees. She tried to open them, to invite him between her legs, but he gently pressed her legs together and looked up at her with heavy-lidded eyes.

"All in due time," he whispered, his voice hoarse. "I want to make you want this as much as I do."

"I do," she told him, her own voice slightly rougher than usual—she had mastered the art of sounding exactly as full of desire as she chose to.

"Not yet. Right now, I am a client you want to please. But I know you, Carra." Her name, her real one, was rich on his tongue, and she longed to kiss it off him, to capture it for herself. For a moment she wondered how it would sound coming from Straid's lips, but she pushed the thought aside; now was not the time to think of her husband.

"You're going to see me as a source of pleasure as well, Carra. The pleasure, the longing, will be mutual. Only then will we begin."

The warmth of his hands as they explored her was exquisite, and she sank into the feeling, letting his magic wash over her. It crackled and sparked, and when he finally brought a hand between her legs she arched into it.

"Do you like that?" Lord Astrea asked, a slight whine to his voice. Like her answer mattered, like he depended on it.

"Yes," said with a smirk that she knew would excite him further.

"What do you want?" he asked.

Typically, she would respond with whatever she knew her client hoped to hear. But with him, she gave him a real answer, knowing he got off on pleasuring her.

"The heat," she said. "Give me more."

And he did.

The warmth had been incredible through the fabric, but as he circled his heated fingers on her bare flesh, Carra feared she would lose herself entirely.

He slid a finger inside her, then another, moving them in and out of her with delicious slowness. Her eyelids fluttered, and she fell back on the bed, which only served to provide a better angle for Lord Astrea's ministrations. He pushed in farther, deeper, faster and faster, and all the while his fingers grew warmer, until finally she couldn't take it anymore and clenched around him, crying out with abandon.

He slowed his attentions but didn't stop until she'd ridden out the orgasm completely, her body spent.

He pressed a kiss to the delicate flesh between her legs, and her body bucked in response.

"Beautiful," he whispered.

Carra raised her head and tried—and failed—to suppress the slow smile that crept across her face. She watched him for a moment, registering his slight panting, and the dilation of his pupils.

"There's a problem," Carra purred. "You just made me feel so good, but…" She bit her lip, glancing down to where his erection clearly strained against the cobalt blue fabric of his pants. "We'll have to take care of that."

"What do you suggest?" he asked, his voice needy. Breathless.

"I want you to take off your pants," she said, sitting up more fully so she could look down at him as he gazed at her rapturously. "And then I want you to show me how you pleasure yourself."

A small moan escaped him, and his eyes fluttered shut as one of his hands twitched toward his cock, almost reflexively. He paused, and his eyes locked on hers. She could see the war in them: to allow someone power over him and get the pleasure he so desperately needed, or to leave here with his dignity—and his erection—intact.

"Please," she murmured. "Please."

He always settled any debts her words incurred before they parted. Words he clearly craved to hear, but never held over her the way most fae would. So she gave them freely, knowing he would say the requisite words to close the contracts incurred before he left. And he would pay handsomely for the privilege.

His hand flew to the waist of his pants, and she could see it moving inside them, stroking his cock before he'd even managed to remove the clothing. Lord Astrea's breathing grew ragged and his eyes, still locked on hers, widened as his brow furrowed in pleasure.

Carra slowly dragged her eyes down his body and grinned at the whiny moan he let out in response.

"Perfect," she whispered, biting her lip when he leaned forward to hear her better.

She locked eyes with him, then trailed her hand down her chest, down her stomach, until it settled between her legs.

"Would you like me to give you something to watch?" she asked.

"Yes. Fuck—yes," Lord Astrea panted.

She dipped a finger between her slick folds, then added a second. Then a third. Lord Astrea's breath grew even more ragged, and his hand pumped faster and faster. She spread her legs further to give him a better view, and he canted forward, burying his face in her sex.

Carra bucked against his mouth, and he lapped at her greedily, his tongue flicking her clitoris at lightning speed. He nuzzled her cunt, breathing deeply, and she spasmed in response.

"You smell..." he breathed.

And then his tongue was on her again, warmer, hotter, the magic building on the motion to create a level of pleasure she could hardly bear.

He moaned into her, then sucked her clit into his mouth. Her body coiled, growing more and more taut, until finally her orgasm took hold of her, ripping its way through her body as she rocked her hips against Lord Astrea's face. Harder and faster until he moaned into her again, long and loud, and she felt his body jerking against her as his own orgasm consumed him.

He remained knelt between her legs for long moments with his head on her thigh, until his breathing slowed. He avoided eye contact with her while he stood and tugged his clothing back into place

"Thank you," he said stiffly.

"Mmm. Thank *you*," she responded. She remembered this, now: the moment when he forced himself to become who he was outside these doors: a lord who would never subjugate himself to such baseless desires.

He'd been the one to seek her out, that first time and every time after. And over the months (or was it years?) she had known him, he'd slowly grown more comfortable, less ashamed as they parted way.

"Thank you, Lord Astrea," she repeated. "This was exactly what I needed."

"I will see myself out."

As he turned away, she caught the ghost of a smile on his lips. He slipped three gold coins onto the table beside the door and murmured a handful of *you're welcome*s as he left, closing out the verbal contracts they had created over the course of their meeting.

She gathered the coins on her way out. Most of her clients paid everything they owed directly into her bank account—and he had paid for this session ahead of time with the perfume—but Lord Astrea always left a little something extra for her: gold, or crystals or, once, she remembered fondly, a gorgeous chicken she had taken home with her.

She wondered at the fate of the chicken: was it being cared for in her absence? Had it been eaten or become a part of the family?

Carra looked out the window into the darkness beyond, willing herself to recall memories that simply would not come.

CHAPTER ELEVEN

Kexxia was well and truly missing. She had left for her sister's home, and then there was no trace of her. No correspondence with her family or friends that hinted at a change in plans. No sign of a struggle in her home or on the route she would have taken to reach her sister's home two towns over. Straid had joined Corlan on a search early this morning, and it had proven utterly fruitless.

Corlan would not talk about his fears, but his willingness to extend the search well beyond dawn was an indication of how determined he was to find Kexxia. Corlan detested sunlight and typically did everything in his power to avoid it. And it had all been for nothing; Kexxia had vanished and left no clues as to where she had gone.

Corlan had declined Straid's invitation for breakfast, returning home instead—one of the very few who would dare. For once, Straid wished his dearest friend felt the same desire to cater to Straid's every whim that other fae exhibited; he worried over his friend and wanted him close. But Straid returned home alone—and was glad he had.

The kitchen was in disarray when he arrived, with flour and fruits strewn about the counters. It looked similar to how it did when he attempted to bake, something he had not done in a very long time—for good reason. But he had expected better from the staff he had hired. There was no reason for the kitchen to ever be in this state, let alone before breakfast.

"Apologies for the state of the kitchen, my lord." Brey dipped into a brief curtsy before pouring a large number of egg yolks from one bowl to another. "Elesina has yet to arrive. She typically handles the cleaning in the mornings while I prepare breakfast."

"What time did you expect her?" He ran a finger through the thick dusting of flour on the nearest countertop.

"Almost two hours ago, my lord." Brey dipped her head in deference to Straid but continued her work, frantically mixing the contents of a bowl with one hand while flipping the pages of a cookbook with the other. "She also helps with some basic preparations. I will do my best to ensure that breakfast is served on time."

"Where is she?" Straid leaned against the counter and crossed his arms in front of his chest. If Elesina had deemed it acceptable to arrive late to work for anything short of an emergency, there would be a problem.

"I don't know, my lord. I have not had time to check."

"Stop."

Brey fell still and looked at him with round, fear-filled eyes.

"My lord," Straid clarified. "Stop using that title."

"But you said you didn't want me to call you—I can't just—"

"That is an order, Brey. In this home I am Straid. Nothing more." Without thinking about it, he flexed his hand, and the air around it chilled. Brey eyed the counter uneasily as frost crept across it, inching toward her. She stumbled back.

"I understand. It will not happen again."

He shook his head and his hand alike, dispelling the cold. "You may resume your work. I will inquire into Elesina's absence."

"I implore you to be easy on her, my—" Brey's mouth

snapped closed. She took a deep breath, then spoke through gritted teeth. "She is grieving an unfathomable loss. I worried the position might be too soon, but she needs this job. Allow me to visit her tonight and see if I can't help her dull the pain enough to work. She is a hard worker, my lord, and one of the best chefs in all the Quarters, as you have tasted for yourself, your—"

"Straid." He growled the word, and Brey flinched.

"Straid," she repeated, her voice shaky.

He watched her from the doorway for long minutes while he considered. Finally, he spoke, sharing the pain he rarely revealed to others.

"I, too, have grieved."

Brey's shoulders sank; she clearly mistook his response as a reproach. But when his world had ended all those years ago, he had withdrawn entirely. There were weeks that had passed by in a blur, and days he had slept through entirely. The grief had consumed him, and nothing outside of it had mattered. The same grief that had led him to saving Anna—the only reason Elesina had been hired to work here in the first place.

"Three days. She may take three days to grieve. Do what you must to ensure that she is here on the fourth."

"Thank you, my—Straid." Desperation mixed with the relief in her voice as she worried over her friend's well-being. For a brief, guilty moment, he wondered if his own friends had been driven to such carelessness with their words in the wake of his own grief.

"You are welcome."

His chest flared warm at her words, and again at his: the closing of the contract she had initiated without second thought. He left her, wide-eyed at his response, and retreated to his study, suddenly restless.

He had no interest in a bond forged from grief, no interest in a contract with such sadness clinging to it. That it was a third party's grief did not matter; he could taste it on Brey's words and had felt the bitterness fade with his own. It was another burden he had been trying to outrun these past fifty years. He had lost his stomach for grief and no longer wanted any dealings tainted with it.

And though most would never admit to it, the fae world teemed with almost as much grief as that of the mortals.

He spent the next hour mired in it: making lists of Kexxia's acquaintances, of anywhere she might have gone. Corlan had compiled an extensive list of anyone who may have meant her harm, but the grievances ranged from mild to moderate, and there was nothing that suggested anyone wished her true harm.

"I wish I could remember anything that would help," Corlan had moaned that morning. "Anything at all. I feel like I'm failing her."

"You might not have known," Straid had reasoned. "Kexxia kept many secrets."

"Not from me. She must have said *something*. I just need to remember."

Now, as he poured over the list, the memory tugged at the back of Straid's mind. One word in particular caught and held firm.

Remember. Memories buried that might hold the key to the answers they sought.

Moments later he found himself pounding on Anna's door.

She opened it blearily, her dark curls mussed with sleep. "What time is it?"

"Morning." He did not know, or care, beyond that. "What do you remember of the night we met?"

"You mean of you fighting the guard?" she asked, her voice heavy and thick, and her brow furrowed in confusion.

"Before that," he insisted. "Why were you in the Quarters? Why were you hurt?"

Anna scowled. "I was here to meet with Lord Astrea. I don't remember anything after leaving his house a few hours before the guard found me. Why?"

"A friend disappeared three days prior. We have tried and failed to discover her whereabouts or anything that happened to her."

Anna's head jerked back, and her eyes were fierce when they met his, with an intensity that stole his breath. "You think it's related. You don't just want me to stay in the house because of general disappearances; you think my memory loss is directly related to all of that."

"Quite possibly, yes."

"You think that—what? She was kidnapped, and someone tried to kidnap me, too? Or kill me?"

Straid had expected her to react with fear, but there was no emotion behind her voice: no fear, or disbelief, or anger. Only a matter-of-fact question. Her reaction piqued his interest, even as a small grain of suspicion wound its way into his gut.

"Perhaps," he said. "People rarely go missing in the Quarters. Humans do not find themselves alone in forbidden areas with me nearby to rescue them. I do not believe in coincidence. The two must be connected. You must remember," he urged her. He recalled Corlan's comment the night of the wedding: *For all you know, it could have been a deliberate attempt to get close to you, and now you've brought her into your home.* He had dismissed his friend's worries. Now that he had gotten to know Anna, he certainly did not believe she had engineered this to grow close with him.

And yet, he could not entirely discount the possibility.

Anna laughed.

It wasn't derisive, or cruel, as he might have expected from a fae. No; her laughter was loud. Energetic. It echoed off the walls behind him, filling his home with a sound he had not heard in entirely too long. And yet, it wasn't mirthful, either. If he had to put a quality to it, he would say it was startled, perhaps.

Or nervous.

"So let me get this straight," Anna gasped between peals of laughter. "I know almost nothing about my life beyond my name and occupation—and I didn't even know those a few days ago. I'm forced to live among the fae for at least the next year. And now you're telling me there's an evil fae entity somewhere out there who tried to kill or kidnap me, and who has succeeded in killing or kidnapping an actual *fae*—maybe multiple. And, because I don't know anything about my own life, I have no way of knowing if mine was a random attack or if I was targeted for some reason. And without my memories of the night, I don't know what I did to escape, or if the person who attacked me is still out there."

Anna sobered, her face settling into a heavy, dazed expression.

"You have recalled your name." It was not the most important thing she had said. Yet his unease grew at the reminder that she used a false name with him while others were privy to her true one.

Her eyes met his, but that fire from earlier had extinguished. They were guarded now. Stony. "Yes."

"Tell me."

She shook her head.

Reflexively, his fingers curled. He breathed deep, tamping his magic down deep. He would not use it to threaten her.

Not yet.

Not unless it became necessary.

"You said you understood why I'm not ready to share it. I know so little about myself, I'd like to keep it to myself for a little longer. Especially since I don't know how you fit into all of this."

"I swore I would not hurt you."

"But you didn't swear that you hadn't already."

"I did not."

"Swear it?"

"I have sworn many things to you already, *Anna*." He emphasized the false name—the only name he had for her—and leaned close when he said it, until their faces were mere inches apart. "I have extended more than enough vows to convince you of my unwillingness to harm you. If you still do not trust in me—in the promises I have made and kept—then another vow will do nothing toward that end. You have pulled more vows from me these few days than most have in my lifetime." It rankled that she would not tell him, and for a moment, rage coursed through him at her defiance. No fae would exhibit the audacity she did, standing before him and demanding yet another vow, from one normally so disinclined to make them. He attempted to force the anger aside, but it lingered, simmering beneath his skin.

"Be careful, mortal." He did not recognize the furious calm in his own voice as he stepped back. "You ask much of those you do not know, and you forget your place in the process. Perhaps *you* should swear to *me* that you mean me no harm."

"I don't think I could harm you if I tried." Her voice was low, breathless, and Straid allowed himself one brief moment to savor the fear in it.

"She knows her limitations," Straid growled approvingly. "Now swear that you would never attempt to cause me harm."

Anna tipped her chin in defiance.

"And yet you ask the same from me. Me, whose vows are worth more than you could fathom, dear wife. No new contracts will exist between us in your favor until I believe you would not harm me if you could."

He made to leave, then paused, and turned back to the mortal woman who would be in his home for the next year. He sent a tendril of cold toward her and watched in satisfaction as it curled around her neck. He kept its touch gentle, so as not to harm her—he could not do so if he tried—but the threat was there all the same. Her eyes widened in alarm.

"Trust me, little one, your assertion was correct: you could not harm me if you tried."

CHAPTER TWELVE

Carra did her best to avoid Straid the next few days.

Their encounter had been a needed reminder that he wasn't human. That the rules were different in the Quarters. He held a power she could never hope to match, and she'd let herself forget that in her first few days here. No longer. She would treat him as the threat that he was, and she would remain on her guard until he proved himself otherwise.

They dined in silence, neither of them willing to be the first to speak, and he disappeared into his study immediately after. Occasionally the man who had conducted their wedding ceremony would stalk into the room behind Straid, but he never joined them for meals or acknowledged Carra's presence.

On the third morning, Carra bit into a scone and spluttered, coughing out a cloud of flour. Straid smiled while she gulped the sweet, honeyed drink that accompanied their breakfasts, but he said nothing.

She tried not to notice that his smile didn't reach his eyes. That even in his newfound disdain of her, a part of him clearly did not delight in her misfortune.

The next morning, she ate breakfast alone.

The table was already laid when she arrived, and she waited

five minutes before eating. He had been the one to decide when breakfast would begin each morning, and if he couldn't make it on time, she saw no reason to wait any longer.

Still, she lingered over her meal and listened for his footsteps in the hall. She couldn't help the pang of worry when she retreated to her room a full hour later with no sign of him. The fae stood on ceremony; even Straid, as relatively relaxed as he had been, held to the conventions that made fae society function. Meals taken at certain times, with formal dress, was one of those conventions. Even though he had told her she could dine in her nightclothes, he had never once appeared at the table in anything that could be considered casual. The closest he had come was the day he had prepared the suite for her—and even then, his clothes had been formal, just dirty.

She forced her worry aside and took the day to explore the house. Straid's tour on the first day had only included the main wing of the second floor and the necessary rooms on the first: the dining hall and the foyer. In the days since, she had explored the rest of the second floor on her own, though it mostly consisted of bedrooms, sitting rooms, and the like. Only one door had refused to open: what she assumed to be Straid's bedroom, tucked in a far corner of the house.

The third floor was largely unremarkable, and the dust lay thick enough up here that she decided not to linger. Once she determined what purpose a room served—salon, ballroom, study—she moved on to the next.

A portrait in the library halted her: a woman with flaming hair who looked both young and old—Carra's age and ancient beyond measure. Power radiated from her so strongly that Carra *felt* it through the portrait, and she wondered if there was some fae magic at play. The golden band threaded through her hair marked her as royalty—the fae queen, perhaps, or a princess.

As she examined the painting, holding her sleeve against her nose to protect against the dust that lay thick in the room, a hazy memory slowly appeared. Her mother had kept a portrait of an old human queen over the hearth, gifted to Carra's great-great-grandmother, who had harbored the royal family when other locals had rioted over her presence in the village.

She returned to her room to write the memory in her diary, then made her way down to the ground floor. She paused outside Straid's study but stopped herself from knocking. If he wanted to explain his absence at breakfast, he could seek her out to do so.

The first few rooms were mostly full of ancient furniture and decorations that were mostly not to her taste: heavy furniture, dark drapes hiding the windows, and wallpaper that seemed to soak up the shadows in the rooms. She gingerly sat on the edge of a settee, sinking deep into the cushion. She ran her hand along the black velvet, wondering what this home had looked like in its prime: had it bustled with children? Had there been parties long into the night? Who had used this room, and what conversations had taken place here?

She continued on, finding more rooms that were similar to one another and unremarkable as a whole.

The final room in this wing of the house, however, left her stunned. She could tell it was different from the moment she approached it. The other doors in the house were of uniform size and made of heavy, dark wood, but the large door at the end of the short hall was lighter, airier, with pieces of glass imbedded across its surface. Faint light shone through the shards, making it appear as though it glowed.

Carra turned the doorknob slowly, strangely nervous to see what lay beyond.

Hazy yellow light filtered through a domed glass ceiling, and dust motes swirled in the slanting beams of light. Ferns crowded the walkway that wound through the room, their tendrils a riotous shade of green clamoring for her attention. They seemed to reach for her, to beckon her nearer, and she followed willingly, drawn by some deep desire she could not name.

The room seemed to grow with each step she took, as though

her mere presence sustained it, *fed* it—just as being in the space nourished her. She inhaled deeply, the rich, loamy scent easing the tension from her body with each breath she took.

The class ceiling arched high above her head, and as she peered up at it, she could scarcely imagine how beautiful it must have been in its prime, before the glass had yellowed and grown thick with grime. Before the plants that crowded the shelves on the walls had withered and died.

The room must had been stunning before it had been discarded.

She lost herself in exploration, her worries forgotten as she drank in every inch of the space.

Piles of threadbare pillows dotted the ground, often paired with low tables made of finely carved wood—though many had seen better days. The wood of one table she bent to examine was worn, with speckles of rot and holes where some insect had burrowed through it.

A shallow channel wound its way across the floor of the room, disappearing at points between the thick tangles of ferns. She bent to inspect it and found it coated in a thick black layer of grime that suggested it had been a creek once. Though the water had long dried, she could almost hear its burbling as she walked along its edge.

Carra was so lost in the abandoned beauty of it all that she didn't hear the footsteps behind her.

"This was my favorite room, once."

She spun, then stumbled backward at Straid's nearness. He didn't reach out a hand to steady her, as he might have done her first few days here, but she accepted his quiet words as the offering of peace that they were.

"It's beautiful," she whispered.

"No. But it used to be, and it could be, once more, with a little care."

"Are you going to give it that care?" she asked, her heart beating fast in the hollow of her throat.

He held her gaze for long seconds, and the sadness in his eyes made her want to reach for him, to do what she could to ease it.

"No, I will not. However, you may, if you would like. There are tools beyond that door." Straid gestured toward the far corner of the room, to a small wooden door that was so well-hidden Carra hadn't noticed it as she explored.

"Why won't you do it, if it was your favorite room?"

"It has not been my favorite room in a very long time."

"Maybe it will be again, once it's restored. We could work on it together?" She held her breath, hoping he would accept her peace offering just as she had accepted his. Long seconds stretched between them, during which she fought the urge to prompt him; she feared that one wrong word would send him running.

Finally, so slowly she almost wondered at first if she imagined it, he nodded.

"Together," he murmured, a strange expression flitting across his face. There one moment and gone the next, but in that brief second, she had seen longing, and loss, but maybe also…hope?

"Together," she agreed. She turned her back to him, not ready to confront whatever she had seen, whatever he was so clearly trying to hide.

By the time she turned back, he was long gone.

Carra's stomach grumbled as she pushed a curl from her face. She stumbled as she stepped back from her work, and only then did she realize that the sky had darkened on the other side of the glass. No wonder she was so unsteady: it was dinnertime, and she hadn't eaten since breakfast. But she had cleared the dead plants from the shelves along one wall of the room, watered the ones that still somehow clung on to a scrap of life, and dusted every surface she had uncovered. Though there was still a long way to go, the area she's worked on already looked much better, and satisfaction tipped the corners of her mouth up into a smile.

Straid had left just after breakfast, and though they had agreed to restore the observatory together, she hadn't been able to help herself; she had slipped into the room moments after he walked through the front door and hadn't left the room since.

"Have you eaten?"

Straid leaned against the doorframe. He looked tired, and as she took a step toward him and brushed the dirt from the pants Niana had laid out for her that morning, she realized that his tiredness—exhaustion, more like—ran deeper than she'd initially thought. He looked wan, depleted, utterly devoid of his usual sparkle.

Not that she would ever call it sparkle to his face. She would choose a word more befitting him, such as charm, or…presence.

"Have you eaten?" Straid asked again, his brows drawing together as he watched her from the doorway.

"Not since breakfast."

"Come. Eat."

She followed him to the dining room and perched on the edge of her chair, cringing at the dust that clung to her, though Straid hardly seemed to notice.

"These clothes are too nice. I need outfits I can work in without ruining them," she said, examining the pants Niana had insisted she wear today. Carra had argued; they were *silk*, hardly appropriate for cleaning or working with dirt. She'd had to move carefully to ensure they didn't rip.

"I would hardly call that clothing nice," Straid said as he pushed a platter of savory pastries toward her. He watched as she chose two for herself, and only then did he add three to his own plate. Carra caught herself smiling at the ceremony of it: of him waiting to serve himself until she had food, even though he had held the dish in his own hands to give it to her. "However, I agree that you need proper clothing; the seams on those trousers are much too delicate for the work you do in the observatory." He frowned at her. "Do you have a preference of fabrics?"

"No; just something less delicate. I'd hate to ruin such beautiful silk."

"You could ruin every piece made by the designer's hands and he would consider himself lucky you had worn them. However, you will receive new shirts and trousers by the end of the week. I shall provide a number of new dresses as well; you have worn all the ones you own multiple times already."

"I can re-wear clothes, Straid. I only have five outfits back home; all my money went to food, or to supporting my family."

She froze with her hand halfway to her mouth. She'd applied the perfume that morning, but my midday it had worn off, washed away by sweat and dirt; it played no role in the surfacing of this knowledge. Maybe the simple passing of time would help restore her memory. She was scared to hope.

"You remembered."

She shook her head. "Not really, no. I just said it. I knew there were five outfits, but I can't picture them. And I can't—I don't remember my family, just that most of my money went to them. Which means they relied on me. They must think I abandoned them."

"Judging by your clientele, you likely earned enough in a month to keep them fed all year. Even a large family—siblings, parents, children"—he stumbled over the last word ever so slightly—"would have been provided for."

"My father." Her stomach clenched as she remembered tinctures and powders pressed into tablets. Medicine, for a sick man. "I can't see his face, but he needed the money. He wouldn't have accepted it if he knew where it came from."

"He would have faulted you—"

She finally met his gaze, drawn by the sharpness in his voice. She appreciated his anger; it made her feel cared for. Protected. But it was misplaced. Her father hadn't derided her job—she wasn't sure he even knew what she did for work. But she could hear her father's voice: *"Prostitution is the oldest occupation in the world. There's no shame in doing something as old as humanity itself."*

"I'm not sure he would have minded what I do for work. Maybe he would have felt differently about his daughter doing it, but he respected prostitutes. No," she said, taking a sip of the wine and savoring the ensuing warmth that spread through her, "It's the fae clientele he would have taken issue with."

"You care for him." Straid's voice was soft, almost tender, and it wrapped itself around her.

She smiled, happy to share this small moment with him. "I do. It's weird, loving someone you don't remember."

"Many have families they would rather forget; you are lucky, to love yours even after you have."

She opened her mouth to ask if he spoke from personal experience, but he continued before she could.

"I will send missives into town. I will ask about a missing woman and find the family that searches for her."

"It'll be easier if you know my name." She said it quietly, almost hoping he wouldn't hear. The thought of sharing her name terrified her, though she couldn't quite pinpoint why; he had saved her life and been understanding about her job. He had made her *vows*, given freely to set her at ease. And the tension of the past few days had eased slightly in the observatory, and further over dinner tonight. If any fae had earned the privilege of learning her name, it was him.

"Yes."

Her heart raced as she opened her mouth. Then closed it again. And then, finally, screwing her eyes shut tight, she forced the word past her lips.

"Carra."

"Carra." He said it quietly, almost reverently, and she nearly melted at the sound.

It was just his strange fae way of putting the inflection on the wrong part of the word, she told herself. His fae formality that somehow made things feel more intimate than they truly were.

But she couldn't lie to herself fully; she couldn't deny that her name on his lips had an effect on her. He said it the way a lover might. With no intention behind it, for no reason other than that he was fae, but her body didn't know the difference.

"I will find your family, Carra." He did not swear it, not with a binding word, but his words settled around her nonetheless, and she knew without a doubt that he would honor it if he could.

"I know you will." It was as close to *thank you* as she was willing to get, so soon after giving her his name, but he locked eyes with her across the table, and the look in his eyes seemed to say *you're welcome*.

CHAPTER THIRTEEN

Carra.

The name replayed in his mind as he lay in bed, a thin shaft of moonlight streaming through the gap between his curtains. It fit her: sharp and strong, but with a delicate fullness to round it out. The way it felt in his mouth…

He rolled over and closed his eyes against the haunting of her name.

There were more important matters to contemplate as he waited for sleep to claim him.

He had given Elesina three days. Three days to grieve, to find someone who could dull the pain enough for her to return to work. A very generous three days; an offer most employers would not have extended.

Today had been the fourth.

Rage had simmered beneath his skin at the sight of the flour coating the kitchen counters: an obvious indication that Elesina had not returned.

"I left her a note." Brey had trembled before him, her eyes downcast. "I told her, three days and then she had to return," Brey said, as he left the kitchen.

He paused. Turned to her. "A note. You did not speak to her directly?"

"She wasn't home. Or she didn't answer. Who could blame her, after losing so much of her family? But I made it clear, my lord. Three days."

He shot a blast of hot air her way and tightened a tendril of it around her, pinning her arms to her side. Her eyes widened as sweat beaded on her brow.

"The next time you use a title for me—that one or any other—you will no longer be welcome in my home. Am I understood?"

She nodded frantically, her mouth clamped shut.

"And the next time I ask you to do something, you will follow the instructions exactly. Elesina has been missing for four days. Had I known you had not spoken with her directly, I would have visited her myself. You better hope," he said, his voice dropping low, "that she is home and well."

Straid strode from the house, and only once the door had closed behind him did he release the air that bound her.

By the time he reached Elesina's home, he was certain he would not find her. Certain the home would be empty, with no trace of where she had gone. Certain that he had another name now to add to the list of the missing.

He wanted desperately to be wrong, but hope refused to take hold.

He stood on her doorstep, his hands thundering against the wood of her door so hard it threatened to splinter. After long minutes, he wrenched the door open and entered uninvited, cursing under his breath as he did so. To simply ignore a ward was a grave power he wished he did not possess, and one he had rarely used. Even now, when he feared she might be dead, when he did it only for her safety, it unsettled him deeply.

The house lay empty and utterly still, devoid of any signs of habitation in recent days: there were no embers in the hearth, no dishes in the sink. There was no fresh scent of perfume, no lingering energy from someone recently departed.

Elesina likely had not been home since he had seen her last.

He left the house as undisturbed as possible during his quick perusal and closed the door gently behind himself as he left. He asked the neighbors if they had any information on her whereabouts, but none had answers; none had seen her since the last day she had worked.

His suspicious had been right, then: Elesina, like Kexxia, had simply disappeared without a trace. Hers was another name to add to the list. Another piece to a puzzle that eluded him and was proving to be bigger than any of them had initially suspected.

The knowledge burdened him all afternoon. Even as he collected his wife for dinner, the weight of it consumed him.

And yet, all he could think of tonight was Carra, her name like a melody that enchanted him, a song that ensnared his very soul.

He dreamed of dancing that night.

Of Carra, in an exquisite ballgown that hugged her every curve and highlighted them: her hips, her breasts, the swell of her stomach. A dress crafted by his own hands, every stitch placed with care. In that dress she commanded the room, demanded that lesser beings, of which he was one, pay their respects.

He dreamed of slow, sensual dances with their bodies pressed together and giddy waltzes that took her away from him only to send her spinning back into his arms. One dance after another, all to that same song, her name threaded through every chord, every step, every stolen glance between them.

As the sun considered peeking above the horizon, the tune shifted. It grew softer, slower, almost hesitant. His partner changed, her curves shrinking, her hair lengthening. He clutched the new partner close, unwilling to look at her, to face the flood of emotions he knew would overwhelm him at the sight of her—

for he knew the feel of this body. He had worshipped it once, had planned to spend his life with the woman it belonged to.

In fifty years, he had not dreamed of her, not once, though he had been desperate to in the wake of her death. And yet, he kept his eyes closed, for fear that looking at her would wake him from the dream. For fear that it would bring the longing flooding back so strongly he would not be able to escape it again.

Somewhere in the back of his mind was a smaller, quieter fear, one he convinced himself was not there at all: that looking at her would cause that first song to fade from his mind entirely. And now that he had heard Carra's song, he was not willing to lose it, too.

So, with his eyes closed against the many truths he was scared to behold, he held Lyenna in his arms, their cheeks pressed together as he embraced his late love one final time.

He awoke with tears on his cheeks and no memory of the dreams that had put them there.

"Elesina." Straid strode into Corlan's house just as dawn burst into being. "My chef. Put her on the list."

"Your chef? I didn't know you had one."

"Two," Straid corrected. "I hired them after Carra came to me. The better of the two failed to appear for work this week."

Corlan ran a hand down his freckled face as Straid relayed the conversation with Brey and his subsequent trip to Elesina's home.

"She was grieving," Corlan said. "Are you sure she didn't go visit family or take some time for herself?"

"She would have informed somebody if that were the case."

"You didn't."

The quiet sadness in his friend's voice wrapped itself around Straid's chest, squeezing tight. "I locked myself away, but you knew where I was all along; my chef has vanished, seemingly without a trace."

Corlan sighed, then pulled a sheaf of paper toward himself. "I'll add her to the list. What was her name?"

"Elesina."

"What do you know about her?

Admittedly not much, though Straid divulged all of the information at his disposal. "We should return to her home together," he suggested. "Perhaps you will notice something that connects her disappearance more clearly with Kexxia's."

"I think it's time to ask—"

"My family is an absolute last resort."

"We've reached the point of the last resort," Corlan countered, his voice quiet. "I think we reached it a while ago, actually, when Kexxia—"

"Corlan." Straid's hand flexed at his side as the air rushed from the room. His friend's face went from golden to pale to bright red in the long seconds before Straid released his magical hold.

Corlan gasped, desperately drawing air into his lungs.

"We will not approach my family until I have deemed it necessary. The time may come soon, but we have not yet reached that point. Perhaps you forget what they did to me. How they treated me, after Lyenna."

Corlan's face clouded. He had been there, had watched as…

"You're right."

Straid couldn't hear the words over the roaring in his ears, but he watched them form on his friend's lips. Watched other words form as well, but he did not care to parse them.

Finally, the roaring subsided, though they sat in silence for long minutes more.

"I'm desperate, Straid." Corlan's voice warbled. "Kexxia is—I know she will likely never feel the same way, but I love her. It's like a piece of my heart is missing with her."

Straid stilled.

"You love her?" He had long suspected romance, or something akin to it, between Corlan and Kexxia. They were suited to each other. Both gave physical affection freely, and both hid behind joviality that almost, *almost,* concealed the pain that lay beneath. But in the nearly seven decades of their friendship, Straid had never known Corlan to speak of love, let alone to claim the phenomenon for himself.

"I love her," Corlan confirmed. "I have loved her for two years now, I think. She's oblivious, of course, and I would never expect her to love me back, so I don't see the point in telling her. But I do. I love her."

Love.

What last resort could there possibly be, if not desperation to save the one you loved?

"I will not involve my mother," he said slowly, his mouth twisting around the words. "Fell or Umber, take your pick."

"Umber?" Corlan raised a brow in disbelief.

"He owes me a favor."

"And you think he would allow this to be it?"

"It was no mere favor; Umber owes me a boon."

"Shit. A boon from Umber. And you'd cash it in for me?"

When Umber had shown up on his doorstep twenty years ago, Straid had almost turned him away. Of his four siblings, Umber was the one he had always liked the least—though young as Straid was, there was ample time for that to change. But the look on Umber's face had made Straid step aside and allow his brother into his home without putting up a fight. And he had been glad for it, too. Umber had needed something so monumental he had had to offer a boon in return: a favor of any size, without question, that Straid could collect on whenever he pleased.

He had meant to save it for something dire, something for which he had no better option than his brother's help.

"I can think of nothing better to use it on," he answered truthfully.

"I couldn't ask you to use Umber's boon on this. Not yet. I know what that means."

"I would not expect—"

"I don't care about what I would owe you! I don't care if I'm indebted to you a thousand times over! Not if it means bringing Kexxia home. But for you to lose a boon over Umber…no. I can't ask that of you."

"I would do so willingly."

Corlan shook his head. "Fell's the better option, anyway. Her skills are much better suited to finding Kexxia."

Straid dipped his head in agreement and relief. "Fell it is."

CHAPTER FOURTEEN

The following weeks passed quickly. Carra spent her days restoring the observatory, joined by Straid on the days he was home. He rarely talked, so she'd found there wasn't much difference whether he was there or not. She had come to enjoy the silence, either way.

Every morning Niana lay out her clothes, though Carra rarely needed help dressing; there was no place for corsets or fanciful ties in the dirty work of restoring an abandoned room. Niana, like Straid, seemed most comfortable in silence: her answers tended toward short and she never initiated conversation. Carra wondered if that was her natural inclination, or if it was a result of her training for her position as a lady's maid.

Every morning Carra asked Niana questions, only one or two each day: about the weather, about town, about the home. She was careful not to ask personal questions that might make Niana uncomfortable—about her or Straid, though those questions burned the brightest, begged the loudest to be asked.

"What happens to the clothes after I've worn them?" Carra asked one morning, fingering the edge of the shirt she had pulled over her head while Niana took inventory of her wardrobe. At first glance the shirt had looked the same as one she had worn two days before, but as it slid over her skin, she'd discovered the fabric was softer, and more textured than the other shirt had been.

"They go to good use," was Niana's only response.

Carra wondered what Straid's, and Niana's, definition of *good use* was. If it was anything like their definition of *casual*, it would differ wildly from her own. Even the clothes she wore with the express purpose of sweating and mucking around in the dirt were nice by her standards. They were certainly nicer than the clothes she'd been wearing the night she met Straid—and she'd met with a *lord* in those clothes; she had to assume they were some of her best.

She had fallen into an easy rhythm these weeks. After being awoken by Niana, Carra would dress, then breakfast with Straid. If he were home for the day, they would walk to the observatory together before parting ways at the door. They each had their own mission: Carra tended to the plants, while Straid focused on cleaning the large, domed glass roof and the glass walls that surrounded the room.

True to his word, he did the work himself, rather than hiring help, and she suspected that he enjoyed it, though it was clear he was not used to doing this kind of labor. She'd had to show him how to wipe the glass so he would not spread the grime on his second pass, and she taught him how to steady the ladder so it would not send him crashing to the floor.

She had been nervous the first time she'd corrected him, scared of how he and his fae pride would respond, but he had taken the direction surprisingly well—as he had every time since. Every time she offered up a critique, he listened and adjusted accordingly.

She gently pried a fern from the ground, teasing its roots from the soil and smiling in satisfaction as they slid free. Under her care, the walkway had slowly become more visible, and ferns now crowded the edges of the room. As she placed the newest fern, she'd unearthed in the wheelbarrow Straid had found in the garden shed, she wondered who had done this work before her—clearly not Straid. A gardener? A team of gardeners? Or had the previous owner of the house sunk their fingers into the earth the way she did now, the feel of soil under her nails centering her.

She wheeled the full barrow across the room, unloading the ferns directly into the holes she had prepared for them along the wall. She mounded dirt around the base of each one and doused the row with water, then lingered, her toes curled in the soil.

Straid worked nearby, cleaning the glass with a rag and a bowl of soapy water. She watched him, marveling at how normal, how *human*, the action made him seem. He wrung the rag and murky water cascaded from it to the bowl below.

"The water's too dirty; the glass won't get any cleaner unless you get fresh water."

He startled, then glanced at the bowl of water beside him as though he hadn't even noticed it was there.

Straid grabbed the bowl and disappeared, returning a few minutes later with fresh water—and a tray of savory pastries, which had become a staple in the household.

"Elesina has disappeared," he'd explained, linking her with the other names on his list. He'd offered to hire a replacement, but Carra had been adamantly opposed; it felt deeply wrong to even consider it. As though doing so would mean they'd given up on her.

"You have not eaten since breakfast." He placed the food on the nearest table, then watched her expectantly.

"It's not that late. And neither have you."

"Eat," he said, sinking onto a pillow. "I will join you."

"In a moment. I just need to..."

She tamped the earth around a fern then stood, brushing her hands on the front of her pants to remove the dirt.

As she turned to Straid, a plant on the nearby shelf caught her attention and she fiddled with it, tucking a long tendril back among the rest of its bushy orange foliage. Straid had ordered hundreds of different varieties of flowers, bushes, and trailing vines, and they'd been arriving over the past week. The shelf where she kept the ones she hadn't yet found a home for was crowded to the point of overflowing, yet new plants arrived every day, and her heart swelled at the sight of each and every one of them. With each passing day, the room grew more spectacular. More *magical*.

She turned another plant on the shelf until the white striations in the leaves caught the light at just the right angle, and only then did she drop onto the floor across from Straid and grab the nearest pastry, rolling her eyes at the indignant sound Straid made over her eating without washing her hands first.

"I've practically been breathing this dirt in all morning. A little more won't hurt me."

"You should take better care. Mortals are fragile."

His words carried an undercurrent of sadness, and she hesitated, worried about overstepping. But they had formed a fragile bond these past few weeks, something akin to a friendship, and she couldn't let him sit with his sadness alone.

"It sounds like you're speaking from experience."

"I have known mortals, yes. I have seen what happens when they get sick or injured. Illnesses my kind consider mild are enough to kill you. I do not want to lose—" he paused. "You are my responsibility. So yes, I do speak from experience."

"Do you—"

"I do not wish to speak of it, no." It was not a rebuke but a plea, his voice quiet and desperate. She longed to take his hand in hers, to hug him, to provide any measure of comfort against his devastation.

"If that ever changes," she said, her eyes on him though he'd looked away, "I'll be here."

He gave a single, tight nod in response.

• • •

"Where do you go when you leave?" Carra asked the next morning. She sat back on her heels, watching Straid clean the final stretch of the walls. Most of the ceiling was still caked in dust and grime, but they had yet to figure out the logistics of getting him high enough to clean it. Even so, with the walls mostly restored to transparency, the room was already much brighter than when she'd first stumbled into it.

He paused his scrubbing and turned to dip the brush in a bucket of steaming water. A streak of something yellow-brown ran across the sharp bridge of his nose. A loose black curl had escaped its binding, and he tucked it behind his ear with long, slender fingers that dripped muddy water. With the early morning light shining behind him, he looked ethereal, even in his dishevelment—the dirt only heightened his otherworldly beauty.

She wondered if he knew how un-coiffed he looked, and whether he would clean himself up immediately if he did. She decided not to say anything; she liked seeing him this way.

"I am helping a friend."

She waited for him to say more, but he let silence fall between them as he resumed his scrubbing. She watched him, ignoring her own task for the moment.

"A friend of his, Kexxia, is one of the missing. Her disappearance is what alerted us to this issue. She disappeared a week before your arrival."

"Have you found anything?"

"Not as of yet, no. Many details of the disappearance are strange. She, Elesina, and the others simply vanished. We continue to search, though so far it has proven to be in vain."

"Is there anything I can do to help?"

"Likely not. I would not expect a human to succeed where two fae have not." He said it blandly, as though he didn't mean offense, but Carra still bristled.

"What have you tried?"

"We have retraced their final days. We have talked to family members, friends, and neighbors. We have sent a missive to my sister, though her response is taking longer than I would have liked."

At that, Carra's head whipped up, but Straid shook his head, correctly interpreting her worry.

"She has not disappeared; my sister simply does things on her own time. There is nothing I can do to hurry her, urgent though the situation may be." His mouth twisted in a grimace.

"Have you talked to any influential people? Guards, or shop-keepers, or other lords? For example, off the top of my head... Lord Astrea? Or maybe not a lord; maybe you need someone who seems to have connections everywhere? Like, for example... Jax?"

"Jax." Straid's voice was flat, and his jaw tight. She could hear the disapproval in his voice.

A week before, they'd taken a walk through the Quarters, perfume heavy on Carra's wrists. Most of their walks revealed nothing, but that night, she had recognized a stately manor on the edge of town. She'd stopped outside its gate, sifting through the memories that had appeared: many visits, and a muscular fae with shaggy blond hair. She'd wanted to knock on the door, to meet the client who lived there and gain new memories at the sight of his face, but Straid had dragged her onward.

"You cannot simply show up at Jax's house uninvited. I cannot be seen there at all."

"Why?" she'd asked, reluctantly following him away from the home. Now that she knew the client's name and where he lived, she could return another day or send a letter asking him to come to her.

"He is a criminal, notorious for his depravity. He has his hands in every unsavory corner of the Quarters"

A shiver ran through her as they turned the corner. "Am I in danger with him?"

Straid halted, his furrowed brow casting shadows over those stark silver eyes. Her heart quickened under the intensity of his gaze. "Truthfully, I do not know."

Straid's unease had given her pause, and she'd resolved to learn—or remember—as much as she could about the other fae before reaching out. But if he really was as well-connected as Straid had said, he could be an asset to the search.

"If I were looking for someone who had gone missing, I think he'd be the first person I asked."

"He would never share his secrets so easily. Even if tortured, nothing could get answers out of Jax that he did not want to share."

Carra couldn't help it; she laughed. Over the past week she had remembered bits and pieces: eyes full of desperation; a broad, muscular chest beneath her hands; someone watching as he had slid inside her. And conversations. She remembered drifting off as his words flowed over her, a torrent of confessions she had sworn to keep.

"Why are you laughing?"

She wiped sweat from her brow, then grimaced as she caught sight of the dirt on her hand. But when she looked back up Straid, he didn't seem to register it.

"Jax is many things, but tight-lipped is not one of them."

"He would not have sustained his *business* for so long if that were the case; secrets are the cornerstone of all that he is."

"He would tell me anything I wanted to know," she countered.

"You are mistaken to think so."

"I don't think so; I *know* so."

"What magic do you presume to have over him?" Straid asked, still disbelieving.

"These." She pressed her arms together, pushing her breasts up between them. Even in this shirt, with its modest neckline, the effect was spectacular. She watched as his eyes dipped to her chest, to the delicate chain that disappeared into her bosom, then lingered there for a beat longer than was strictly necessary. When he made eye contact again, she could swear his pupils were dilated. He blinked, and his brow smoothed.

And then, ever so slowly, he smiled. It was barely there, a ghost of a thing, but she grinned back regardless.

"You truly believe you could convince him to share anything he might know?"

"Definitely. And not just him; I'll ask everyone." She had been compiling a list of her own. Every night, she wrote down any detail she could remember about her clients. Names, faces, snippets of conversations. The work was slow, and arduous, but she had four names now, and had met with three: Lord Astrea, Retyiao, and Gureig. So far, Lord Astrea was the only client who had resumed their appointments, but Gureig was schedule to come the following week.

"This matter—"

"Is delicate, I'm sure," she cut in. "If people are going missing, you probably don't know who you can trust. I'm good at delicate."

"Mortal standards of delicacy do not align with fae standards of delicacy."

"And I can meet the fae standards. Easily. Try me."

Straid watched her for long moments before dipping his head slightly. "Name your clients."

"Too easy. I *can't* name the ones you haven't met yet, so it's not a challenge not to. And your question is too direct. If you want to test me, then *test me*."

"For a true test, the answers must be hidden within conversation."

"Then talk to me. Surely you know how to have a simple conversation with your own wife." She softened her eyes and smiled slowly. It was a look she typically reserved for her clients, but Straid reacted just as they might: his pupils flared, and his gaze dropped to her lips. When he spoke, the words were rough.

"Tell me what you remember of your life."

"Only if you'll also tell me about yours." She softened her voice, made it just the tiniest bit husky, and preened as he swallowed thickly before turning away.

They traded questions and barbs alike as they worked side by side: Carra arranging pots along the shelves and planting flowers between the ferns, and Straid cleaning the windows and the walkways.

"Tell me of the necklace you wear," Straid prompted as he swept dirt from the path she knelt beside.

Her hand rose to the pendant that hadn't left her body since she'd arrived in the Quarters. "I don't remember anything about it, even with the perfume's help. It feels important, like it was a gift from someone I loved. But that's just speculation; I don't know why it matters so much to me. Do you have any jewelry that's important to you?"

She'd seen him wear rings and earrings, but he seemed to switch them out without any apparent preference for one or another.

"None that I care to wear; there are family heirlooms I would rather not claim. And a ring that..." he said the last portion so quietly she almost missed it. The sadness was back on his brow, and she knew that if she pushed, she would lose him.

"You're not close with your family, then?"

"No. We should eat."

With clean hands and a plate of fruit and pastries before her, Carra resumed her questioning. "Why do you love this room so much?"

"My mother used to throw parties here when I was very young. I was not strictly allowed, but I would sneak in and marvel at the gowns and tailored jackets her guests wore. As the night wore on, I would find a corner, tucked out of sight, and fall asleep staring at the stars."

"What happened to this place, if it was once so loved?"

"On our first walk in the gardens, you said that nature reclaims everything. You asked if I had lost someone." He fiddled with the pastry in his hand, his perfect mouth puckering into a frown. "In my grief, I allowed nature to reclaim this room. I am glad you prompted me to restore it. Shall we continue?"

The conversation turned to lighter matters, and Carra found herself laughing a handful of times. Though Straid never joined in, his face was practically an array of emotion—by his standards, anyway. He had frowned, and glowered, and that ghost of a smile had even made an appearance more than once. Halfway through the day, Carra realized he was enjoying it every bit as much as she was, and she found herself hoping they would have more days like this: the teasing and lighthearted sparring, rather than the silence that had slowly built between them before.

"And that was with you knowing what I was doing," she crowed over dinner, her hand darting out to grab the last of a succulent green vegetable she didn't know the name of. Straid paused with his hand in the air and watched as she gleefully sucked the innards from the reedy exterior.

"I will admit you did very well," he said slowly. "However, I still worry."

"They won't know what hit them," she said with a grin.

"It is not your approach that worries me; I fear many of them will be unwilling to speak about such matters under my roof, and I would not have you walk the Quarters alone, even where permitted, due to recent events."

"They won't care. They know about you, and it hasn't stopped any of them. Well, except for Retyiao. That was more about my memory loss than about you, though." She frowned. He had been one of her most loyal clients—and the only one who'd refused to keep seeing her; the others had all been eager to resume their regular sessions.

"I expected more of your clients to refuse to see you under my roof, and I expect that most will be less forthcoming here. My presence often makes others uneasy."

"Why is that?" she asked.

"There are many reasons."

It was as enigmatic a response as ever. She had grown used to the openness he'd displayed today, but a part of her found his returned reticence comforting. It had become familiar in the short time they had known each other.

"Your powers?"

He stilled, his eyes dropping to her throat. Her own hand rose to trace the spot where he had wrapped his power around it.

"Carra," he said, his voice strangled.

"I get it," she whispered back. She cleared her throat. "Just don't do it again."

He nodded tightly.

"How old are you? You must be ancient, to have powers like that."

"Lesson number one of dealing with the fae: never ask a fae their age." His voice was low, deadly, such a quick shift that she couldn't help but shiver. She pushed aside the current of fear running through her and forced another question between her lips to give her mouth something to do other than beg forgiveness for the slight.

"How powerful are you, then?"

"Very."

This time the danger in his voice was richer. Deeper. And it touched a part of her that danger rarely did.

Carra forced herself to chew normally, to swallow her food, even as warmth flooded between her legs from the sudden, deep longing that wrapped itself around her core.

"Well, so am I," she said, forcing her voice to be light. "In a different way, maybe. But I'd bet I'm just as powerful as you."

Her chest grew tight, like a thread was being pulled from it, and she immediately regretted her words. He had gotten her flustered and she had made one of the biggest blunders of her life: betting a fae.

"I do not accept the wager," Straid said, standing from the

table and looking down at her with stormy eyes. "You did so well today—until this moment. Be glad I decided I would accept no more contracts between the two of us. Be glad I spoke that decision out loud. Because that is a wager you would lose, little one, and due to the nature of the bargain, your punishment would not be gentle."

CHAPTER FIFTEEN

"You should really let me prepare the rooms for you to meet with your clients," Niana chided as she dabbed makeup on Carra's face. She'd been freer with her words these past weeks, as though Straid's openness had paved the way for her own.

"No. Each of them wants something slightly different, and it's easier for me to do it than to explain it all to you. Besides, it helps me get into the right mindset. I like doing it." They'd had this conversation every time she met with a client—the first time Lord Astrea visited, Jax's first and second visits, Lord Astrea's second appointment, and Gureig's first, and so far only, one.

"It's improper."

"Is it the cleaning you have an issue with, or the prostitution?" She met Niana's gaze with an arched brow. She'd chosen her words intentionally; people could hide their true feelings if she offered a euphemism. But prostitution, direct and to the point, left nothing for them to hide behind.

"The cleaning," Niana said firmly, her eyes steady on Carra. "Men—whether fae or human—will look at you and want you and give you attention regardless. You may as well make it be on your own terms and charge them for the privilege. But cleaning is *my* job; you should not be doing it yourself."

"I'm not going to change my mind about this. For their sake and for mine, I need to be the one who prepares the rooms. That's non-negotiable."

She regretted her stance the moment she stepped into the room. Something was off about it, but she couldn't quite put her finger on what. She set to work, laying out the pillows just how she wanted them, and had just drawn the curtains when it struck her: the room was larger than it had been before. Not by much. The difference was small enough that it had taken her almost half an hour to pinpoint what was wrong, but it unsettled her nonetheless.

"It's just some fae trick," she muttered, giving the room one last look before backing out quickly. But the unease followed her down the hall to Straid's study, where she knocked for long enough it became clear he wasn't there.

It was fine, she told herself. It didn't matter that the room had changed; she would just—

She shuddered. She couldn't face the room. At the very least, she would be too distracted, too uneasy, to perform the way she needed to. She would pick another room for today, then. Make up some excuse, if Jax asked.

By the time Jax arrived she had prepared a parlor a few doors down from her own room. She'd chosen the room that needed the least amount of work, but it still left her with only a few minutes until his arrival.

She waited for him in the foyer, and he smiled widely as she opened the door to him.

When she had finally written him a letter he'd responded instantly, arriving within the hour to meet with Straid. Based on Straid's commentary she had expected tension, perhaps even a fight, but Jax had sat silently and agreed to every one of Straid's rules. Pleasant and polite, he had shaken Straid's hand on the way out and kissed Carra's cheek.

The few memories that had surfaced as she'd spoken with Straid had given her some idea of what to expect, but the perfume on her wrist at that meeting filled in much-needed gaps. The audience she'd remembered was something he requested often—and paid handsomely enough for that Carra readily agreed most times.

More importantly for the sake of their meetings, she remembered that his enthusiasm did not translate into ability, and she had stocked the wardrobe with a lubricating oil in anticipation of their appointments.

What she had initially assumed to be confidence when he met Straid proved to be well-leashed disquiet, and he'd shown obvious relief at Straid's absence since. He'd grown less skittish with each visit to the house, but she could still see traces of anxiety tightening his lips and eyes.

"We're not going to your rooms?" he asked, as she paused outside the parlor door. She shivered. "What's wrong?"

"Nothing," she purred, throwing him a sultry glance over her shoulder. "I'm just thinking about what you're going to do to me. I thought it would be fun to use a different room today."

Jax pressed himself against her, hard and firm at her back. She moaned, pitched just the way he liked it, and he ground his erection against her. "And it'll be private, still?"

She almost didn't hear the slight disappointment in his voice; if she hadn't known any better, she might have thought he was seeking reassuring that Straid would not find them. She pretended to misunderstand.

"Everyone knows not to disturb us." Carra spun, letting her hips drag across his erection, and stood on her toes to brush her lips softly against his ear. "What are you going to do, now that you have me all alone?"

He gripped the back of her neck and drew her in, sliding his tongue across her bottom lip. "First, your mouth is going to work its magic on me. And once I am thoroughly satisfied, I will return the favor. I will drive you wild as I always do and make you beg for more."

Carra bit her lip and peered up at him from lowered lashes, her face betraying none of the thoughts that ran through her mind. She typically didn't expect the experiences with her clients to be particularly pleasurable—it was work, after all, with a clear focus on *their* needs—but Jax had never brought her anywhere close to orgasm. Not like some of her clients. Not like Lord Astrea, whose whole focus was often on that one goal—and who always achieved it, often more than once.

"The way you bite your lip drives me wild," Jax said, tripping into the room after her as she tugged on the waistband of his pants. She had begun playing a game with herself the first time he'd come to the house: she kept a running tally of the number of times he mentioned either of them driving the other wild. If he said it more than ten times during a single session, she could buy herself a new set of lingerie, for her own personal use.

Her collection was already at two, and she had a feeling the streak would not be broken today.

She dropped to her knees and took her time unlacing the front of his pants. He bucked with every motion of her hands and by the time she drew the fabric down his thighs he was throbbing, the tip of his cock glistening and pointing straight toward her.

Slowly, she leaned forward and licked the moisture from it, and Jax spasmed in response.

"Fuck," he groaned. And then he repeated it when she drew him into her mouth, pressing her tongue against the vein that ran along the underside of his cock as she took him farther and farther into her mouth.

She barely had time to cup him in the way he liked before he jerked his hips and spurted his seed down her throat.

When he'd fully spent himself, she drew back and licked her

lips. "How was that?" she asked, peering up at him through her lashes.

"Amazing. Your mouth drives me wild."

She attempted to rise but he shook his head, gesturing for her to lay back on the floor. His hands found her thighs the moment her back hit the plush carpet, and he made short work of pushing her dress around her waist and drawing her white lace panties down her legs.

Jax slid a finger inside her, groaning at the feeling. "The way your body prepares so thoroughly for me drives me wild."

That's four, Carra tallied. "It's all for you," she murmured as huskily as she could. "Look at what you do to me."

Him and the lubrication she had replenished on her last trip to town, at least—Jax had never managed to inspire quite enough of that response in her.

A second finger joined the first and he pumped them hard and fast.

"Come undone for me, beautiful," he growled, and seconds later she clenched her thighs together, letting out a breathy moan. Jax withdrew his fingers almost immediately—too soon even if the orgasm had been real— and lay beside her, part of his face disappearing as it sank into the carpet.

"How do you want me to take you today? What would drive you wild?" He traced a hand down her arm, sweet and gentle.

A part of her felt bad for him, that he so clearly wanted to bring her pleasure but did not understand how. But he wasn't paying for her pleasure; he was paying for his own, and for the illusion of competency. She could give him that. "Here, on the floor."

Jax stilled at her words, at her decisive tone. It was one she didn't usually take with him, but the carpet felt nice against her skin, and he loved to take her from behind. She sat up and quickly pulled her dress over her head, leaving her completely bare before him.

She dropped onto her hands and knees, facing away from

him, then turned to look at Jax over her shoulder. "Take me from behind. Show me how much you want me. Let me drive you wild."

His eyes fluttered shut at her usage of his signature phrase.

"Take me, Jax. Fuck me while I'm on my knees for you."

Seconds later he pressed his broad thighs pressed hers, his cock at her entrance. His hands gripped her hips, hard, and she found herself wondering if they would bruise. She wouldn't mind. When he did leave them, they never truly hurt. She had outlined, up front, exactly where the limits lay, and he honored them every time—if he'd crossed the line even once, she would have dropped him as a client.

Jax slid into her, and she rocked against him, drawing him deeper.

"Fuck, you know that drives me wild," he said, slamming his hips forward to fully sheath his cock in her in one swift move. "Keep fucking me just like that."

Carra drew forward and gasped as his cock almost slipped out of her, then rocked back toward him, moaning as he slid back in. She repeated the motion a few times, until Jax gripped her hips tighter and took over, pistoning his hips to take her hard and fast.

This was always the way it went: quick fellatio followed by a lackluster attempt from him to reciprocate—but only ever with his fingers—and then a marathon session of his cock in her cunt. Once the first orgasm was out of the way, Jax could last for hours.

Jax drew her backward, pulling her upright until she was flush against his chest, and the angle, combined with his thickness, was almost enough to give her real pleasure. She dropped a hand between her legs, her fingers finding that sensitive spot that Jax always ignored. Slowly at first, she circled the nub, but that only served to drive her frustration higher. When Jax sped his pace, so did she, moving her fingers directly to her clit and rubbing hard and fast.

Jax whispered something against her ear, but between the friction and his heavy breathing and the moans she was making for his benefit, she couldn't quite what he said. He nipped her ear, and she gave him another moan in response.

"Fuck. Fuck!" he groaned, release her so she dropped back to the ground, both her hands planted firmly on the carpet. He gripped the front of her hips, so close to where she needed his fingers, and she hummed in frustration.

"Touch yourself again," he commanded. And she did.

Her eyes closed as she provided herself with the pleasure she so deeply sought, while Jax sought his own within her. She didn't know how long they stayed like that, fucking in a frenzy on the floor of the parlor, while she chased a release she wouldn't find until after he had left.

A creaking sound caught her attention, and she glanced up through half-lidded eyes.

Straid stood in the doorway in front of her, a halo of light surrounding him.

She could barely make out his face in the shadows—save for his eyes, shining silver in the darkness.

Eyes that were locked on her.

His gaze sent heat pooling between her legs, and she panted, her fingers speeding up almost of their own accord.

Behind her, Jax moved faster, harder, almost desperately, and Carra knew that he had noticed Straid in the open doorway, as well. Not just that he'd noticed; that he *enjoyed* it, as he always did the rare times they had an audience. She could feel his excitement: his cock swelled inside her and his motions grew more erratic as he swiftly approached his climax, much quicker than usual.

She had never minded an audience, but it had never felt like *this*, like it was the piece she had been missing. With Straid's eyes locked on her she felt...exposed. Wanton. Delirious with need.

Seconds later her desire came to a head, and a powerful

orgasm ripped through her body. She cried out as wave after wave of pleasure tore through her. This was the first time she'd ever orgasmed with Jax, and she knew the man inside her had nothing to do with it; it was Straid, with his clenched jaw and his burning eyes locked on her, who had sent her over the edge. Straid whose silent attention drove her to waves of pleasure beyond any she'd experienced before.

Her eyes fell shut as she rode out her release.

When she opened them again, Straid was gone, the door swinging shut behind him.

Behind her, Jax let out a deep, guttural groan, pumping into her hard and fast, then holding her tight against him he shuddered one last time, fully spent.

CHAPTER SIXTEEN

"I regret my earlier actions," Straid said stiffly at dinner that night. He bit back the apology on his tongue, though a large part of him wanted to owe her. A dark part of him wanted her to demand her recompense in the form of something akin to what he'd walked into, but he knew better than to hope for that. "I did not realize you would be in there."

"I thought you were out. You usually don't come back much before dinner."

"I was out. I came home early. It will not happen again."

"It's your home," she countered with a shrug. "You can come whenever you'd like. Come home. You can come home whenever you'd like." She took a bite of her food and smoothed her features, but he caught the hint of a blush on her cheeks and knew that it would feature into his fantasies later that night, against his better judgment.

"I meant to leave, but shock stilled my feet." He did not know why he was confessing this to her, though it was only half of the truth. He had been shocked, yes, but seeing Carra like that, seeing the body he had dreamed of bared before him, had stirred the desire he had been so desperately attempting to keep at bay. He had not meant to stay, it was true, but neither had he wanted to leave.

He could not stop thinking of it.

The sounds she had made. The look on her face.

She was a professional, he reasoned. Damned good at her job, if her client list was any indication. And yet even knowing that, it had sounded so real, had *looked* so real. And with her eyes locked on his…

He cleared his throat. "I regret to cut this dinner short, but my work is waiting for me. Sleep well, Carra. I will see you in the morning."

He swept from the room, uncaring of his rudeness. He could not look at her for another second, not with that image still so fresh in his mind. Not with the resulting desire burning underneath his skin.

The second the door of his study fell shut behind him, he freed his hard length from his breeches. He gripped the tautness at his base, squeezing as he rocked into his hand, gasping and moaning as if this fantasy were real, as if Carra were here in the room with him.

Like a man possessed, he stroked himself hard and fast, imagining it was Carra's hands touching him, imagining her lips on him; that look on her face, her sounds filling the room.

The pressure in his cock mounted painfully, but he could find no release. He only grew painfully stiffer as he imagined dropping to his knees and worshiping her with his tongue.

If he had his way, he would trace her collarbone with one finger, trailing it down her body slowly to feel her every curve. The other hand, he would slide between her legs. Find that bundle of nerves nestled between her thighs and circle it with his thumb. He would pull pleasure from her like she'd never felt before and only then would he sink himself into her.

He gasped, then bit his lip to keep from crying out as his pleasure mounted higher and higher, but still, he could not find release. He bucked, then swayed, falling to the floor. But he was desperate, so close, and he thrust into the air, into his hand, unable to stop the frustrated cries that fell from his mouth.

Long minutes later, exhausted and sweaty and no closer to finding release, his head fell back against the ground and his hand dropped listlessly beside him.

He was spent, in every way but the one that mattered. His breath came in ragged bursts, his throat raw from groaning. He needed to shower, to collapse into his bed, but he could not summon the energy.

He longed to call her into the room, to take her as Jax had. He had no doubt he would find his release buried within her.

But he had promised her, and himself, that he expected nothing from her. It was a vow he would have held to even if not bound by fae rules; he wanted her, desperately, but he knew that he could never have her, that he would never cross that line.

He fell asleep on the floor of his study, his mind on the woman across the hall who held more power over him than anyone ever had.

He arranged his features to be perfectly blank the next morning as they walked down to breakfast together and silenced the treacherous parts of him that replayed that moment in the parlor.

This day was just like any other, he told himself. Nothing had changed. He was imagining the heat in her eyes during their morning meal and the way her eyes lingered on his longer than usual at dinner. That moment had not affected her as it had him. It could not have.

Two interminably long days later, at the end of a long day spent trying to make sense of the notes and diagrams he and Corlan had compiled, he found a note under his door.

Jax tonight. We'll be in the library at 8:00.

He clenched his jaw as his cock sprung to attention at the mere thought of the coupling. The room was rarely used: he couldn't remember the last time he had been in there. He did not know why she had abandoned the suite he had prepared for her, but she clearly had done her best to choose a room he would not stumble into today.

He found his eyes drifting to the clock all evening, and his cock stiffened as the hands inched ever closer to the specified time.

At 8:00 he fought the battle against his control and slid his trousers off, fisting his cock and stroking it hard.

He imagined the soft flesh of her thighs against his own, driving him into his leather chair. A low, guttural sound spilled from him, one he'd never made before, and he pumped harder, wishing Carra could see what she did to him. Wishing he could bring her as much pleasure as just the thought of her brought him.

He groaned, his cock throbbing as he gripped it harder, chasing his pleasure until his energy was depleted and he slumped over his desk, cock still so hard it pained him.

CHAPTER SEVENTEEN

*H*e hadn't come.

She had hoped against hope that he would be there—and she knew Jax had hoped for an audience, as well, though in his case, any audience (as long as they were discreet) would do. Though a part of her had known Straid wouldn't come, the possibility of it hanging over them had made tonight one of the best sessions she'd ever had with Jax—for both of them. Jax felt that way about any audience.

She specifically wanted Straid.

Carra bathed quickly, then donned her favorite set of lingerie: hand-spun silk the same silver as Straid's eyes.

She dimmed the lights until she could barely see anything in the room, then lay back on her bed. She trailed her hands along her body, pretending they were Straid's instead of her own. She'd known he was attractive, of course, and her thoughts had drifted to him before, on occasion. But these past three nights he had consumed her fantasies, and she gasped his name as her fingers slid beneath the lace across her hips, wishing she had his company.

The next morning, Carra ate breakfast alone. Straid had left a note that he would be out, but she still found herself looking up at every sound, hoping it would be him. Even now, as she knelt in the dirt along the far wall of the observatory, pruning the plants she had lovingly installed earlier in the week, she listened for signs that he might finally be coming to talk to her. She didn't know what she would say to him, only that the silence growing between them—again—was killing her. She needed to speak to him, to acknowledge what had happened. To apologize for sliding the note beneath his door. Clearly, it had crossed a line and made him uncomfortable.

He had said, from the beginning, that he wouldn't fuck her. He'd used more delicate words, of course: words befitting a fae lord. She scoffed at herself. She had married a fae lord who had promised he would never sleep with her, and now she was disappointed to find that honor actually meant something to him.

She laughed aloud at her own foolishness.

"What are you so amused by?"

She hadn't heard him enter, and she fumbled the plant in her hand, cursing when she discovered that she had accidentally snapped off one of the tiny emerald-green leaves she had meant to preserve. Its soft scent wafted to her nose: delicate, almost floral. Somehow it *smelled* green, the scent an embodiment of the color itself. She pinched the stem at its base to ensure the plant would waste no vital resources thanks to her careless mistake.

"The fact that, of all the men in my life, it's the one I'm *not* sleeping with that I seem to find myself in an awkward situation with." She brushed a wayward curl from her face and stood to face him.

"Awkward?"

"Oh, come on. You feel it, too. Ever since you walked in the other night—"

"I should apologize for that." His voice was low, and his eyes were steady on hers, his brow furrowed—it seemed he genuinely felt bad about it. But still, he'd phrased it in a way that avoided an actual apology, a trick of the fae.

She supposed she shouldn't be upset about it, not while she was playing the same game with him. Not when he had made it clear he would not incur any more debts to her.

And yet, heat flooded between her legs, and disappointment warmed her cheeks.

She shrugged. "Oh, there's no need. Jax was thrilled; he tipped *very* well," she said with a wicked grin, hoping that her face would project the confidence she didn't feel.

"And you?"

Carra shrugged again, though this time there was no accompanying smile, no hint of flirtation. "That night isn't what I wanted to focus on. I wanted to apologize for the note I left you." *Wanted* to apologize; just like his *should*, it was a careful avoidance of a fae bargain.

"Why would you apologize for that?" He seemed genuinely confused, and the realization made her falter.

"Because it clearly made you uncomfortable?" She hadn't meant to make the words a question, but she pushed on. "You said from the beginning that you wouldn't sleep with me. You made that explicitly clear. I should have kept that in mind and refrained from inviting you."

"Inviting me…" Straid stilled.

Then, slowly, ever so slowly, he stalked toward her.

"That was an invitation?" His voice had gone deadly quiet, and low.

So, so low.

"What else would it have been?" Her voice came out breathy, but she held his gaze even as his nearness sent shivers through her.

"A warning to stay away." His voice was tight, his face completely blank, and she yearned for some indication of how he felt. If he burned as she did. She closed her eyes, willing herself to be brave.

"No. I—we—*I* wanted you to know where we were. Jax has always loved an audience, and I…"

"You…"

"I had never explored the side of myself that clearly feels the same way. I'd never even considered it, really. We've had audiences before, but it never felt like…that."

"Like what?"

Carra drew in a deep breath to steady herself. "Like my body was on fire, under your gaze. Like you were the piece I was missing to find my release. It—it was a charged moment. But that's all it was, and I should not have sent that invitation afterward."

"I was not aware it was an invitation."

Her eyes flew open at the tightness in his voice. He sounded…like he was losing his grip on the tightly controlled restraint that seemed to govern him. He sounded like he would have come if he had known.

His eyes darkened, growing stormy and so intense she feared she would fall into them.

He leaned close.

Closer…

"Good night, Carra," he whispered, his breath feathering against her lips.

He turned on his heel, but she refused to let him walk away so easily. Not with the confusion and *lust* roiling within her.

"What would you have done if you had known?" she challenged, following on his heel and almost crashing into him when he stopped abruptly.

He turned, slowly, his every move taut, controlled.

Dangerous.

He lowered his eyes to her lips, letting them linger for long seconds before dragging them up to meet her gaze, and by the time his eyes landed on hers, she knew.

"Nothing."

The word doused the flames growing in her, and she bristled. "Nothing? That look you just gave me suggests otherwise."

"I would not have come to the library that night, even had I known. I told you the night we met that I would not expect husbandly…privileges."

His voice faltered on the final word, his perfect facade crumbling for one exquisite second, and Carra felt a thrill of triumph thrum through her. She opened her mouth to call him on it, but he spoke before she had a chance to.

"I would have acted exactly as I did last night. When we married, I told you I expected nothing from you in that regard—and your agreement to marry me, to stay, was contingent on that. Do not deny it," he added, as she opened her mouth once again to argue. "I saw how the assertion eased your mind. Your need to hear me say those words, and my doing so in the face of such strong need, was a contract in itself."

"Not a binding one."

"Not a fae contract," he corrected, leaning in close enough that his eyes were the only thing she could see, rich pools of silver that swirled with longing and frustration, "but one I am bound to nonetheless. I would not betray your trust, nor take advantage of a situation you had no choice but to find yourself in."

"I had a choice!" She leaned closer, until their noses brushed, and she felt the slight hitch in his breath at the contact. "And I chose this. You. Maybe I didn't imagine this then, but I've imagined it plenty ever since. I. Chose. This."

"A choice between marriage and death is not a true choice, Carra." She shivered at the sound of her voice on lips, the way his mouth seemed to caress the word. His eyes flares in response, and she *heard* him swallow thickly. "I married you to save your life. I was under no illusion the marriage would include physical relations. If you will remember, I specifically told you I was not offering them."

"Well, I am."

"And I am declining. Tell me, would you deny me the right to decline your advances?"

She deflated, defeated, and took a small step back. Even if

she knew he was bluffing, even if she knew he wanted her every bit as much as she wanted him, he had a right to deny her. A right that she would not violate, no matter the circumstance. "No. Never."

"Then goodnight, Carra." Straid pulled back, but his eyes lingered on her for long seconds before he finally turned and left her standing alone in the conservatory.

He wanted her. She had seen it in his eyes, plain as day. It wasn't just surprise that had widened them as he'd stood in that doorway, and it wasn't refusal that had caused them to go stormy now; it was lust. Longing.

And yet…he was saying no. And she could not, *would* not, dishonor that.

She stalked to her room and dropped into the warm bath that awaited her, drawn by Niana sometime in her absence.

"No more," she said aloud to herself. "No more," she whispered again, the vow hanging heavy on the steam.

If he wanted to deny her, fine. But then she would stop pretending there might be a chance she could get him in her bed —or get into his. She would stop imagining what it might be like to feel his hands on her skin, his length inside her. She would shut down any inkling of the fantasies that had plagued her ever since that night and do her best to put Straid from her mind as much as she possibly could.

She dragged herself to bed and fell into a fitful sleep and dreamed of Straid leaving on one of his many mysterious trips. In the dream, she waited, unable to eat or drink until he returned. When he finally did, a chasm opened between them, widening with every second, until she could do nothing but look at him across the vast expanse, her hunger and thirst growing as he moved ever farther out of her reach.

CHAPTER EIGHTEEN

*D*enying Carra was the hardest thing Straid had done in fifty years. The look on her face had almost shaken his resolve, which had been tenuous to begin with. But he stood by his decision and by every word he had said. He would not take advantage of the position he had put her in, no matter how much she believed she wanted it.

She is a grown woman, a traitorous part of his mind reminded him.

A human woman, he countered. *Barely older than you and Lyenna were, and you were little more than a child.*

She knows her own mind.

No.

He would not cross that line. Perhaps when this was all over, when she returned to the mortal realm. Perhaps on one of her trips back to the Quarters, he would allow himself to accept her proposition if she extended it again, but as long as she was under his care, all but trapped in his home, he would not. Could not.

He left before breakfast again the following morning, cursing himself for his cowardice. But he could not face her, not yet. The revelation that her note had been an *invitation*…he hardened again at the mere thought. He needed to get himself under control before facing her again.

A light, misting rain dampened his skin as he crossed the house's threshold, growing into a full thunderous downpour by the time he reached the gate at the far end of the gardens. He had only a vague idea of where he was going, but by the time he reached his destination, he had long resolved himself to it.

Roughly two miles beyond the border of the Quarters, he arrived at the old graveyard, full of headstones that had mostly seen better days. The first few years after Lyenna's death he had visited daily, each trip easing the pain in his chest.

Worse than the emotional pain had been the physical, a result of each bond between them snapping at once. It had left him weak and feverish, and his journey to her had taken days, rather than hours, as he had forced himself to run, to walk, to *crawl* to the woman he'd loved. Her family hadn't recognized him, ruined as his mind and body had become.

He'd slept at her grave for three days, desperate to be as close to her as possible, until Corlan and Fell had dragged him away, and his mother had threatened to relocate her body if he did not pull himself together.

His visits had dwindled over the decades, and this was the first since he had married Carra. His guilt had kept him away; it had felt like a betrayal, as though in marrying Carra, he was denying what he and Lyenna had had. What they *should* have had.

He sat before her gravestone, forgoing the traditional fae rites of grave visitation. She would not have minded. The fae customs had never mattered to her. And he had been ready to leave them all behind—the ones he could, at any rate—to provide her with any life she desired.

It felt fitting, that his first visitation in so many months would be accompanied by rain. Lyenna had shared with him the human belief that rain was merely the sky crying, its tears falling to the ground below, and he allowed himself, for a moment, to pretend he believed in the notion.

It took mere seconds for his own tears to mix with those of the sky. The pain was still fresh; fifty years was barely enough time to begin to heal.

A wreath of yellow flowers lay on her gravestone, carefully braided. They were fresh, barely wilted, probably left here yesterday or the day before at the earliest. He wondered who had left them, who would have taken the time to grieve for her here, after all these years. Her parents likely would have died by now. He found himself guilty that he did not know; that he had left them to their grief as he had tended to his own.

Even her siblings would be nearing the ends of their lives now, and nieces or nephews would have no reason to pay respects to a woman they had never met, not so long after she had left the mortal realm.

You would have lost her soon, regardless, a traitorous part of his mind whispered. She would have been seventy, nearing the end of her life. He had known from the beginning that he would outlive her—that she would die of age before he reached full adulthood. But he could not help but think that the sting of losing her would have been softened by the time they had spent together, the love that would have had a chance to grow and blossom and shape who he was.

Her death had left him to be shaped by grief, instead.

The drizzle slowed, then stopped, and tentatively, as though it did not want to intrude on his sorrow, the sun began to peek from behind the heavy clouds—and still, Straid sat in silence at his dead love's grave.

Hours later his stomach rumbled, and he rose. Straid reached into his pocket, retrieving the figurine he had carried with him these last few decades. They had stumbled across a faire their first spring together. Lyenna had dragged him through the crowds, her eyes sparkling, then stopped short at the sight of a booth teeming with glass baubles.

She had stopped, fascinated, her easy smile replaced with deep longing at the beauty before her. Straid had bought her a rose, cloudy pink with clear green leaves, and an identical piece for himself.

"So I will have you with me, even when you are not at my side," he had murmured, pressing a kiss to her lips.

He had found her rose in his room after returning from her grave, that first time, and he had never moved it in all the years since; it lay on the table beside his bed, safe from the world. His own had remained on his person, transferred from one pocket to the next; he could not bear to feel it against his skin.

He pressed his lips to the small rose made of glass and ash and crushed petals, then lay it on her gravestone.

When he turned once more to leave, he found an old mortal woman watching him. Her gray hair was pulled back from her face, and her right hand rested on a wooden cane. She watched him curiously before her eyes flicked to the gravestone that now lay behind him.

"Paying your respects to a human?" she asked.

"She and I were acquainted."

"You have anything to do with her death?"

"No."

The woman nodded, satisfied. He was fae, after all; he could not lie outright.

"Did you love her?"

Straid did not hesitate in his response. "I did. I loved her deeply."

"You still miss her, even though she died a long time ago." It was a statement, an assessment from the old woman, not a question at all.

"Fifty years is not so long, for a fae."

The woman smiled, though her smile was tinged with sadness. "It's not so long for a human, either. Oh, it was most of my life," she added, at Straid's quiet scoff, "but there are things that don't get easier. I lost my husband three years ago. He's buried over there." She raised a shaky hand to point at a gravestone two rows from Lyenna's. "We lost our child around the same time Lyenna passed—a year after she died, almost to the day. I miss my boy every single day. People say it gets easier, but I have not found that to be the case. My only consolation is that I won't have to live with the pain for hundreds of years.

"Many people think mortality is a curse," the woman continued, "and I would agree with them: my child passed well before his years, and if that's not a curse, then I don't know what is. But mortality is also a blessing: I know I'll be able to join him, and my husband, in the afterlife soon enough."

"Another blessing of mortality: belief in the afterlife." Straid envied the mortals and their foolish notion that something waited for them beyond death. He wished he could believe that he would see Lyenna again, but he knew his body would return to the earth and his soul would fracture, taken on the wind.

"Ah. That's not a blessing of mortality. It's a blessing of faith. You could believe in something more for yourself, too; you simply choose not to. Plenty of mortals feel the same way you do, but I know there's more out there. I know that I will be reunited with the loved ones I've lost. And if I'm wrong, well… my hope has eased the burden of grief and carried me through the years."

The old woman's words stayed with him as he slowly walked back to the Quarters. Though he knew it was foolish, a part of him clung to the idea that Lyenna might still be out there somewhere: that one day, their souls would be reunited.

And that she would forgive him for wanting another in her absence.

CHAPTER NINETEEN

"I'm going to need a bodyguard," Carra informed Straid over breakfast. His absence the day before had given her time to think, and to decide how to approach the conversation. She needed space from him, time to clear her head, and that was hard to do when she lived in his house and only left it at his side—when she still remembered so little of her life and depended on him to learn more.

She hadn't minded it, but now that things had shifted between them, it felt stifling.

And lonely.

"I am happy to take you wherever you must go."

"Someone who isn't you."

"Why?" She must be imagining the confusion and hurt in his voice. He'd mentioned hiring someone when she'd first arrived, and it wasn't like he'd ever sought out her company.

She couldn't imagine he'd start now.

"Callad won't meet me at the house, and I have to assume Retyiao would be more comfortable with me going to him, as well. Having you be the one to accompany me to their homes would defeat the purpose, don't you think?

"Besides, you disappear so much—what if I need to leave the

house while you're gone, and I have no way of reaching you? I need someone who can escort me wherever I need to go, *when*ever I need to go. Unless I am, in fact, a prisoner in your home?" She quirked a single brow at him, and he watched her impassively from across the table.

Finally, after three excruciatingly slow bites, he spoke. "No. You are not a prisoner. I will find someone suitable."

"Soon."

"As soon as I am able."

"Within the next few days," she pressed.

"You seem desperate to get away." He took a sip from his flute of sparkling nectar, and she watched his throat bob as he swallowed.

"Yes."

She wanted to say more, wanted to explain. But if he was going to be distant and secretive, then so would she. And if her vague response hurt him, well, then maybe he should learn to communicate better, and they could avoid these games he had given her no choice but to play.

"Someone will be here tomorrow to be used at your disposal."

"Good."

Even after all these weeks, she had to fight the urge to thank him. Her response felt cold and unnatural, but he didn't seem to notice. Of course not; distance came naturally to the fae.

Still, he watched him closely for the rest of the meal, willing him to give some indication that he wanted her as much as she did him. That denying her had caused him some bit of the discordance it had provoked in her.

But Straid appeared maddeningly unaffected, and they finished the meal in silence.

The bodyguard was stationed outside the dining room door the next morning, and he ignored her as she walked through the doorway and took her usual place at the table.

"Bodyguards don't get to eat?" she asked, dropping inelegantly into her chair.

"Not with us."

"Feels kind of self-important," Carra mumbled, sinking her teeth into a flaky pastry that exploded with a light, citrusy flavor.

"The other servants do not eat with us; the bodyguard is no different."

"Maybe they should," she challenged. She had dreamed of him last night, her unconscious mind lingering on thoughts she refused to entertain during the day. The Straid of her dreams had murmured wicked things she could not imagine falling from his lips, before turning his tongue to other, more intimate matters.

She'd awoken flushed and panting, then drawn a cold bath, desperate to hold to the promise she'd made herself. The cold had helped, but not enough, and she had slid her hand between her thighs, cursing her own weakness.

"I'm leaving after breakfast," she declared, unable to meet his eye as the fantasies she'd conjured during her bath danced through her mind.

"Where are you going?"

"To try to get back a client I lost."

"Retyiao."

"Yes." It was an easy guess; she had only lost two clients outright, and the other was missing.

"Use caution with him."

"I can handle myself."

"Carra. This is not a moment for flippancy; Retyiao requires care."

Carra snorted. "Between the two of us, I think we'll trust the one who's professionally fucked him *multiple* times to know exactly how much care he requires." She held his gaze as she said it, and the slight flare in Straid's brought a smile to her lips.

Fueled by her frustration, she reached for words she typically would not use with Straid. "Now, would you like to explain just how I should care for him? What parts of my body to use, how to touch him in the exact right way to make him beg, or scream, or come so hard he sees stars? Or will you leave me to my job—one that I am *very* good at, I might add—while you go off doing whatever the hell it is you do all day when you disappear?"

Straid clenched his jaw. Then, in the greatest show of defeat she had ever seen from him, he slowly stood and walked out of the room.

She relished in the victory, in the longing that had burned in his eyes as he'd torn his eyes away from hers, but a part of her railed against his retreat. She wanted him to stay, to fight, to make her forget about her clients for a day.

She forced herself to finish her pastry, then approached the guard outside the dining room door, smoothing her features to erase all trace of Straid's influence from them.

When she'd asked for a bodyguard, she had expected someone tall and muscular—someone whose brawn could easily kill anyone who meant her harm, and whose appearance would warn them away before they even attempted.

But the guard standing in front of her was slender, and just a hair shorter than her. He was paler than she would have thought possible—and a closer look revealed that his skin was actually translucent. She could make out the color of the veins under his skin, and she could also distinctly see the muscles when he moved. It was an unsettling effect, up close, and she pulled away slightly, all of her focus on keeping her face blank so she wouldn't react and offend the person responsible for keeping her alive.

"What's your name?" she asked.

"My name is irrelevant."

"I'd like to know it."

"My name is irrelevant," he repeated.

"How could it be irrelevant? It's your *name*. That matters. It does to me, anyway. I'm not the kind of employer who thinks I'm somehow better than the people who work for me. What's your name?"

"It is irrelevant."

"Well, I need something to call you." He remained silent, and Carra frowned, an idea taking hold. "Fine. I guess I'll have to take you at your word. So, Irrelevant, are you ready to accompany me to a client's house?"

"Yes." He spoke the single word sharply, and she fought the instinct to wince. She supposed it was good he was so singularly focused on his job, but it unsettled her nonetheless.

"I just need to change, and then I'll meet you back down here."

Niana tied the laces up the back of Carra's dress while Carra quickly applied some simple color to her face. Minutes later, she met her guard in the foyer, and they set off with him a step behind her as they walked the path that lined the side of the house.

"What do you think about the front door being in the back of the house?" she asked. "It took me a while to get used to."

"I do not think anything of it."

"You're allowed to have opinions," she said gently.

"I would rather not."

The air felt heavy with the promise of rain, so Carra hurried forward, eager to arrive before the skies opened. Even at a faster clip, it would take them the better part of half an hour to reach their destination.

She and Straid had walked past Retyiao's house on a few of their walks, but he'd had to point it out to her the first time; it seemed Straid was right about Retyiao being immune to the perfume's power. Not a single memory of the house or the fae within had surfaced, no matter how long she lingered.

"How long have you been a bodyguard?" she asked, taking a quick step back to draw level with him.

He said nothing.

In fact, that was his response to every question she asked him: just a wall of silence that practically radiated off him. She kept up a steady stream of questions along the way, determined to eventually wear him down, but he did not utter a single word from the moment they stepped through the gate at home until their arrival at Retyiao's doorstep. She would keep trying every time they left the house. Like Niana, like Straid, she would coax words out of him soon enough.

Carra pressed her hand to the front door, wincing slightly as she felt the wards flare to life, heating the oak beneath her fingers to an uncomfortable temperature before the door finally swung open and let her through.

Her bodyguard attempted to follow her, but rebounded off the invisible wards, stumbling back a couple steps.

"You cannot go in there without me," he said, standing as close to the wards as he could without triggering them.

"Oh, you do speak." Carra raised a brow. "I'm perfectly safe in here; I just needed an escort. Feel free to go into town if you don't want to wait here for me."

"Neither of those options is acceptable. What business do you have with him that you could not conduct with me present?"

"My client is under no obligation to welcome you into his home, nor would I ask him to. Our business is between him and me."

"Well said." Retyiao's voice slithered from behind her, and she turned to him with a broad smile. His long tongue snaked from his mouth, tasting the air around her.

She hadn't noticed how long his tongue was when he'd come to the house, and until this moment she had forgotten that that it was one of his reptilian features. But with it darting around her, other memories came drifting back—not as clear as the ones triggered by the perfume, but what she did remember sent heat flooding between her legs, and Retyiao smiled as he retracted his tongue.

"Beautiful." Retyiao turned to her guard, his reptilian eyes narrowing at the sight of him. "I do not make a habit of welcoming strangers into my home. I appreciate your willingness to accompany Carra here, but the doorstep is as far as you go. You may wait in the yard or return in…two hours?" he turned to Carra. "Does that work?"

"Yes. Two hours," she echoed.

"Straid will not be pleased," the bodyguard informed Carra.

"He'll be fine. His concern was with me being out on the streets alone; he was never worried about what might happen once I got here. I'm safely tucked into Retyiao's house now, where nothing can hurt me. Your services won't be needed until I'm ready to be walked home."

"Yes. I typically do not enjoy an audience." Retyiao's face was impassive as he said it, but a second later his tongue slithered from his mouth, just the barest amount, and Carra couldn't help but smile, even as her mind went to another client, and the audience that had caught all three of them by surprise.

"I'll handle Straid. But trust me, he won't be upset that you left me here; he expected it. As long as you walk me home, he'll be happy."

"I *will* be walking you home." Her guard's jaw clenched, and his eyes narrowed as they shifted back to Retyiao.

"Then there's no need for you to worry about Straid's response. I'll see you in two hours." Carra stepped forward and closed the door in his scowling face, then spun around to Retyiao, giving him the most dazzling smile she could muster.

"I've missed you," she said, taking a few steps forward to close the gap between them and sliding her hands up his chest.

Retyiao hissed faintly, the sound warming Carra to her core.

"You remember enough of yourself to make this decision?"

"I don't remember everything," she confessed, "but I remember enough, yes."

"Truly?"

"Truly."

He watched her for a long moment, his mouth slightly open. She wondered if he could taste the truth on her words. Finally, he nodded, apparently pleased with whatever he had learned from her scent. "Then perhaps we should retreat to my rooms."

Retyiao took her hand in his and pressed a kiss to her knuckles. At the feel of it, a hazy memory of the first time they met filtered in. She couldn't remember who had referred her to him, only that she'd been apprehensive at the sight of the offaedia.

The other fae she'd worked with had all appeared human at a distance; if not for the pointed ears and the unearthly beauty, they each could have been mortal. But Retyiao, though he had arms and legs like a person, was unmistakably serpentine: he had oblong pupils set in yellow-green eyes, and when he blinked, his eyes closed from the sides. He had no hair, and his ears lay flat against his head. His skin glistened with tiny iridescent green scales, which she'd found, to her delight, were ever so slightly rough to the touch. His tongue was easily five times the length of a human's and forked at the end.

The way he moved was reptilian, as well: he didn't walk straight forward, like a human or the other fae she knew did. Instead, he swayed, his gait shifting side to side in a manner that looked distinctly snakelike.

But he had been polite, and seemed kind, and he had offered her enough money to set aside her reservations. She'd learned later, from their discussions, that he was ruthless in business; that those who crossed him always regretted it. But here, with her, there was no sign of his legendary retribution; he was kind, and attentive, and had never made her feel for a moment that she was in any danger, or that she was anything less than a cherished guest.

Aside from his attitude, and the fact that he paid more than double her next most generous client, the sex was some of the best she had ever experienced—starting with the pheromones he was already emitting in small doses, just enough to make her knees weak. Even if he had been less skilled in his endeavors, even if he focused solely on his own pleasure, those pheromones would have ensured she found her own release every time. And yet, he was attentive and thorough and incredibly skilled.

He gestured for her to climb the stairs, and he followed behind her, his tongue darting out to caress the back of her neck. With each touch, he released more pheromones, and each dose brought forth a memory of their coupling. Between the memories and the pheromones themselves, her legs threatened to buckle beneath her by the time he guided her to the bedroom.

She fumbled with the laces along the back of her dress, and by the time she'd loosened them enough to let the dress slither to the floor, Retyiao stood before her, naked. He backed her toward the bed, and she dropped onto it, biting her lip as he swayed closer to her.

"Spread your legs for me," he murmured.

His tongue flicked out the moment she complied, tasing the air between her legs, but not making contact. Still, it was enough to make her whimper as another heady dose of pheromones flooded her system.

He repeated the action again and again, never making contact with her thighs—or the part of her that ached for his touch. Her pleasure rose higher, and it took every ounce of her will not to slide her hand between her legs and provide the release he kept just out of reach.

He hissed softly as he watched her squirm, his own arousal evident as he stiffened impossibly before her. He stroked himself slowly, his eyes never leaving her as he brought her closer and closer to her peak.

"Retyiao," she finally gasped, and he hissed in pleasure at the sound of her desperate plea. Finally, *finally*, his tongue landed between her legs, and the force of it against her clitoris made Carra scream out as she came.

She shuddered as he gently laved at her, caressing her sensitive flesh. She jerked with each touch, until he had licked her clean.

Retyiao dropped into bed beside her, tasting the air every now and then as they lay side by side, neither of them talking. She wondered what scents he found: her arousal, or her sweat? Or her own pheromones, beyond her ability to sense?

After a few long minutes he began releasing the pheromone again. Not that she needed it: she was still wound tight, never far from her release, and she could feel her pulse between her legs, fast and strong, and aching. Without moving from her side, he began flicking his tongue over her body. Mostly, he teased her, moving lower and lower over her body, his tongue so close she could feel the whisper of air as it danced above her.

Her breasts tingled in anticipation, and she gasped when his tongue made contact with one of her nipples, which instantly tightened under its touch. His tongue wandered ever lower, hovering over her ribs, the swell of her stomach, her hips, her cunt.

Whenever he made contact, he released a flood of pheromones, and she arched into the sensation, writhing beside him.

"Ret—" she began, but his tongue gently caressed her clitoris, and she cut herself off with a gasp. He turned to her, his eyes bright with desire mere inches from her own, as he plundered her aching depths. He pressed his forehead against hers, his hisses mingling with her gasps until she couldn't quite be sure who made which noises.

Retyiao withdrew, trailing gentle licks up her body, then pressed his lips to hers.

"May I enter you?"

She nodded, smiling at the formality.

He moved atop her, lighter than he looked, and kissed her deeply as he notched himself against her entrance. She pushed her hips toward him, and he hissed, his eyes falling shut as she hooked her legs around him and drew him inside her inch by excruciatingly delicious inch.

He moved slowly, almost reverently, and shivered as she trailed her hands along his scales.

"I'm close," she panted against his lips long minutes later, and he immediately released a flood of pheromones that had her crying out and clenching around him.

"Beautiful," he murmured when the waves of pleasure had subsided. "Absolutely beautiful." He began to move inside her once more, impossibly stiff in the wake of her orgasm. "Watching you brings me such pleasure," he added, speeding his pace. She ached, and yet she craved more. His tongue darted out to catch a bead of sweat that threatened to drip into her eyes, and he hissed at the taste of it.

"Carra," he groaned. "I cannot hold back much longer. I cannot—the things you do to me. I am—oh" He hissed, all trace of his decorum gone as he clung to her, and she followed as he tumbled over the edge.

CHAPTER TWENTY

Straid had been preoccupied since Carra's little challenge at the breakfast table. When she had talked about her job, about using her body to bring pleasure to others, he had imagined her doing those things to him. And once his imagination had begun, it would not stop.

He had extricated himself from the situation. Clumsily, indelicately, but it was better than staying and inadvertently letting her know just how deeply her words had affected him.

He spent the late morning attempting to banish her from his mind to no avail. He had just decided to take matters into his own hands when the wards alerted him to Corlan entering the home. Hastily, he retied the laces on his breeches and met his friend in the foyer, where he lounged in one of the chairs meant for waiting guests. Corlan raised a brow at his disheveled state but Straid found himself unable to meet his friend's eyes. His shame burrowed, secret and low in his belly.

"Have you heard anything?" Corlan asked.

"No. Fell has yet to respond." His sister was not known for her promptness; she would send a response—or simply appear at his door—when it suited her. Due to her ability to visualize the threads that connected all things to each other, her timing, though often frustrating, always proved apt.

Corlan frowned. "I know she has her whole…thing, but I wish she'd at least acknowledge people before the threads converge, or however she says it."

"Her threads do, on occasion, get quite tedious, yes," Straid agreed. "One would think she would have the ability to acknowledge her brother and dear friend, even if the threads did not dictate she do so."

"At least your gift is straightforward," Corlan mumbled. "Control the air. Heat it, cool it, move it. Easy."

Straid worked to keep his face neutral, but a part of him prickled with unease. At face value, yes, his gift did seem straightforward. However, there were aspects to it that he had never divulged to anybody, including his closest friend. Aspects that even he had not fully explored. Corlan had almost witnessed the depth of his power in the wake of Lyenna's death, but Straid had quelled it, terrified of his own capabilities, and his friend had been none the wiser. Providing heat or stealing the air from a person's lungs had their uses, but his gifts went much further—and he had yet to experience his first Ousilie's comet, had yet to come into his full power; he still possessed the magical strength of a mere child. If others discovered the extent of his gift, they would fear him, as they did his eldest sister and brother alike.

One of the many reasons Straid had left his old life behind was that he did not desire fear, did not enjoy holding it over others. The guard had been an exception, one that had turned his stomach. The *only* exception since the night he had fled his family's home and taken this one as his residence.

So he hid his deepest secrets from everyone in his life. Even Lyenna had never known, had never so much as suspected the secret he had carried since his childhood. It was the only piece of information he had ever kept from his love; his closest friend; and his favorite sister alike.

"It might be redundant with Fell joining the case soon, but we should update the list of everything we know," Corlan suggested. "Anything that might help at all, even if it doesn't seem that relevant. Names, families, species, last known locations of the victims. Connections between them, if we can find any. Putting it all in writing might help us find something that we've missed. At the very least, it'll give us something to do."

Three hours later, they had rewritten the list. It was as futile as Straid had suspected it would be, but his friend seemed less distraught than when he had arrived. For that reason alone, Straid was glad they had done it.

"I need a break," Corlan said, stretching. "Let's take a walk."

The overcast sky and light drizzle matched Straid's mood perfectly, and he scowled as they crossed the threshold of the property, leaving behind the place that had become his sanctuary.

"So, where's your bride?" Corlan asked as they approached town. "I didn't hear her moving around like I usually do." Corlan, with his superior hearing, would have been able to hear her in any room of the house that wasn't spelled to keep sound in.

"With a client." His response was terse, harsh even to his ears, and he inwardly winced.

"You're jealous?" Corlan's open surprise rankled, and Straid scoffed in response.

"I am not jealous of lesser fae who have been deemed worthy to pay for the right to lay with her. Her business is her own." A month ago, he would have meant it. Now, he was not entirely sure.

He could have her as well; she had told him as much. And yet, the line drawn between them was almost tangible. With her clients, she had a mutually agreed upon transaction that benefitted both parties, with clear rules and boundaries in place. Her lack of choice in marrying him precluded the same being true for any relationship with Straid. Many fae would take her word over their own hesitations, and perhaps they would not be wrong to do so. But she had been so desperate the night they had married, had clung to him as her only option, and that desperation flashed in his mind every time he found himself almost giving in. The circumstances leading to their marriage hung between them, an unwelcome third party in their relationship, and he saw no way around them, not if he wanted to still respect himself after.

Perhaps if he paid her…

He wondered if she would see that as an insult or a compliment. If it would further muddy the waters. Reluctant husband-and-wife carried enough complications; would adding a clientele aspect to the relationship empower her to say no, or would it trap her even further?

"Straid!"

He glanced at his friend, who watched him with a smirk.

"Yeah, I don't believe for a second that you're not jealous. Just talk to her. Tell her how you feel. Husband to wife." Corlan shrugged, with a glint in his eye.

"I do not harbor secret feelings for my wife."

His friend snorted.

"There are…complications."

"Like that?" Corlan asked, pointing ahead of them. Straid followed his friend's finger and there she was, stopped on the street and arguing with the fae he had hired as her bodyguard. A steep personal favor had been redeemed to acquire his services him at such short notice, but the scene before him indicated he may have to call in another.

As they drew nearer, Carra's words became clearer, and Straid's jaw tightened at what he heard.

"You have no right to judge me. It is none of your business what I do, or who I do it with." She caught sight of Straid and whirled toward him, fury sparking in her eyes as her disdainful gaze landed on him. "If you want me to have a bodyguard, you'll need to find a different one."

He stepped closer, cognizant of multiple pairs of eyes straying their way. He stood tall and proud and spoke quietly for only her to hear.

"Come, let's discuss this at home." He angled his head slightly toward the passersby, and she nodded once, a sharp, terse jerk of her head. "Corlan, I will join you later."

Straid took Carra by the elbow and traveled her home, leaving the guard—whose name he had barely bothered learning, and which he had a feeling he would forget entirely soon—to follow behind them.

"What happened?" he asked, the moment they breached the wards.

Carra drew away from him, her eyes flashing as she yanked her arm from his grasp. "He tried to follow me into my client's home and argued when I refused. Which, I shouldn't have to remind you, is my right. My *clients'* right. My job requires privacy that he seemed determined not to give me. And then—" She advanced toward him, and the fury rolling off her was so palpable he took a step backward. "He found out what it is I do for work, and he had a lot of opinions about that."

"He is not paid to have opinions."

Carra snorted. "Well, clearly he didn't get the memo. He was worried about your reputation, and your feelings about my 'infidelity.'"

"There cannot be infidelity in the absence of an expectation of—"

"I know that!" Carra yelled. "But somehow you neglected to tell my bodyguard that, so I had to spend the whole walk back being lectured and shamed for a job that I love and that I am frankly *very* good at. Don't you ever fucking assign someone to me without discussing my job and the terms of our arrangement ever again," she spat.

"Understood."

"That means," she emphasized, stalking forward, "that you tell them I'm a prostitute. You use the word clearly. That means you tell them that you are not fucking me yourself. That means—"

The wards alerted Straid to the guard's presence a second before the guard strode through the doors. Carra whirled, anger flashing in her eyes as she registered his presence.

"Your services will no longer be needed." Straid barely glanced at the guard as he revoked his access to the house. By the time the guard flew backward, swiftly removed by the wards that now recognized him as an intruder, Straid's gaze had settled back on Carra. "It will not happen again," he assured her.

Carra merely glared at him, then stormed to her room, slamming the door behind her. He followed and knocked gently but was met with silence.

"I will ensure that any future guards understand the nature of their assignments," he said, hoping she was listening through the door. "If you would be more comfortable conducting the interview yourself, that can be arranged."

There was no response.

She skipped dinner, electing for the food to be sent to her room instead, and he did his best to ignore the unease that rose in him. She had every right to be angry. *He* was angry, and he had not been the one slighted. A significant part of him wanted to track the guard down, to unleash the power he had long kept leashed, and make the guard regret his actions.

He knocked on her door one final time, lingering until he could be certain it would not open.

"I will make this right," he vowed, his forehead pressed against the door. "Whatever I must do—I will make this right."

CHAPTER TWENTY-ONE

"New guards are waiting to be interviewed. You may do the honors or leave it to me...if you trust me with it."

Carra had been stiff all morning, on edge after the guard's attitude toward her last night. It wasn't that she couldn't handle herself, but she shouldn't have had to. It stung, made all the worse by how unexpected it had been, and she had a feeling it would be a while before the pain and anger faded. Now, she glared at Straid across the table. Of course she didn't trust him to find her a new bodyguard; the last one had shamed her, had tried to make her feel like it was wrong to take money for sex. Had tried to make her feel bad for sleeping with someone other than her husband, who wouldn't even allow her into his bed though they both wanted it. How could she trust his judgment on a replacement?

"Every candidate is aware of what, exactly, your job is, and they are also aware that I do not expect you to give it up simply because we are married. Two candidates left, sworn to never speak of our conversation or disparage you in any way. Many fae do not ascribe to the monogamous ways of the mortals. The fact that they expect differently from my wife is not something they should hold against you."

"Why do they expect different from your wife?"

Straid shifted, his eyes flitting away from hers, and she knew that whatever he said next, it would not be the truth. It wouldn't be an outright lie; he was fae, after all. But he would find a loophole for his words to settle into.

"You are mortal; I am fae. Aside from that, I earned a reputation in my youth as someone who believes in true, deep, romantic love. Many assume I would expect all needs to be met within a romantic relationship. While that *is* my own preference, I understand that the same is not true of everyone."

His words rang true, even if she suspected was more to it. But she simply nodded; her focus today needed to be on finding a new guard, not on uncovering his secrets. There would be plenty of time for that in the months ahead.

"I'll interview them."

He inclined his head. "Would you appreciate my presence, or would you prefer to do this alone?"

"You can come with me. You'll technically be the one hiring them, after all."

Straid frowned over his steepled fingers. "Does that bother you?"

She hesitated. Did it?

No.

It did, however, make something in her chest ache, and the gentle, remorseful look in his eye only worsened it.

"You may hire them if you wish," he continued, his eyes softening further, making that thing in her chest splinter. "Judging by your clientele, I assume you could afford their fees. By all means, do so if it would make you more comfortable. However, I assure you that no harm will come from letting me be the one to pay for their services."

"It doesn't bother me. I'm just not…" She trailed off, not wanting to add vulnerability to the strange, strained mess between them. *I'm just not used to you being so careful with me anymore.*

Carra sighed. "Come on, let's get it over with."

Eight hours later, she had a new guard, one she already felt much more comfortable with than…it bothered her that she still didn't know the old guard's name.

She had led the interviews, with Straid only chiming in occasionally, and this candidate—Jesson—was the clear frontrunner. He had given her a slight smile when she'd pushed back on something Straid had said, and didn't react when she had mentioned her job. One of the candidates had looked at her with so much desire in his eyes that she had immediately rankled and dismissed him without further thought.

But Jesson had been softer than the others, his stoicism falling away more than once, and he had answered all of the questions that she and Straid had asked. The thing that really solidified her choice, though, was that he directed his answers to her every time, even when Straid was the one who had asked a question, a clear sign that Jesson understood he would ultimately work for her.

"So, Jesson, are you staying for dinner?" she asked him.

He hesitated. "Is that an invitation?"

"Yes." She glanced at Straid, who gave her a tight smile and then one single nod. She didn't know if his agreement was because she had already extended the invitation or because he felt bad about the first guard. It didn't matter either way; she planned to use tonight as a steppingstone to inviting all of the servants to eat with them. "I'd like to get to know you a little better before you start actually guarding me. And I can tell you a little about my work. Things you need to know for each client."

"Is that something you and I should be alone for?" Jesson asked, not so much as glancing at Straid. Carra shrugged in return.

"Straid already knows everything I'm going to tell you. It's just the basics, nothing too intimate. Come on, let's eat."

She led the way to the dining hall and was pleased to find Brey there, setting the table when they arrived. Carra smiled at the fae woman, but the moment she opened her mouth to invite her to join them, Brey disappeared. Not tonight, then. But soon. And tomorrow she would start working to get Niana to have breakfast with them.

"Before we begin, you said you'd already sworn the candidates to secrecy?" she asked Straid.

"Yes. I also took the liberty of informing your clients that whomever we chose would need access to your client list."

She looked up, shocked. "When did you do that?"

"Last night," he said softly. "I needed to be sure you were protected. Each of your clients agreed; your safety matters above all else.

She swallowed thickly, suddenly overwhelmed. She'd been so angry yesterday, so hurt, and he had taken measures greater than she could have expected to right the wrong. She blinked away the tears that swam in her eyes and bowed her head in thanks.

Not for the first time, she wished he wasn't fae, so she could properly thank him for what he had done.

"Shall we proceed?" he asked, his voice gruff.

She cleared her throat and turned to Jesson, grateful to have something to take her mind off Straid's kindness. "I met with Retyiao yesterday. He won't want you to enter his house, so you'll have to wait outside in the garden, or go into town and come back at the specified time. He can get a bit…possessive of me, I suppose, but I'm perfectly safe with him. He takes *very* good care of me."

"Understood. Do you have a preference?" Jesson hadn't touched any of his food, and with a start, Carra realized that neither had she.

"A preference for what?" she asked, biting into one of the

small, crescent-shaped, chicken pastries on her plate. A burst of lemon hit her tongue, followed by the milder taste of dill, and she closed her eyes in appreciation.

"Whether I wait or come back for you."

Carra shrugged. "No, although I think Retyiao would rather you stay—it shows that I'm taken care of, and he likes that."

"Noted."

"Now, Lord Astrea, on the other hand, you should definitely leave, if I ever go to him. He might invite you in just to get you off the street, but I think he'd prefer you not be there at all. If I go to his house at any point, it might be best if you stop at the end of the street and let me walk the rest of the way on my own."

"I can do that," Jesson said.

"Jax would honestly probably prefer you be in the room with us, but in the interest of professionalism between you and me, I'd suggest otherwise." Across from her, Straid stilled, and she willed herself not to look in his direction. She couldn't bear *whatever* expression she might find on his face. "If you are interested in that possibility, we can certainly discuss it, though I would insist that you and I do a trial run beforehand."

"What would that entail, exactly?" Jesson asked.

"I would talk you through some specifics of what you might witness in the room. I'd probably also take my clothes off, just to get that initial shock out of the way before you have to encounter that—and much more—with a client involved." She smiled at the slight widening of Jesson's eyes. "Like I said, I'd suggest we not go down that avenue, at least for the time being."

"That would probably be for the best," he agreed weakly.

She sat back, satisfied that Jesson would not create a repeat of the behavior she'd faced from the previous guard. "For Jax, you can just walk me to the door or wait inside—whatever makes you most comfortable." Carra frowned, considering what she knew of Jax.

"You being there specifically to protect me might heighten his excitement. I don't want to involve you in that, so to keep things simple Jax will always come to me."

Carra glanced at Straid, despite trying her very hardest not to. At the talk of Jax, her mind flashed to seeing Straid in the doorway that night, and she wondered, for a moment, if the same was true for Straid. But when she looked at him, the expression on his face wasn't lust, or disgust, or any of the other things she might have expected to see; no, the look on his face was a sort of intrigued thoughtfulness.

CHAPTER TWENTY-TWO

A week later, Carra knocked softly on the study door and Straid bade her enter, much to Corlan's astonishment. His friend had raised a brow as Carra settled into the chair beside him in silent question, and Straid gave a subtle shake of his head.

He had not told Carra how he felt.

He *would* not tell Carra how he felt.

Corlan raised a brow and Straid wondered, idly, if his friend might take it upon himself to tell Carra in his stead.

"Carra has been helping with our investigation. She told me this evening that she had something to share, and I asked her to wait to divulge the information until you were here. Carra, we have some new information that must be shared with you, as well."

"Do you want to go first or should I?" she asked.

"Why don't you go first?" Corlan suggested before Straid could respond. The edge in his friend's voice suggested unease, and Straid hoped Carra's information would reassure him.

"Okay," she began, her eyes darting to Corlan before settling on Straid. "I was with…a client…today. He mentioned that someone he has regular business dealings with had lost her memory. She showed up at his house, convinced they were supposed to meet. The meeting she'd come for had already happened, a month before. She didn't remember anything since then—a whole month was missing from her memory." She blanched, and Straid gripped the chair beneath him to keep from going to her.

"Is she human or fae?" Corlan asked, dipping his pen in the ink pot on Straid's desk.

"Fae."

"Did your client give you a name?"

"Myrtle. She's a tree fae—a dryad, I think. She's safe now; he sent her home with security who's watching her every hour of the day. But she was found wandering the Quarters alone, missing her memories. It has to be connected to what happened to me, right?"

"How much of your memory were you missing?" Corlan asked, bent over the parchment before him.

"All of it." At Carra's soft response, Corlan's head whipped toward her, and Straid's chest ached. This information was not new to him, but it pained him all the same.

"All of it?" Corlan asked.

"I remembered nothing," Carra confirmed. "I didn't even know my own name."

"How much of your memory has come back?"

"Not enough," Straid and Carra answered in unison. He caught her eye, but she looked away quickly.

"That must be hard."

"It is," she murmured.

"All this time, I thought...I know we haven't spent much time together, but I thought you were hiding something. I didn't realize it was hidden even from you."

Carra shrugged, but Straid could see the depth of emotion behind the simple motion.

"I had help recovering my memories, and I remembered enough about my job to be reasonably sure I've recovered my entire client list—aside from the one who's on *your* list. I can't tell you any more about him than that," she said in response to Corlan's raised brow. "I remember most of my life in the Quarters. But I don't remember anything about my family or my home—my *actual* life.

"I don't even remember the moment the guard saw me; the *only* thing I knew that night was that I'd be killed if I was caught."

"Shit." Corlan closed his eyes. "Speaking of the guard, though...there's new information on that front. And I think Straid is right; it's something you probably need to hear. Straid, I think you should be the one to tell her."

"Fine." Straid cleared his throat, preparing himself to relay the information he had only learned this evening. "I will deliver the news, then."

His gaze landed on Carra, and he softened at the sight of the apprehension on her face: the tightness around her eyes, her teeth worrying her bottom lip. He did not know whether what he was about to say would set her mind at ease or scare her further; all he knew was that he felt, deeply, that she deserved to know, that she *needed* to know.

"The night you were found," he began, gritting his teeth at the image of her on the ground, looking so weak, so broken, so terrified, "a guard was found dead. I was not aware of this until recently, but another had reported the death. It is rare for guards to die on duty, although not entirely unheard of, and his death was not reported outside the ranks of the guards. This is typical," he added, at the look on Carra's face. "The guards are the Quarters' show of strength; we do not want the citizens to panic over the thought that something could overpower one. The official policy to conceal their deaths keeps the citizens of the Quarters safe from themselves. Fear breeds unrest. Panic breeds riots. I have seen what happens when the general population hears of the death of a guard, and it is not something I would wish to see again."

He grimaced. He had been a child, expected to stay in his rooms, but he had snuck out his bedroom window and watched the rioting city from the roof. Fell had discovered him and pulled him back into his room, but not before he watched the panic claim two lives. Four more had been lost after he had returned to his bed.

"Our recent investigation revealed that the guard who died the night you and I met was the same guard who found you in the Quarters. The one who threatened to report your transgression and call for your execution."

"The one you saved me from."

He bowed his head in acknowledgement.

"His throat was slit, and his tongue carved from his body."

"That's horrible." Carra paled, her breath speeding a fraction. "Do you think they did it because he let me go?"

Straid hesitated, fear roiling in his gut.

"Tell her," Corlan urged as the silence stretched too long. Straid steeled himself.

"He was found nearly a half hour before your encounter with him. The guard who discovered his body ran to summon help. When he returned, the body was missing, as was all evidence of the crime.

"He had disappeared—only to reappear seven streets over, throat and tongue intact, attempting to arrest you."

Carra gasped, and her eyes grew wider. "That's not possible, is it?"

Corlan cleared his throat. "It's not…*im*possible. There were rumors of a similar occurrence roughly four hundred years ago. I need to look into it more; so far, I've found nothing but a name: a witness who fled into the human world not long after and was never heard from again. I think, with the right resources, I can find him. When I do, I'll visit him and ask what he knows. If he's still alive."

"In the meantime," Straid began, fighting the fear—the *panic*

—that rose at the thought, "you are in more danger than I realized."

"Do you think they'll target after me again?"

"We have no way of knowing. Perhaps you were a victim of convenience who has been forgotten in the weeks since. Perhaps there is an unseen pattern between the attacks, and you are unsafe even now. The fact you have not been attacked since brings some level of comfort, but I would not risk your life again."

"I appreciate that." She met his gaze with a half-hearted smile.

"I will help Corlan search for the witness."

"It'll take some time. I think we might need Fell on this one," his friend admitted. "I'll keep looking, but his name doesn't even appear in the documents I've found."

"I am certain she will thrill at the challenge."

"I'd like to help." Carra sat forward in her chair, a fierce fire suddenly burning in her eyes. Straid's heart fluttered at the sight of it. He ignored the feeling as best he could; now was not the time. "I want to help however I can. I want to come with you when you find him."

"You cannot."

Carra bristled at Straid's words, and he sighed. "He resides in the mortal world now, and due to the constraints of our marriage contract, you may not return for months yet." He could only hope they would find the witness before then.

"What happens if I break that part of the contract?" she challenged.

"Then you die." He forced them from his mouth, though he wanted nothing less than to utter the possibility. He had watched one woman he loved die before her time. He would not —*could* not—do it again.

"You must stay in the Quarters," Straid entreated. "You have helped already, bringing us another name. Continue speaking with your clients. Information is vital. The urgency of the situation has increased, and I would ask that your probing do so, as well."

"Is there anything specific you need me to find out?"

"Are you sure you can handle it?" Corlan's question sent pinpricks of anger down Straid's spine.

Carra held his friend's gaze for long seconds. Then slowly, she crumbled.

She folded in on herself, her shoulders dropping and her face crumpling into a mask of fear and sadness. "I heard that people have gone missing. *Fae*, even, not just humans. I—I'm scared to leave the house." She hiccupped a sob and Straid rose from behind the desk, ready to comfort her, but she continued on, her eyes wide and pleading. "Straid says I have nothing to worry about, that he'll keep me safe, but he has a tendency to tell me what he thinks I want to hear. I know you'll tell me the truth, without dancing through loopholes: am I safe? Is there someone, or some*thing*"—she shuddered—"out there that might want to hurt me?"

Tears shone in her eyes, but she blinked them furiously away. He had never seen her so openly vulnerable. Even that first night, she had been defiant; tonight, she seemed fragile. The speed with which she had seemed to break took him aback, and he froze, uncertain whether she would want him to comfort her or leave her to her emotions.

Corlan merely gaped at her, the three of them frozen in place.

Until Carra broke the silence. She laughed, brushed the tears from her eyes, and settled back in her chair, all trace of her fear gone. "I don't know, Corlan; do *you* think I can handle it? If I eased into that, in a moment when your guard was already down, do you think you'd overshare in an effort to comfort me? My guess is yes."

Straid dropped into his chair with a weak smile, but his heart still galloped like a spooked horse, and his chest still ached from the sight of her distress, false though it had been.

"Fuck," Corlan breathed, awed. "You can handle it."

For the first time since Straid had brought Carra into his life all those weeks ago, he saw begrudging respect on Corlan's face, aimed at her. Respect that Corlan did not give easily—not even to Straid, who had earned it time and time again.

"So. Again," Carra pressed, "what do you need me to ask?"

The three of them talked long into the night, until Corlan slipped out, claiming exhaustion. He glanced meaningfully between Straid and Carra as he crossed the threshold of the study, though Straid pretended not to see.

He settled back in his chair as the door snicked closed.

"You should eat," he murmured. "You missed dinner."

"I don't think I can; I'm suddenly exhausted." Carra yawned, her mouth stretching wide.

"You need to eat." The thought of her going to bed without supper upset him. He had come to love watching her eat, had even on occasion asked Brey to use ingredients he knew she loved on the days he had to miss a meal, simply so he could imagine her eating them.

It had been decades since he had allowed himself to care about someone's well-being. However, at the sight of her heavy eyes, a warring part of him yearned to tuck her into bed, food be damned.

"I will bring food to your door. Something small before bed."

She nodded and rose to unsteady feet. He followed her out of the study, turning left toward the stairs as she crossed the expansive hallway to her room.

Minutes later he knocked on the door, and his heart clenched at the sleepy "Come in" that sounded from the other side of the door.

He stepped inside for the first time since the night he found her and placed the tray on the table beside her bed.

Only her head was visible above the blankets, her wild mass of dark brown curls spilling over the cream satin pillowcase beneath her head. His heart stuttered at the sight.

"I'm too sleepy to eat," she mumbled softly.

"Just a few bites," he coaxed. "I brought the rosemary jam you love."

She opened one eye at that, and he chuckled at the sight, catching him by surprise. He could not remember the last time he had laughed so freely.

"Come, I will feed you." He did not know what compelled him to make the offer, but when she opened her mouth, he slathered the jam on a cracker and slipped it between her lips. Her lazy smile in return might have been the most beautiful thing in the world. She opened her mouth again and he dutifully fed her another cracker, then another, until the pot of jam was empty and Carra's eyelashes fluttered against her cheeks.

"More?" she whispered, her lips formed into a pout.

"You have eaten everything I brought, but I could fetch you more." He rose, but her hand landed on his knee, stilling him.

"Stay."

He did not have the strength to do so but allowed himself one final indulgence: he gently skimmed his fingertips across her forehead, then pressed a tender kiss to the soft skin of her cheek.

"Goodnight," he whispered.

"Goodnight," she mumbled back, her words slurred with sleep.

He slid into his own bed mere minutes later, still feeling the warmth of her skin against his lips as he drifted into the soundest sleep he had experienced in a long while.

CHAPTER TWENTY-THREE

*C*arra met with every one of her clients that next week—all but Ichold, whose name she pictured on Corlan's list. She wondered where it was in relation to Myrtle's, how many names lay between theirs now.

Anything of note—anything she even suspected might be relevant—she passed on to Straid, who in turn passed it onto Corlan. As she questioned her clients, the list grew by three more names, all from the past year. She made note of their names, where they'd last been seen, and any other information she could coax out of her clients.

She had always enjoyed her work, but as the days passed it became a careful dance of pleasure and prying. Gureig bristled at her questions, and she finished the session without asking another. She spent their next session soothing him and planning a new approach that wouldn't set him on edge.

She changed her mind about only meeting with Jax at the house; she went to him—leaving Jesson at the end of the street—and suggested an audience. He had eagerly complied, and afterward had spilled more secrets than she knew what to do with: names of people he had business dealings with, the value of his most recent shipments, and information she could not even begin to understand but filed away for later regardless.

They lay together on the floor of his living room at the end of one session, having dismissed the fae whom he had invited to watch. The audience, as usual, did nothing to heighten her pleasure—Straid remained the only person whose presence had done so—but in the wake of it, Jax was even freer with his information than normal.

"It sounds like you have a lot on your plate," she murmured, trailing her finger across Jax's chest. He had sent the guests away and they lay now on a plush rug, Carra caged in his arms as they talked.

"Almost more than I can bear," he responded, tightening the arm he had wrapped around her. "The burden grows heavier each day, and I fear that I may crumble beneath it soon."

She nuzzled closer to him and pressed a light kiss to his shoulder. He only spoke in such a formal way when work overwhelmed him; usually his speech patterns were much closer to hers than to Straid's. He needed extra attention when he was like this. Extra care. She found herself glad for the audience for his sake, not just hers.

Guilt flared in her belly, and she did her best to ignore it. She hated using his vulnerability to probe for answers. Hated lulling him into a sense of security just so she could exploit his ease, his comfort with her, for her own purposes.

I'm doing this to save missing people, she reminded herself. *To prevent more from going missing.* This wasn't some selfish act of hers; what she was doing could save lives. It could prevent others from losing their memories, just as she had.

Straid and Corlan had been adamant that she not ask her clients anything too directly, reasoning that someone powerful must be behind the disappearances. When she'd insisted that none of her clients were behind the disappearances, Straid had readily taken her at her word.

"However, they may decide to do their own investigations,

which could interfere with ours," Straid had said. "Or they may decide they want nothing to do with it—once they know, they become complicit, which many may not be able to afford to do. If we want their help, it must be done in secret."

She'd seen the logic in his words, and reminded herself of it now, as she cupped Jax's jaw and pressed a kiss to his lips.

Straid's initial meetings with her clients proved useful: his insistence that Carra be allowed to share with him any potential threat to her safety had created a perfect loophole. She was able to share the information her clients divulged freely with Straid.

The fact she could only do so because her life might still be in danger was not lost on either of them.

"Is there anything I can do to help ease things?" she asked Jax, dropping her voice low. "Would talking about it more help?"

"Yes." The relief in his voice was palpable, and Carra had to stop herself from flinching at the sound of it. "You are, perhaps, the only person with whom I can speak freely."

"Unburden yourself. Tell me anything you need to get off your chest."

"You are certainly not one of my burdens," he said, turning them slightly so he lay on his back, with her head on his chest. "Right here is exactly where you should be."

He spoke for the next few minutes about things she didn't understand, and though she listened for anything that might help with the missing fae, nothing stood out to her—until he mentioned a business partner of his failing to show up for an important meeting.

"She has never failed me, not once," Jax said, his words already becoming more casual as his stress melted away with each sentence. "She's young: not yet two hundred years old. But she's cunning and shrewd, and I knew from the moment I met her that I wanted to do business with her. She dines with the royals and the criminals alike, and though everyone knows this about her, she is accepted in both of their worlds. Exactly who someone like me needs on their team.

"I have always been able to rely on her, but she missed a very important meeting four days ago. Luckily, I managed to salvage things, but when I called on her, she wasn't home. She's highly secretive, and often disappears for days or weeks at a time for reasons not always known to me, but she had never missed a meeting. Something must be deeply wrong for her to do so now."

"What's her name?" Carra asked, careful to keep her voice low and inquisitive, careful to keep the thrum of excitement she felt out of it.

"Kexxia. Perhaps you've heard of her?"

Carra shook her head, even as her mind raced. "I don't think so." She found herself glad, not for the first time, that she was human. Glad she could lie. It made her job much easier, and she suspected that was part of why her clients chose her: she could tell them exactly what they wanted to hear, no matter how she truly felt, something another fae would not be able to provide in her position.

"This is out of character for her, then?" Carra tilted her head to look more directly at Jax, but he kept his face pointed toward the ceiling, and his eyes remained closed.

"Very. It's been months since I've seen her, but that's not unusual. She mentioned that she would be gone for much of autumn, so I hadn't had occasion to see her before last week."

"Did she say where she was going? Maybe the journey back took longer than expected."

"No," Jax said, his voice tight. "She did not say. But I'd think that if she were merely delayed, she'd send word. Missing a meeting can get dangerous very quickly in our line of work.

"She's entitled to her secrets, of course. We all are. I suspect that keeping her secrets has kept her alive on numerous occasions. But she knows better than to miss a meeting. Her reputation and mine hinge on being dependable. I'm telling you, something is terribly, terribly wrong. I've asked after her this week, but the contacts I've spoken with have as little information as I do. As for the guards…they would not help me. I am not very well respected in the Quarters, Carra."

"If people saw the side of you that I see, you would be," Carra said, pressing a kiss to his cheek. "You're kind, and dependable, and you clearly care about her."

"I am a criminal." He stated the fact plainly, devoid of emotion.

"That doesn't make you a bad person. There are places I would be considered a criminal because of what we do together; does that mean I don't deserve respect or help when I need it?"

"Your profession should be honored above all others." Jax's voice took on a steel edge. "You provide valuable services, ones that those like me need in order to get through the day. The sex is incredible, of course," he said, "but this, as well. The space you create to safely be vulnerable is perhaps the most important job anyone has ever done. And you do it well. Nobody should ever make you feel lesser for any part of your job."

"They don't," she assured him. Not since the first guard had been dispensed with, anyway. Somewhere in the back of her mind another memory fought to make itself known: insults hurled at her, words she'd rather not repeat, even in her own mind. She couldn't remember who had said those things to her, for which she was glad; she had no interest in remembering the painful moments if she didn't have many happy memories to balance them out.

"I wish I could do something to help." She sighed, and had to fight a smile when, moments later, Jax responded to her careful delivery. She spun her words so they were regretful and hopeful, with just the right level of naivety to make men—whether human or fae—seek to give her whatever she wanted.

"I will keep you informed. And if you truly mean it, I will let you know if there comes a time I could use your help."

"Please do," Carra said, hoping she didn't sound too earnest. "I want to help you. I want to help *her*."

"You are so good, Carra," Jax murmured, tightening his arms

around her. "Never let anybody take that from you. The world needs more people like you."

Jesson met her at the end of the street, and they made easy conversation as they walked into town.

Her guard waited at the door as she slipped into The Meadow, greeting Sky as she entered. The faerie had warmed to her these past months, even going so far as to set aside pieces she thought Carra might want.

"Three new pieces I think you'd like," Sky trilled, leading Carra to the case in the back where she kept the special pieces locked away.

Carra knew before seeing them that she would purchase all three; Sky, like Carra, understood exactly what her clients wanted. Each of the three pieces was perfect: a dusky orange set with matching stockings that Lord Astrea would love; a cerulean slip that rippled as it moved, which would be perfect to wear with Retyiao; and a lavender piece made of straps and clasps that would take careful attention to remove—perfect for Callad, who loved a challenge.

As she made her way back to the counter to pay, a display along the wall caught her eye. Tucked behind a trickling waterfall, a brassiere sat nestled in a bed of moss. She peered closer, admiring the soft silvery shimmer of the material.

"Touch it," Sky commanded beside her.

"How? It's behind the waterfall."

"It's designed to get wet. Go on."

Warm water cascaded over her hand as she reached for the brassiere. Even after Sky's reassurance, she hesitated before touching it.

A bead of water dripped from her finger and Carra watched with bated breath as it landed on the fabric—which came alive in a riot of colors that spread from that single drop of water, until the entire garment shimmered an iridescent rainbow.

"It's beautiful," Carra whispered.

"Nobody has noticed it before. It's been here since the shop opened, a hundred generations ago. We age much faster than the high fae," she explained at Carra's curious look. "Faster even than humans. My family opened this store around the time Queen Zialania took the throne. A little over five hundred years, now. And in all that time, this display has not caught anybody's eye."

"How can that be?" Carra asked, awed. "It's stunning."

Sky shrugged. "The lore has been distorted as it passed from one generation to the next, so none of us know which stories are true. But it's yours to take."

"Oh, I'm not—"

"It's yours," Sky repeated firmly. "Whichever story is true, there's one part that never changes. The customer who's drawn to these pieces takes them free of charge."

"These pieces?" Carra looked closer, but there was only the brassiere nestled behind the waterfall; no matching panties or anything else.

"It's a matching set, separately hidden. The panties have yet to be found. Come, I'll wrap this up for you."

Carra stepped out of the store, dazed.

"What's wrong?" Jesson asked, following at her heel.

"Nothing. I was just gifted a beautiful piece. Nothing's wrong."

Jesson delivered her to the door, declining her invitation to join them for dinner.

"One of these days, you're going to accept."

"One of them," he answered with a smile. She grinned, struck by how easy it was to spend time with him. "Good evening, Carra."

She stood in the open doorway, watching him disappear around the side of the house.

"Welcome home."

She startled, whirling toward Straid as her heart raced. "Where did you come from?"

"I spent the afternoon in the observatory. I felt your absence greatly." His eyes widened slightly, like he hadn't meant to say it, and Carra's belly fluttered at the admission.

"Do you have anything to share from today's appointment?" he asked, stepping aside so she could enter the home.

"What do you want to know about?" she asked, with a teasing grin. The acknowledgement that Straid had missed her made her bold. "I'm not sure the privacy loophole will allow me to tell you about his favorite positions, although…" The familiar pressure that usually occurred in her mouth when she came too close to divulging secret information wasn't there. "Although it seems like he might be fine with that, actually. Is that what you were asking about?"

She smiled innocently, and a thrill coursed through her as Straid clenched his jaw, refusing to rise to her bait.

"You know why I am asking," Straid said, his voice quiet. But his eyes burned, and they dropped to her lips for the span of a single breath. Her eyes caught his and silence stretched between them for long minutes, growing so charged she could feel her temperature rise in response.

"Actually, yes." She cleared her throat and took as step back, dragging her mind back to the information Jax had shared with her. "He works with Kexxia. He said she missed a meeting a few days ago and he hasn't heard from her. He's worried, and when I offered to help, he said he would let me know if there was anything I could do."

Straid's eyebrows rose slightly—an expression that, from him, suggested utter shock.

"He's worried about her—so much so that I felt bad asking." She told him everything she remembered from their conversation, using Jax's exact phrasing whenever she could.

"You did very well."

She grinned. "I told you I would."

"Yes, you did." He regarded her with an inscrutable look.

"What?"

"I think—I am proud of you, Carra," he said softly, before

turning abruptly and walking away, leaving her alone in the foyer.

She watched him leave, pleased and disappointed in equal measure—she valued his pride but wished he had stayed. With a sigh, she turned to the stairs.

He caught up with her after only a few steps.

"Take these." Straid handed her a napkin, and when she unfolded it, she found two pastries inside. "They are made with orange and a spice I think you will enjoy." He slipped past her without another word, closing himself in his study and leaving her to stare after him in surprise.

She sank into a hot bath and bit into the first pastry, not even trying to fight the moan she made in response. He was right; the spice was sharp and made her tongue tingle ever so slightly, and she already wanted to ask Brey for more.

She didn't think about what it meant that he had paid such close attention to her tastes or that he had gone to the kitchen himself for the scones. She didn't think about the softness in his eyes as he had handed them to her.

No, she didn't think about those things at all.

CHAPTER TWENTY-FOUR

Straid organized the papers on his desk one final time in anticipation of Fell's impending arrival. None of his siblings had been to this home in years: only Umber had come—and only the one time—since the house had passed into Straid's sole possession. Fell had been only since Lyenna's death, and Straid had behaved abominably on that occasion.

Of his siblings, Fell was the least likely to make overt judgements, and yet Straid could not help but measure himself by the standards with which they had been raised. Standards he had always fallen short of, even before losing Lyenna—before *meeting* her, even. Her note, sparse as it was, had ignited the feelings of inferiority, though she was the only member of the family who had never made him feel less than enough.

He startled when the doorbell rang and swept down the stairs, hoping Carra would honor her agreement to stay out of sight. News of their marriage must have reached his family—everything did, typically fairly quickly—but he did not wish to introduce her to the family yet. Or ever, if at all possible.

Lyenna had been treated as a flightful fancy, a youthful obsession that his family had tolerated until it had become clear that he was serious about his love for her, at which point his mother had made it clear Lyenna was no longer welcome at the family's primary residence.

"She's beneath you," she'd hissed, her fingers tight on Straid's upper arm. "Mortals are fine for a dalliance here and there, but *love*? You might as well denounce your title and move to town."

He had moved to the townhome that day, though his mother had refused to allow him to leave the title behind. "You'll regret it someday," she'd said, her hand on the family book. "I will not strike your name from the ledger. You are barely in your second year—little more than a child; you do not yet know your own mind."

What little tolerance his family had had for Lyenna had disappeared the moment Straid had declared his intentions. He had to assume Carra would be extended much less grace as his wife. Even if Fell was the compassionate one, the only one who had planned on attending the wedding that had never happened...still, her understanding could only go so far.

He braced himself as he opened the door, steeling himself against Fell's inevitable reproach.

Fell flew forward the moment the door opened, wrapping her arms around him and squeezing so tightly it forced the air from his lungs. He stiffened under the hug, frozen, and she simply laughed, pulled back, then kissed him on both cheeks.

"You invited me back into your life, Straid. You had to know that would come with hugs and kisses. Affection is the price of working with me." She grinned, and he felt the corner of his mouth lift ever so slightly in response.

In relief, yes, but also in *joy*.

"See, I told you he could still smile," Fell tossed over her shoulder.

Corlan stepped into view. "Rarely. I didn't think he would react favorably to such a wanton display of affection." He chuckled.

"A wanton display of affection?" Fell scoffed.

"By his standards, yes."

Straid stepped aside to let his sister and friend enter his home, already regretting his decision to meet with the two of them. The three had been close in their youth, but he had aged immeasurably since then, while Fell and Corlan had not yet lost their exuberance.

He ushered them up the stairs, silently cursing himself when he saw Fell's gaze linger on Carra's door, then slowly shift across the hall to his study, no doubt parsing the invisible threads that linked them—threads only Fell could see.

He should have kept her far from Carra's rooms. Far from anything to do with her. Simply asking Carra to stay in the observatory for the duration of the meeting was not enough.

Fell's smirk as he closed the door and gestured for her to sit made his skin crawl: as though she knew something he would rather keep secret, some connection between him and Carra that, if he were to examine it closer, he would find was stronger than he had ever intended it to become.

"Why did it take so long for you to bring this to me?" Fell demanded, once Straid and Corlan had filled in the, admittedly very few, gaps in her knowledge.

Straid simply raised a brow.

"It took *me* so long to respond because I was looking into things, you ass. It might not have taken me so long if you had reached out to me sooner—by the time I got your letter the threads were already old. Do you know how much harder weak threads are to read after a few weeks? I'm not the one to blame here. Why *didn't* you come to me sooner?"

"He didn't want the family involved," Corlan answered, before Straid could.

"I'm hardly 'the family,'" Fell scoffed. "Aside from being your literal sister, I am nothing like the rest of them. Which you'd know, if you would spend time with me. Something you should remember from the days we used to spend together."

Straid could hear the undercurrent of hurt in her words; she did nothing to hide them. He wondered, for a moment, if he had been too hasty in cutting contact with her. At first, he had not wanted anyone around—save for Lyenna, the one person whose company he could no longer seek. As the years passed, it had simply become easier to keep to himself. To ignore the missives that came less frequently with each passing decade.

"I was grieving," he said quietly. "I could not face anybody."

"Except Corlan," she challenged.

"He turned me away for over two years before I finally wore him down," his friend corrected. "Even then, he only talked to me under duress for the better part of a decade. I still can't get him to attend a party."

"I attended one." The party at which he had met Kexxia.

"You came late, you left early, and you spent the entire time alone in the gardens."

"Precisely. I attended."

His lips twinged as he fought a smile—and lost the battle when Corlan and Fell made eye contact one another and laughed.

He had missed this. Had missed them.

Fell insisted on visiting Kexxia's home that night, and Straid agreed that would be the best course of action. He sent Fell and Corlan ahead, then detoured to the observatory to inform Carra he would miss dinner.

When he reached the room, the sight of her working stopped him short.

She moved pots and planters with precision, tucking them into alcoves, then shaking her head and swapping one plant for another. Occasionally, she wiped sweat from her brow with the back of a hand, and he found his eyes tracking the glistening drops that clung to her fingers as she returned to her task. There was a beauty to the way she moved, and he found himself utterly entranced.

"Straid? Are you coming?"

He whirled at the sound of his sister's voice, inwardly

cursing himself for the distraction—and for the fact that he had failed to notice that the wards had remained silent. He glanced back at Carra, hoping she had not heard his sister's query, but of course he could not be so lucky.

She looked their way with a broad smile on her face and gave them a small wave. She tilted her head at Straid, as if to ask who this was, and if she would be getting an introduction. He had told her he would have a guest; he had not divulged who it would be.

Behind him Fell snickered.

"I see why you tried to keep her away from me, dear brother," she murmured. She stepped around him before he could respond, and in a few short strides Fell reached Carra.

"I'm Fell," she said, with the smile that made men and women alike fall at her feet—and he noted with a start that Carra was not immune to her charms. "Straid's sister. You must be the wife."

"I'm Carra."

"Beautiful name," his sister said, looking his wife over. "It suits you."

Straid strode forward and clasped Fell's upper arm, gently tugging her away from Carra. She allowed him to pull her backward until they stood side-by-side, and he thanked the universe for the small mercy of her acquiescence. It was too much to hope that she would forget about Carra, that she would let the matter drop, but perhaps she would follow him out of the house without a fight.

"We must leave," he reminded her. He turned to Carra. "I came to inform you that I will be absent for dinner. We will be investigating Kexxia's disappearance."

"Straid." Beside him, Fell had gone very still. "Say that again," she urged him. He did.

His sister's eyes darted between him, Corlan, and, maddeningly, Carra. He fought the urge to sweep his wife from the room in order to protect her from whatever his sister said next.

"She's coming with us," Fell declared. "You're coming with us," she repeated, turning to Carra.

"Fell."

"When you mentioned Kexxia's disappearance, I saw something, Straid. A thread, between your words and Carra. Bringing her along could help."

He did not like the idea, but Carra had already set aside the pot she had been holding. "Do I have time to change?"

"I'll help you." Fell stepped forward and reached out a hand, which Carra took, and before he knew it the two of them had retreated to Carra's rooms.

"Lost control of that situation," Corlan said with a snort.

"I should have known that I would. Fell is a force to be reckoned with, and—"

"So is Carra." Corlan finished his sentence for him, and the two shared a brief smile.

One which Straid quickly forced into a frown. If he was not careful, he would lose control of much more than just this situation.

Would that really be so bad? a part of him wondered. He had not realized, these fifty years, how lonely the house had become. How painful the silence he once sought had now become.

A silence that was immediately broken by the return of Fell and Carra.

Carra, who wore trousers that clung to her every curve and sent wicked thoughts through his mind. Thoughts of the hands that had crafted them ripping the fabric to shreds in his haste to remove them.

"Ready?" Fell asked him with a smirk, and he quickly turned his mind to other matters, though it was too late. His sister clearly saw the connection growing between him and Carra. And, judging by the look on her face, she knew exactly how he wanted to act on it, exactly what he hoped might change between them.

All of that fell away once they reached Kexxia's home. Fell

walked through the space slowly, her discerning gaze landing on every item. She touched nothing on the first walkthrough; she merely looked closely at the threads that only she could see.

Once she had closely examined every room of the house, she repeated the process, though this time she touched everything: she brushed her hands against the clothes in the dresser; unstacked then restacked the plates in the kitchen cupboard; and lay her hands on many items Straid did not understand the significance of.

None of the others spoke; they watched her work in silence until finally, more than an hour after they had arrived, Fell dropped onto the cushions on the floor of the visitation room with a sigh.

"I don't understand."

"What do you not understand?" Straid asked. Something about his sister's expression set his heart racing, and when she turned her gaze on him, it only became worse.

"The connections. They don't make sense. It's almost as if..."

She trailed off, her eyes growing glassy. Carra tensed at his side, but Straid subtly shook his head at her. This happened with Fell's gift, at times.

"The connections here run deep," Fell murmured. "They are multi-layered: none of them exist on their own. At least four distinct threads—no, five, I think. But some of them blur together, and some of them...even when they're clear, they don't make sense."

"Tell us." Corlan's voice was strained, anxious, and Fell aimed a gentle smile his way.

"Two of the threads in particular are giving me pause: one of someone who's long dead, and one of someone I've only felt—" She stiffened, her mouth snapping shut and her jaw going rigid.

"Something you vowed not to speak about."

Fell nodded, her face crumpling as her eyes darted to Straid.

"What can you tell us?" Corlan asked, inching closer to Fell. "Anything at all. Please."

"The first thread is of—" She faltered again, and as her eyes settled on Straid's, a deep sense of unease roiled in his gut. "Did she ever meet Kexxia?"

"Did who ever meet Kexxia?"

His sister hesitated, and in that moment, Straid knew. Numbness flooded his body and Fell's words were far away as she answered.

"Lyenna."

"No. They did not know each other." Straid shook his head, certain.

"Perhaps the same illness that claimed her, then? Sometimes the connections are tenuous, or murky. And her threads are faint. I can't quite tell *how* they are connected, but they are."

"You said there were more threads," Corlan urged.

Fell clenched her jaw, the strain of her vow evident. She shook her head, then took a deep breath. "The first thread is Lyenna. I—I can't talk about the second. The third is yours, Corlan. You are all over this house. In the bedroom, which I would have expected. But you're in her wardrobe, and her garden, too. You're everywhere."

"I didn't exactly keep my feelings secret." Corlan's voice was quiet, subdued, and Straid strained to hear it over the roaring in his ears.

There was no evidence Kexxia had been ill. No evidence the illness that had claimed Lyenna even affected fae. For Lyenna's threads to be here, so long after her death…she must have come here often. The two women must have been close. How that would have happened without Straid's knowledge eluded him.

"No, you didn't," his sister was saying. "I'm happy for you, Corlan. I hope we can find her." She gazed at Corlan's face for long seconds. "You're worried. I won't lie; I definitely think you have cause to be. But as far as I can tell, she's alive. She was when she left, and the connections are strong. Stronger than I would expect if she were dead; her threads are shining. I would bet my life that she's alive right now."

Corlan crumpled. His face and his body both, and his loud, shuddering breaths were the only sound in the place. Fell moved to his side, throwing an arm around him and murmuring words that Straid could not hear.

Beside him, Straid could feel Carra's gaze on his face. He dared not meet her eyes.

"There's a thread unaccounted for." Straid said instead.

"Your cook, I think. Elesina, was that her name? I didn't spend enough time in your kitchen to be sure, but I think it was her."

"And the connection between Kexxia and Carra?" Straid asked.

"It's stronger," Fell whispered, her eyes dancing across the mortal woman's face. "Stronger than Carra's connections are to you, in this moment."

"What does that mean?" Carra breathed.

"It means—"

But the rest of his sentence went unsaid as a blast shook the home. He dove toward Carra out of instinct, his body shielding her from whatever threat had appeared. He made to check her for injuries, but as he raised his head, movement caught his eye, a person moving swiftly through the door, away from the scene. Straid did not think; he simply ran.

CHAPTER TWENTY-FIVE

Carra didn't think; she just ran after Straid.

He was always so calm, so measured. If something was making him run, then she probably should, too.

She realized her error two blocks over, as he grew farther with every step. He was tall, and fae; she should have known she wouldn't be able to keep up with him.

She made it to the edge of town before losing him entirely. Each breath felt like knives against her throat and lungs, and she tasted metal on the back of her tongue. She paused to catch her breath, bracing herself against a nearby wall.

Seconds later, Corlan appeared at her side.

"Lost him?" he asked.

"I did. I think I got far enough away, though."

Corlan quirked a brow, and she explained. "In case there's another blast. We should be safe here."

"He wasn't running *from* anything," Fell said, sauntering down the street like their lives weren't all in danger. "He saw something."

Of course he had; Straid was too measured to bolt like that. If he was running, it would be toward something, not away from it; it felt obvious now that she thought about it.

"What did he see?" Carra asked. Her breath was finally starting to slow, though her heart still raced.

"Something that's not my place to divulge," Fell responded, though she exchanged a glance with Corlan that suggested he likely also knew.

Everyone was privy to this information but her, then.

"You said there were connections to me. This is related to what happened the night Straid and I met. It's related to why I can't remember anything about my life from prior to a few months ago." Her voice had grown steely, and she raised herself to her full height, squaring her shoulders. "I deserve to know about threats to my own life. You. Will. Tell. Me." She took a step forward, and was met with a sharp smile from Fell.

"Good," Fell said with an approving nod. "You're going to need that fire, if I'm right. And I usually am."

"About what?"

"One of the threads is someone from Straid's past. Someone he will have to tell you about himself. I will not betray him by sharing." Fell's voice left no room for argument. "But ask him," she said, more softly. "He needs to talk about it, and at this point, you need to know.

"Somehow, it's all connected," Fell continued. "Her, Kexxia, Elesina…you. I don't know much, yet. The threads are weak, and sparse; someone has gone through a lot of trouble to conceal them. But I do know that you need to be careful. Don't leave the house if you can help it, and make sure you always have someone with you if you do. Someone strong. You're in danger."

"We should continue this conversation at the house." Corlan scanned the street, his face tight. Fell agreed, looking at Carra expectantly.

"What about Straid?"

"He will return home when he's ready. It could be a while, given…the nature of things."

Corlan reached a hand out to Carra, who took it, bracing herself. She felt a tug in her stomach and a *wrongness* tingling across her skin, and she squeezed her eyes tight against the sensation. When she opened her eyes, the house loomed before her.

She stumbled away from Corlan, gasping.

"It is a rather unpleasant feeling, isn't it? It's over now, though," she said, gazing up at the house with a frown.

Carra peered at the house as Corlan fumbled with the gate, struck as she always was by how much smaller the house looked from the street. She'd asked Straid about it on one of their walks, but he'd given an enigmatic response that did little to answer her question: "I do not wish to have visitors, as a rule."

As they walked the stone path that skirted the house, Carra noticed chips in the blue-gray paint, and weeds growing through the cracks at the base of the house. She'd never paid much attention to the side of the house, but she was certain the house had been in better shape even the day before.

"It didn't look this way this morning," Fell said quietly.

"No, it didn't," Carra agreed.

"Fae magic." Fell's eyes narrowed as she stopped to examine the house. "The house doesn't look great on a normal day, but it never looks this bad. He's hurt," she added softly. "The house is in poor condition because he is as well."

"We should get inside." Corlan ushered them along the path, his anxiety palpable.

"Shouldn't someone go after Straid?"

"He'll be fine." Fell shrugged. "He's tough. And he has... ways of defending himself."

"The thing he does with his hands." Even through her anxiety, an image of Straid's hands flashed through her mind, doing things they'd only done in her fantasies, and she flushed. "The air thing, I mean."

Fell smirked at her, and Carra looked to Corlan for help, but he just watched her with an inscrutable expression on his face. There had been moments where she could almost believe he liked her. Other times, like now, she wondered how much effort he put into simply tolerating her.

"He used the power to save you?" Fell asked.

"He did. The guard was threatening me. He was well within his rights to, if I'm being honest. I don't remember why I took that particular route, but I was somewhere I shouldn't have been, and I *knew* I wasn't allowed there. Straid stepped in and protected me. The guard didn't want to let me leave with him, but Straid forced him to. He…he cut off his air supply, I think. Without ever touching him. He then promised no harm would come to me from his hand." Carra laughed. "Needless to say, I wasn't exactly comforted by that. I'd just watched him harm someone without using his hands, and I assumed he'd phrased it that way to exploit a loophole. I wouldn't go with him. So he promised he wouldn't hurt me at all."

"He said that? He *promised* it?"

"He swore it, actually." Carra's voice softened, and she didn't try to hide it. "It's what made me trust him. What finally made me realize I was safe with this stranger who had saved me, even if I still didn't know why I was in the Quarters. I didn't even know my own name. But I had just watched him hurt someone in order to protect me, and then swear he would never hurt me."

"Well, damn."

"Yeah. Damn," she agreed quietly.

Night had long fallen, dinner had long passed, and still, the three of them waited for Straid.

And then, finally, the front door flew open with a loud bang, and Straid stumbled into the foyer. He listed to the right, his hand pressed to his side, and as Carra drew closer she caught sight of his hand, glistening red.

"What happened?" She slipped an arm around him, and he allowed her to take his weight without complaint. Something he would normally be much too proud to do. Her blood chilled.

"A trap. I thought I saw—but it was not her. Whoever it was knew I would follow someone who bore a resemblance to her. I was ambushed, roughly an hour beyond the Quarters."

"I'll take care of it," Fell said, standing.

"There is no need. There were no survivors."

"Just you," Carra whispered.

Straid shook his head, and her vision tunneled.

"What do you mean? How badly are you hurt?"

"I cannot heal it myself." Straid sagged, and she struggled under his weight until Corlan gently led him to a nearby chair. Straid dropped into the chair with a groan, all trace of his usual grace gone. "I believe I will live. I very nearly did not."

Carra breathed a shaky sigh of relief. She told herself it was because her own future would be unclear if Straid died, but the truth was she had come to enjoy spending time with him. She had come to enjoy the hours they spent in the observatory. The peaceful silence that fell between them—even the tense barbs they had lobbed at one another. She could not imagine her life in the Quarters—or her life *at all*—without him.

"You'd fucking better live," she found herself saying, and for once she didn't care about the emotion that crept into her voice and betrayed the riot of feelings inside her. "What do you need?"

"Rest."

"Then let's get you to bed."

Carra rose, and across from her, so did Fell and Corlan.

"I appreciate your help today," Straid said, the words slightly slurred. He moved his hand to the arm of the chair, as if to brace himself for standing up. "Corlan, I will call on you as soon as I am well enough to continue the investigation. Fell, I will endeavor to communicate more."

"I'm not leaving," Fell challenged, her eyes flashing.

"Yes, you are. I am perfectly capable of getting myself to my own bed." As if to accentuate his point, Straid stood.

He swayed.

Carra rushed to his side, ignoring his scoff as she slipped an arm around him, careful to avoid the blood blossoming on his side.

"I'll help you," she murmured.

"Let us help, Straid," Fell agreed.

"One is enough. I am not so injured that I must have three attendants escort me through my own home. I would accept the help if it were needed, Fell."

She pursed her lips, watching him for long seconds before she finally relented with a nod, though the tension in her jaw betrayed just how much she didn't want to honor her brother's wishes.

"Come on, Corlan. Let's go."

And suddenly Carra was alone with the injured husband she could no longer deny she had feelings for.

CHAPTER TWENTY-SIX

The wound in his side burned. Seven hours, and still it had not healed. He allowed Carra to lead him up the stairs, too weak to fight; too weak to feel shame over his need for help. She paused at the entryway to his room and shifted her weight, as if to extricate herself from him, but he gripped her shoulder with what little strength he had left.

"You may enter."

Four months and she had never entered his room. He had dreamt of her in there, but to actually cross that line…he had thought, when the time came, it would be for very different reasons.

He hissed as she eased him onto the edge of his bed. He needed rest, and then he could attempt another healing in the morning. Until then, though it pained him to admit it, he needed her.

"Sit with me."

She did and took the cloth as he attempted to clean his own wound.

"Let me."

He hissed, then clamped his mouth shut. He had shown

enough weakness tonight already. He caught her hand and squeezed her fingers, pouring his thanks into the gesture.

Sometime later her hand slipped from his and opened his eyes, pulled from a fitful sleep. His gaze found her in the darkness. "Stay for a little while," he entreated.

He breathed deep, the wound in his side screaming. But he needed strength for his next word, a gift to the woman he could not live without.

"Please."

Carra's eyes widened, even as she took a tentative step toward him. "You said there would be no new open contracts between us—"

"Until I trusted you. In all honesty, I have trusted you for some time now. My life was in your hands tonight, and you chose to preserve it."

"Maybe it's payback for you saving me all those months ago," she said softly, too tenderly for the words to carry any bite. "Maybe I'm secretly plotting your demise."

"No." He met her gaze, wished he could vanquish the tears swimming in her eyes. "You cared for me. You…care for me."

"Yes. I do." She cleared her throat. "What do you need? Bandages? Medicine? How can I help you?"

He directed her to the kitchen and told her what to bring: the medicinal herbs, a clean bowl, hot water, and bandages. Though he winced when she laid the marinated bandages on his wound, the pain retreated almost instantly. Her ministrations were soft, careful—but attentive. He could imagine no one better to tend to him in this state—and he had once had the best doctors in all the Quarters at his disposal.

She lingered when she was done, and he did not ask her to leave. Instead, he watched as her curiosity got the better of her and she surveyed the room.

First the bed, with its deep blue silks, then the window that overlooked the gardens where he had married her four months prior, when he had been unsure whether he was making the right decision, yet certain he could not make any other. And then her eyes landed on the small table beside his bed: the water pitcher, the book, the glass rose figurine, and…

"This is who Fell mentioned, tonight?"

"Yes."

"Tell me about her."

Straid closed his eyes, unable to watch Carra examine the portrait of Lyenna.

"No." He meant to say it with finality, but his voice betrayed him; weakened as he was by the wound, he could not keep the hesitation from it, or the pain.

"She was beautiful. She must have meant a lot to you."

He could not talk about her. Not here, not with *her*.

Yet, somehow, he felt the words begin to spill from his mouth, and he was powerless to stop them in the wake of the memories of his first—his only—love.

"Her name was Lyenna." He kept his eyes closed, unable to face her as he recounted his most sacred memories. "She was radiant: the most beautiful woman I had ever met, in every way. We were the same age—I was impossibly young, for a fae, and she was mortal. I did not care that we would only have a few short decades together; I only cared that I would share a portion of my life with her. It would not be enough time, but our love was worth taking whatever short years she had to give.

"And then she fell ill on a visit to her family, when I had only known her two years. I wanted to stay at her side, but she sent me away. She had become convinced there was a way I could save her: that I could somehow transfer a piece of my immortality to her so we could be together forever. I knew better, but her hope infected me, and I left. My research was fruitless, of course, and by the time I returned, it was too late; her family had already buried her."

"That's awful."

"It was the worst day of my life. I returned home, utterly devastated, only to find a parcel waiting for me. Her wedding dress. She never had a chance to wear it."

"Oh, Straid." He felt a hand on his shoulder and allowed himself to take comfort from it for a brief moment. He closed his eyes against the tears that threatened to spill at the tenderness, in the face of such pain. "Marrying me must have been so hard," Carra whispered.

"It was no true choice; it was easy enough, to save a life."

"You did have a choice," came Carra's rebuttal. "You didn't know me. I was just some human woman where she wasn't supposed to be. Everyone knows the punishment for a mortal found in that part of the Quarters alone."

"I would have wanted someone to intervene, had it been her alone in the Quarters. I would have wanted someone to save her, no matter the cost. I will never be able to bring her back, or replace her, but I was able to do this one small thing in her honor."

"I appreciate it," Carra said, pressing a kiss to his temple. Her hand tightened on his shoulder, and he took comfort in the weight of it. Solid, steady. Reassuring. "How long ago did it happen?"

"Fifty years. She likely would have still been alive today if she had not fallen ill. She would have been old, for a mortal, with gray hair and a lined face, and the signs of her age would have terrified and mesmerized me in equal measure."

"You're a lot younger than I thought."

"I am quite young, yes. I will be seventy in the spring. I have yet to attend my first Ousilie's Ball."

"What's that?"

"I will show you." The words were out of his mouth before he had given it any real consideration, but he found that he meant them. What better way to show her she had saved his life as much as he had saved hers than to bring her to the most sacred of fae traditions? As his wife, she would be...not entirely welcome but allowed to attend. He found that he wanted her there, by his side.

"If you ever want to talk about her…"

"No. This was more than I have said about her in half a century. That is enough."

CHAPTER TWENTY-SEVEN

The next morning Carra knocked on Straid's bedroom door, but he wouldn't allow her in his room. Sometime during the night, his pride had returned in full force. If she hadn't heart him stirring on the other side of the door, she would have found a way to pry it open. But with confirmation that he was alive, she had to assume his solitude was a sign he was recovering well enough to return to his typical reticence.

She spent the morning in the observatory, but her mind kept straying upstairs. The plants, purchased by Straid the moment she'd communicated a desire for more, reminded her of him. The glass, cleaned by his hands until it shone clear enough to provide a pristine view of the gardens, reminded her of him. The pillows where they'd shared meals, the walkway where they had so nearly kissed, so nearly acknowledged this thing growing between them—it all dragged her mind back to him.

She sighed, closing the observatory door gently behind her. She lingered outside Straid's bedroom, but couldn't bring herself to knock again, not when she knew he would simply ignore her again. So, after a few interminably long minutes, she turned her attention to the rest of the house. Her explorations took her to a library, three parlors, a ballroom she had barely explored on her first foray to the third floor. After a quick lunch eaten alone, she wandered the second floor.

She'd avoided the suite since that fateful day—easily done, once she'd begun going to her clients' homes instead of receiving them here. But now she found herself drawn to it, curious as to whether it was still larger than the first few times she'd been in there.

She had meant to ask Straid what magic made the room seem bigger than it had before, but his witnessing her and Jax together had banished all thought of the room from her mind.

Now, Carra paused with her hand on the door, remembering the chill that had run through her at the unsettling *wrongness* of the room the last time she was in there. But she was curious, so she took a deep breath and slowly turned the doorknob. The door swung open, and she stepped inside hesitantly, her heart thundering in her chest.

It was normal.

The size it had always been.

Perhaps she had imagined it growing larger before.

Relief slammed through her, and she sagged against the wall. There was nothing to fear here, no magic that wormed its way through the room and left her unsettled. Nothing at all was amiss.

The next day, she returned to tidy it up, though it would likely be weeks, or months, until she used the room for its intended purpose. Still, she needed something to do, and this room had been the first thing that crossed her mind.

She stepped into the room and her blood ran cold.

When the room grew, the change was subtle, and it had taken her long minutes to pinpoint the change. But now she could tell, from the moment she opened the door, that the room had shrunk —to nearly half the size it was yesterday.

She slammed the door in her panic, her vision clouding with fear as she ran to Straid's room.

She pounded on his door, then tried the handle when there

was no answer. She considered yelling, demanding that he let her in, or come out to her, and explain what the hell was going on with his house. But then she thought of his wound, of how hurt he had been, and she stalked to her room, fear still prickling the back of her neck.

She returned to her room and poured her fears into her diary, writing until her hands stopped shaking and her heart slowed to a normal speed.

Carra stopped her explorations after that, fearful of what she might find—of how the room might be shifting in her absence.

Instead, she spent her time in the kitchen, learning from Brey as the chef walked her through the pastry-making process. Carra's creations were lopsided, and often too dense, but Brey praised her nonetheless, and Carra accepted the praise with a grateful smile. It felt good to be doing something as she waited for Straid to appear.

"I can take this to Straid." Carra lifted the tray, laden with her misshapen attempts and Brey's perfect ones alike.

"There's no need. Put it down and watch."

Carra complied, and second later, the tray vanished, transported to Straid's room by magic.

Niana entered the kitchen and froze at the sight of Carra, who aimed an apologetic smile her way. Niana tutted, but her face softened into a smile. "You're cooking?"

"Brey's teaching me," she said, pulling three plates out of the cupboard and setting them on the counter. She motioned for the fae women to join her.

"You should eat at the table," Brey chided. But she dropped a cheese and onion scone onto Carra's plate and slid onto the stool beside her.

"Only if you eat with me."

"It isn't proper."

"Neither is me eating alone. There's got to be some fae custom against it, right? You can't make a guest dine alone at the fancy table."

"It would be more proper than this," Brey argued.

"Join me, and I'll start eating in there again. Both of you."

"I could not," Brey countered, appalled.

But the next morning the table was laid for three, and Niana took the seat across from Carra. Brey joined only once it became apparent the two would not eat without her.

After breakfast something caught her eye in the foyer: smooth wall, where a door had been. She approached it cautiously, running her hand over the wood—but the room where Straid had met with her clients had vanished without a trace.

She stumbled at the top of the stairs, her foot seeking the final step—but it, too, had disappeared. The threw out a hand to catch herself, and it landed on paneled walls, where there should have been air; the hallway had narrowed by almost a foot.

"What's happening to the house?" she whispered to Niana as the fae woman brushed her hair that evening.

"I cannot say. I am forbidden from speaking of it, even with you."

"Give me a hint. Find a loophole," Carra begged.

"I cannot." But the tightness in her eyes only confirmed Carra's suspicion that whatever it was could not be good.

On the fourth day of total silence from Straid, Carra finally gave in and pounded on his door again, resolved not to leave until she had answers—about his condition, and about the house. It took almost ten minutes for the door to swing slowly open, and Straid stood in front of her, pallid, his forehead glistening with sweat. He wore only a pair of black pants slung low over his hips, and his chest, like his brow, was slick with sweat.

"You're...how are you feeling?" She examined him quickly. His skin had taken on a yellow pallor, but the bandage covering his side was pristine white, and she breathed a sigh of relief at the lack of blood. "You don't look good."

"I am unwell." Straid frowned slightly, then swayed on his

feet, stumbling into the hallway. Carra rushed forward and slid an arm around his back to steady him.

"What do you need?"

"Rest."

"What else?" she asked, taking a step forward. But something stopped her: an invisible barrier across his doorway that she could not cross. The wards.

Straid mumbled something under his breath and the barrier fell away, allowing her to guide him into his bedroom and gently ease him onto the bed.

She had expected pride and stoicism when she finally saw him again, but the man before her exhibited neither; he was weak, ragged. She cursed herself for allowing him to stay hidden away the past few days; clearly, he needed help.

Perched on the edge of the bed, Carra brushed a hand across Straid's forehead, and he shuddered at the touch. "What can I get you?" she murmured. "Let me take care of you." She almost added a *please*, but caught herself at the last moment, and the word sat unsaid on her tongue.

"You. I just want you," he rasped, pressing his head into her hand. "Stay with me," he mumbled.

The lights flickered.

She glanced down to see that his mouth was pinched and his eyes shut tight. He gritted his teeth and blanched—and the lights flickered again.

"What's wrong with the house?" she asked, threading her fingers through his hair and lightly scratching his scalp. He was her primary concern, but if the house was failing around them, she needed to know. She would carry him out if she had to.

"Nothing."

"It's shrinking, and the lights just flickered," she countered, but her voice lacked any of its usual fire. *She* lacked any of her usual fire.

"Nothing is wrong with the house; something is wrong with me." He spoke slowly, as though every word pained him.

Carra frowned. "What do you mean?"

"I cannot heal. This wound…should be better by now." Each word was heavier than the last, and he drew deep breaths between them. She shushed him, but he pressed his head into her hand and kept explaining. "The house is tied to the owner, fueled by their magic. I am in pain, so the house is as well. I cannot heal as I should, so the house is offering its energy to me. Certain…sacrifices must be made."

"You need a doctor. If only for the house's sake."

A sound escaped Straid that was somewhere between a laugh and a scoff—though even it was rife with pain. "I cannot bring a doctor here."

"Why not?"

"Word would spread. My family…"

"You think Fell would rather you lie here in pain than bring a doctor in to help? From the afternoon I spent with her, I can tell you that is absolutely not true."

He shook his head. "Not Fell. The rest. They…do not understand certain choices I have made. They would see it as proof of my weakness, and draw me back in."

"You don't get along with your family?"

"They disapproved of Lyenna. She was not the only aspect of my life of which they disapproved, but she was the worst of it. They had qualms about me dedicating my life to a mortal."

"Oh."

The unspoken words hung between them: that his family would disapprove of her, too. It shouldn't bother her; the marriage had never been about anything but keeping her alive. But still, the idea that her husband's family would not consider her good enough for him, without even having met her, rankled.

"And there's no way you could get a doctor here without them knowing?"

Straid shook his head. "My family has ways of knowing everything. They would immediately discover my weakness and leverage it against me."

A ridiculous part of her wanted to ask if he was referring to his injury or to her. Instead, she fell silent, stroking his head in contemplative silence.

"What can I do?" she finally asked. "There must be something I can do to help. Changing your bandages, or—or—something. You saved my life, Straid. Let me do whatever I can to help you."

"I cannot. I owe you too much already."

"I need something to do. Think of it as payment on one of the bonds between us. You owe me, so let me take care of you. For my sake." She hesitated, rolling her next word around in her mouth, building her courage to say it until finally, gently, she let it free. "Please."

Straid shuddered against her, his eyes squeezing shut. "Fine. The bandage."

She eased him into a seated position, then gently traced the edge of the bandage. He tensed for a moment, then gritted his teeth, nodding at her to begin.

"I'm going to take this off, wash the wound, and then put a new bandage on," she murmured. He nodded, the motion a little softer, a bit less controlled, than normal. It was that, more than anything, that made her nervous as she gently peeled the edges of the bandage from his skin.

She gasped, stifling a cry at what lay beneath.

"Sorry," she murmured, looking away. "You need a doctor, Straid."

"No."

"Straid."

She steeled herself, then leaned closer to inspect his abdomen, forcing herself to ignore the roiling in her stomach at the sight of it. The wound was angry, the edges bright red and puckered, like the skin was pulling away from the gaping hole in his side. The hole itself contained were more colors than she could count. Yellow and green oozed from the bloody mess, and spots of white and black clung to his flesh.

"Straid," she ground out, "this is so much worse than I thought. I don't know about fae healing—I don't know what it should look like by now, but I know this is—this is bad. It's infected. If you don't get a doctor here soon, I think you might die." She forced the words through her rising panic.

Straid groaned beside her, but he didn't argue. A chill ran down Carra's spine at his tacit confirmation.

"Call a doctor," she pleaded again.

"I cannot."

"Fine, then I'll make it about me again. What happens to me if you die? What do I do then? You made a promise to keep me safe that night, and dying would be going back on that promise. Are you really going to do that?"

"I will not die."

"Straid."

"You may clean the wound, if you are so concerned."

She gritted her teeth.

"I will accept your help, if the offer still stands. I will not call for a doctor."

Carra started to argue, but the weary desperation in his eyes stopped her short. "Fine. I'll do it, but only for tonight." She reached for the bowl of water beside his bed, wincing when she discovered it was cold. She didn't like the thought of leaving him alone again, but she couldn't properly clean the wound with cold water. She stood to leave, but the bowl grew warm in her hands, and she nearly dropped it in surprise.

"Stay," Straid said, in a tone that sounded suspiciously close to pleading.

She dipped a clean cloth in the bowl and wrung it out, her fingers stinging from the warmth of the water. "Tell me about your ability—your gift, I think you called it?"

"As you clean."

He hissed when she pressed the cloth to his side, his eyes falling shut. She gently rubbed at the edges of his wound as he spoke, his words peppered with barely-suppressed reactions to her touch. She didn't adjust her approach at the sound of his pain.

If he wanted gentler hands, he could call for a doctor.

CHAPTER TWENTY-EIGHT

"I have dominion over the air." He was almost happy for the conversation, as it served to distract him from the blinding pain in his side. Carra's hands were gentle, yet the sensation threatened to overwhelm him.

He had lost consciousness more times than he could count while changing his own bandages, and he found himself grateful for the help; he had initially refused out of pride and an attempt to spare her from the sight, nothing more.

"You saw what I did to the guard the night we met." He could still remember the fear on Carra's face when he had approached her afterward, the way she had backed away from him. He had cursed himself, at the time, for drawing the air from the guard's lungs in front of a woman he was attempting to save, a woman who would be wise not to trust him after witnessing such an act. "I can direct the air where I want it to go. As you witnessed, I can steal it from a person's lungs, for example. I can do more mundane things, as well: heat the air, cool it."

"Not just air; you heated the water in this bowl."

"I heated the air within the water." The thing nobody seemed to realize about his gift—the thing even *he* had not realized until after Lyenna's death—was that there was air in everything. To control the air was to control all things. He shut his eyes against the horror of it, pushing aside the memory he could not face.

"How did you get the gift?" she asked, her fingers soft against his skin. "I know some fae have special abilities, but how is it determined? Or is it random? Retyiao has his pheromone, but that seems to be standard for the offaedia, as far as I can tell. Same with Sky and her flying. But controlling the air seems to be specific to you. Why is that?"

He had been dreading the question since that first night, had known it was coming, but still felt thoroughly unprepared. He cast about for some semblance of truth, a kernel he could weave into an answer without divulging the secrets he still kept.

"It runs in the family," he finally said, grimacing at the pain as she dabbed at the wound once more. "My siblings and I each have a gift. My mother, as well."

"Not your father?"

"None of our fathers do."

Carra cocked her head, but refrained from asking the question he knew was on her mind. He answered it anyway.

"There are five of us. Ash and Umber are the eldest, Ash preceding Umber by mere minutes. After them came Rowan, then Fell, and finally me. Each of us has a different father, save for Ash and Umber. Aside from the twins, our paternal parentage is unknown by all except our mother."

"Oh. Is that…Was that hard for you, growing up?"

Straid chuckled despite himself, then winced at the sharp pain that lanced through his side. "I am still growing up, Carra. I am not even a hundred years old. In the span of fae lives, mine has barely begun. My family lives to be hundreds, even thousands of years old. But to answer your question, no. It has not been difficult. As a child, it never mattered; I was surrounded by family, and servants—there were so many people I likely would not have noticed one more. And now…I have fallen out with my family; had I known my father, he would likely have been another person I lost in the wake of Lyenna."

"You didn't lose your whole family; you still have Fell."

"Fell and I had not spoken in decades, until the day you met her. But I am grateful that she is in my life once more."

"So you get your gifts from your mother." Carra set the bowl aside and dried the wound. She moved slowly, methodically, a welcome change from his own clumsy attempts as he had rushed to finish before losing consciousness. He inwardly chided himself for not accepting her help sooner.

"Yes. Her bloodline is strong, and carries the gift in it, though it manifests differently in each of us."

"You can control the air, and Fell sees threads that show her how things are connected. What about the others?"

"The gifts are personal; they are not mine to share." He spoke the truth, but he had his own reasons for keeping the information from her, as well. She would balk at Ash's gift, and Umber's… Straid clenched his jaw at the mere thought. Umber's refusal to halt time in Lyenna's final days, to stop the illness from progressing, still infuriated him. When Umber had appeared on his doorstep begging a favor a mere thirty years later, Straid had relished in forcing his brother to offer a boon, the largest debt a fae could incur.

"Ash, as the eldest, will pass the gift on to any children she may bear."

"Is she the only one who'll pass it on?"

Straid hissed as Carra spread ointment on his wound. It tingled—burned. But he knew without it, the pain would be far greater.

"As the heir, Ash is the only one guaranteed to pass the gift to any children she may have, assuming she…assuming certain circumstances do not change. I am, of course, the least likely to impart it upon my future children, even were I to consider procreating."

"You don't want kids?"

He had considered it once, when Lyenna was alive, although the likelihood of conception between fae and human was low.

His mother could have used her gift to make it happen, but he would not have asked; she never would have considered such a union suitable for creating children.

"I fear my time for children has passed," he murmured.

"You said you're still young for a fae."

"It is not my age that makes me say so. I wanted children, once. The chances of having them with her would have been low, but we were both interested in trying. Now… Perhaps I will change my mind, one day. But for now, I do not see myself having children without the love of my life being the mother."

"Her loss must have been hard on you."

"It was. I lost everything: Lyenna; what little of my family I had left; even my will to live, for a time."

It felt good to speak, to shirk the silence that had ruled his life for so long. Carra's presence relaxed him, and he found that sharing brought him less pain than he had anticipated. Or perhaps the pain dulled in comparison to the wound in his side, and Carra was merely a witness.

"All done." Carra whispered. She straightened, shifting away from him, but she remained perched on the edge of his bed.

He lay back, wincing as the wound protested the movement, then turned his head toward her. "I appreciate what you have done for me today."

"I did it for me, remember?" she teased, but her eyes held only worry as she frowned down at him.

"Is there anything else you would like to know?"

She shook her head. "Not right now. But maybe next time I change your bandages?"

He nodded his assent as his eyes drifted closed. If the past few days were any indication, he would not be awake for much longer.

"I'll bring you your food when it's ready," Carra promised as the pressure on the side of his bed disappeared, leaving him with an odd feeling of loneliness. It dawned on him that he had not experienced that particular emotion in months—even when things were strained between them, having Carra around had kept the loneliness at bay and given him something to look forward to every day.

"Stay," he mumbled, barely aware of the word as he said it.

"Until you fall asleep," she agreed. His addled mind imagined fondness in her voice, and he smiled at the sound of it.

Too soon, sleep claimed him, and he dreamt of her fingers on his forehead and her words in his ear, telling him beautiful things he knew would never spill from her lips.

He clung to the dreams as he drifted in and out of sleep. Sometimes she was there; sometimes he was alone. But her presence lingered, and for the first time in a very long while, Straid found himself glad for the company. He felt cared for, in a way he was certain he had never truly experienced.

CHAPTER TWENTY-NINE

he house stayed unchanged the following day. Assured that the shrinking hadn't been sinister, and concerned over Straid's well-being, Carra checked every room, and didn't relax until she'd confirmed that nothing had deteriorated further. The house remained quiet and still in the early dawn light, as though holding its breath, but it seemed *whole*. She only hoped that meant her ministrations the day before had helped, and that, with enough time, it would return to its former splendor.

"Will you tell Brey I'll take Straid his breakfast?" she asked when Niana entered her room to lay out her clothes for the day. Carra typically slept through Niana's preparations, only waking once she returned to help Carra dress for breakfast, but today Carra had already been awake for hours, reassuring herself that the house—that *Straid*—was okay.

Niana slipped from the room, and Carra finished getting dressed on her own. The dress she wore today was simple, easy to get into and out of on her own, but she had grown used to Niana's company in the morning, and she felt her absence in the few minutes it took her to dress.

Maybe people who employed servants weren't incapable of

doing things on their own; maybe they were simply lonely and relished having someone to talk to each day.

Breakfast was a tense affair, the fae looking to her for answers, but she didn't have any to give. Straid was alive, and the wound was worse than she'd expected. But she wasn't a doctor; she couldn't assure them that he would be okay, not when she shared their worries.

She knocked on Straid's bedroom door and sagged in relief when he bade her to enter. Even through the door, she could hear more strength in his voice than there had been yesterday.

"The house didn't shrink overnight," she told him, setting the tray across his lap. "Does that mean you didn't get any worse?"

She wondered what would happen if it did shrink again— were there protection in place to ensure it wouldn't eliminate occupied rooms? Could she wake up one morning removed from the house? From *existence*? She shivered at the thought, then balanced the tray when it threatened to overturn.

"You cleaned the wound much better than I have been able to. I was able to preserve more of my own energy for healing. It is thanks to you that the house did not suffer further. It is thanks to you that *I* did not suffer further."

Carra blushed, busying herself with the fresh wound dressings in an attempt to avoid his gaze.

"It looks better," she said, inspecting it closely.

"The famous mortal ability to lie."

"I'm serious. It's still bloody and more colorful than it should be, but the spots of white and black have both receded. I'm no doctor, but that has to be a good sign, right?" Carra bit her lip, and her heart stuttered when she noticed his gaze lingering on her mouth.

"Yes."

"Can you feel when the house shrinks?" She wiped the wound with a wet cloth, and he winced. She grimaced in sympathy.

"Yes."

"Is it uncomfortable?"

He frowned. "I suppose it is. In light of the injury, I barely notice it, but if I were to focus on the feeling…it is not a good one." An odd look crossed his face, and he cursed under his breath. "My sister is at the front door."

"Do you want me to let her in?"

Straid sighed. "I do not. But I suppose you should. Bring her up here."

The sound of heavy knocking reached her ears as Carra walked down the long hallway, and by the time she'd descended the stairs, it was deafening.

When she pulled the door open, Fell stood before her, panting. Carra stepped aside and the fae woman swept past her.

"Where is he?" she demanded, her eyes wild. "Where is my brother? I tried to respect his space, but I haven't heard from him. And then, today—Is he okay?" She paused, then glanced around the foyer. "Shit. I can feel that the house is smaller. He's hurt. Bad."

"He is. I convinced him to let me take over changing his bandages, and I think that's helping—the house didn't shrink overnight."

"He's accepting help?"

Carra nodded.

"Oh, that's bad. Not that you're helping him," Fell rushed to clarify. "I am grateful that you're here to help. But he doesn't accept help easily; the fact that he's letting you means…"

"We should be worried about the severity of the injury," Carra murmured, her strength finally failing her. She'd had to suppress her panic to care for Straid, and she had been so exhausted last night that she had simply collapsed straight into bed. But now, she couldn't keep her emotions at bay. "I tried to get him to see a doctor, but he refused."

"He wouldn't want our mother to know. I get it. A doctor would complicate things. As much as I hate that he's recovering from such a serious injury without one, he's doing the right thing, making sure this doesn't reach our mother's ears. Where is he?"

"He's in his room. He said to bring you to him."

Together, the two women hurried to Straid's room, the mortal a step ahead of the fae, and the wards did nothing to keep them out; Straid must have dropped them for Fell while Carra was gone.

Carra stood aside and watched as Fell raced to her brother's side.

She hadn't had a chance to replace the bandage yet; she'd been halfway through cleaning the wound when Straid sent her downstairs, and she watched as Fell paled at the sight of it.

"Shit." Fell trembled, slumping to her knees beside her brother's bed. "Shit, Straid."

"I am recovering."

"That's not...Look, the wound is bad, and I came here prepared to freak out about that. But, fuck. The threads."

Straid shifted, his eyes suddenly alert, and looked down at his sister.

"Tell me."

"She's all over them, obviously. But...so is Umber."

"Carra, leave us for a moment."

She wanted to protest, but the looks on both Straid's face and Fell's stopped her short. Reluctantly, she left the room. After ten minutes of pacing the hallway, she retreated to the observatory, seeking the serenity she often found in the room.

A small measure of calm settled around her the moment she stepped inside. Plants crowded every corner, every shelf, and though the glass ceiling provided a clear view to the skies above, the foliage had become the focus of the room. She wondered if Straid minded that she had turned his observatory into a greenhouse. He had been the one to purchase the plants, but did he mind that she had transformed his favorite room so thoroughly?

A traitorous part of her wondered if he would even see the room again. If one night without worsening was enough to have hope. She chastised herself for even entertaining the idea. He was healing, even the house itself was proof of that. If he took issue with how drastically the room had changed, they could fight about it once he recovered.

Over an hour later damp soil clung to her knees, sweat streaked her face, and her fingernails were caked in loam. And that was how Fell found her: on her knees, covered in dirt, doing her best to distract herself from the fact that her husband might be dying. From the fact that, even now, he deemed his secrets too big to share with her.

"That took longer than expected," Fell said, sinking gracefully onto a pillow on the floor a few feet from Carra.

"Was Umber behind this? Why would his own brother want to hurt Straid?"

"Umber has always had a certain danger to him. He's the second eldest—the younger of the twins. He missed being the heir by mere minutes. I've always wondered if he'd go after Ash. But I don't understand why he would go after *Straid*." Fell trailed off. "He's tied to this. The thread is thinner; he's not the one who stabbed Straid. But he had a hand in it. I've always been a bit wary of Umber, but I never thought he would do something like this."

"A thinner thread means he wasn't directly connected?"

"Yes. Or that his connection happened a while ago, or that he's dead now—which he isn't. But threads fade over time. In his case, it looked recent, just tenuous.

"Your threads were all over his wound, which makes sense if you've been dressing it. Your threads were gentler, tender. Umber's…There was intention in the threads. It was faint; he might not have known who the target was, but he knew the knife would be used for harm. He might not have intended to play a part in murdering his own brother, but he intended to play a part in murdering *somebody*."

"What are you going to do?"

Fell shook her head. "Nothing."

Carra bristled. "You can't do nothing. You can't just let him get away with it. Find him and figure out why Straid isn't healing the way he says he should."

"If I reach out to Umber directly, he'll know that I know something, and he won't answer any of my questions. We've only spoken twice this decade. I have to live my life as normal and find a way to draw the two of us together. Umber requires… a delicate touch. Ash keeps guards with her at all times, just in case Umber ever decides he's ready to become the heir."

"So he has a history of attacking people?"

"No, but he missed being heir by mere minutes, and it's no secret that bothers him greatly. He's power hungry but willing to bide his time, which makes him all the more dangerous. He's been fairly quiet the past few decades, which some people took as a sign of him finally settling down. But I know my brother. He wouldn't give up that easily, and there were no threads of his anywhere for a long time. I don't know what he is planning, but it's big and, knowing him, it's bad."

CHAPTER THIRTY

The three weeks that followed passed with excruciating slowness. Straid's wound healed, though some days the improvement was imperceptible, and there were moments it seemed as though the infection might return. Carra reported only two more rooms shrinking, and none disappearing entirely: a miracle, considering the extent of his injury. Under her careful care, his pain receded, and the infection ebbed.

He found himself looking forward to the time she spent with him each day.

Not so happy were the moments Fell stopped by the house. Her visits were limited to once a week, with no prior warning. She worried that someone might be watching, Umber, and perhaps another. For the first two weeks, she had nothing to report; she followed threads, making connections of her own to create a chance encounter with their eldest brother.

With four hundred and five years between them, there had always been some amount of distance between the brothers—and Straid was fairly certain his eldest brother had never truly been close with anyone. But Umber's involvement in the attack surprised him; hatred typically required a closer connection than the two of them shared.

And yet, Fell's threads had linked Umber to the wound, irrefutable proof of his involvement.

Meanwhile, the investigation into Kexxia's whereabouts had stagnated. Corlan had exhausted every avenue for his search, and even Fell's threads were fading, so long after Kexxia's disappearance.

"It's a good thing you're stuck here," Fell told him, stealing a pastry from the tray beside his bed, brought by Carra that morning. "Otherwise, you would ruin everything."

Straid protested, but she shushed him, and he fell quiet; he did not have the energy to fight her.

"The trap is closing. I think by next week I'll have met with him. I should have some answers for you soon."

"Next week is not soon enough," he growled.

"If you want to be the one to talk to him, by all means, go for it and watch him shut down and refuse to talk to any of us. If you want me to do it my way, then you have to actually *let me do it my way*. And that takes time. It'll happen soon, though."

"Do not let him use his gift."

"I know, Straid." His sister rolled her eyes, and Straid was struck by how young she seemed; by how young she *was*: only a hundred and twenty years old. "Trust me, he won't have any idea that I'm up to anything."

Two days later, Carra gently guided him down the steps to the observatory. They had taken slow walks down the hallway together every day for a week now, and this morning she had declared him ready for the stairs.

He leaned heavily on her as they descended the steps and did his best to fight the rising humiliation at how much help he needed, even now, a full month out from the injury. But she simply smiled and continued to encourage him, and by the time they reached the observatory he had gained a new appreciation for his ability to make it so far, even as heavily aided as he was.

Carra guided him to a chair she had set just within the room's bounds—they had agreed that maneuvering to the floor was beyond his capability at present. As he examined the room around him, he realized that *observatory* was perhaps no longer the best name for the space. An observatory was cold, a place to step outside oneself and examine celestial bodies millions of miles away. This room had become the opposite of that entirely. The plants seemed to engulf him in an earthy embrace, and the creek, now restored, bubbled merrily. Before, it had served to reflect the heavens; now, he closed his eyes and listened to its music.

Carra helped him settle on the heavily cushioned chair, then fetched a tray of fruit and cheese, setting it on the table beside him.

"Congratulations on walking down the stairs. Let's hope you can get back up them later." Carra settled into the chair beside his and reached for a piece of cheese.

"You have done much for me this month."

"You saved my life; I owed you. And, if I'm being honest, I didn't want you to die. I didn't want to know you were in pain and do nothing about it. I know our marriage isn't...real, or anything, but I care about you. As much as you sometimes drive me crazy, you're the closest thing I have to a friend in the Quarters."

"You have done more for me than I ever could have expected. I appreciate it." He held her gaze, and felt himself smile as a blush rose on her cheeks. "The Ousilie's Ball is in five weeks. Let me bring you, as a way to acknowledge all that you have done for me."

"You mentioned the ball the night you were hurt. Tell me about it."

"The ball occurs once every hundred years, when Ousilie's comet is visible in the winter sky. Various celebrations take place across the Quarters—all fae celebrate the comet's appearance, as it strengthens our magic. Fae of a certain status are invited to a ball held deep in the royal woods. They gather to watch the comet and communally accept the gift of magic bestowed upon them. Attendance is a rite of passage, and the first Ousilie's comet in a fae's lifetime marks their coming into their power. Those born nearer to the comet's appearance are blessed with strengthened power in their infancy; I, at seventy years, will be older than most.

"I've seen what you can do. You're saying this is what you're capable of without being at full strength?"

"Each passing of the comet deepens the well from which our magic is drawn, but the first brings the greatest change. What I am capable of now pales in comparison to what I will be capable of one month from now." The notion terrified him, and he turned his mind to the ball itself. "The royal woods are beautiful, and perhaps best in the winter. I look forward to sharing them with you."

"The royal woods? We'll be in the presence of fae royalty? I've barely left the house since I married you. I don't know how I'd do—"

"You hold your own admirably with both me and your clients." As a rule, he never interrupted others, but he could not stand the thought of allowing her self-doubt to continue to be voiced. "You will be perfect."

"What does one wear to a ball in the royal woods? Should I go shopping, or is that something Niana will provide?"

"If you will permit me, I would like to provide your dress myself."

"Oh. Yes, sure. Of course. Just tell me how much it costs, and I can—"

"Carra," he gently chided, "I will provide your dress."

Already, he imagined the silk that would cling to her every curve, the green that would contrast so beautifully with her skin. If he dedicated himself to the task, five weeks would be enough time to make the dress; it had to be.

"You need not worry about the ball," he murmured at the wild-eyed stare she leveled his way. "You will charm them all. Trust me."

The night they had met, he had wanted her trust because she had reminded him, however tenuously, of Lyenna. Now, he wanted her trust simply because he wanted...her.

He closed his eyes against the feeling blooming in his chest. After letting her care for him, and sharing quiet, tender, *vulnerable* moments with her, his feelings for her had become impossible to ignore. Likewise, it was harder to hold onto his reasons for doing so. They seemed foolish now; Carra was a grown woman, capable of making her own choices. And if she wanted to extend any amount of intimacy toward him, in whatever form she offered it, he struggled to remember why he had insisted on rebuffing her.

He would bare his feelings the night of the comet's return. He would plainly tell her that he wanted her and allow her to choose whether to accept him or maintain the distance he had cultivated between them.

Until then, he would slowly break down the remaining walls he had built around himself. He would inch toward that moment of full vulnerability so as not to overwhelm her when he finally lay his heart bare. And in five weeks' time he would offer her his heart, free to do with as she pleased.

Three days later, as he blundered his way through recounting a childhood story, the wards alerted him to Corlan's presence at the front door. He had half a mind to turn his friend away, but Carra chided him. So, with a sigh, he cut his story short, their conversation stalling as he slowly walked to the door with his wife at his side ensuring he did not fall.

"Fell sent me," Corlan said breathlessly, the moment the door shut behind him. "Let's go somewhere private."

Carra made to leave his side, but Straid shook his head and took her by the hand, keeping her at his side as they made their way to the study. He expected Corlan to object, but his friend did not so much as frown as he followed them into the room.

"Umber gave Lyenna the knife that stabbed you," Corlan said the moment the study door closed. "He knew the knife was meant to kill, though Fell suspects Umber didn't know you were the target."

Straid stumbled, grateful for Carra's presence at his side as she took his weight and steadied him. His stomach soured, and he feared he might be sick. He had loved Lyenna—still loved her, all these years later.

And she had intended to murder him.

"Lyenna." His vision blurred. "Did—did he mean for her to kill me before the wedding?"

Corlan shook his head, and Straid's stomach roiled even further.

"*At* the wedding, then? Did she agree to the plan? Did Fell say? Please, Corlan..."

"He didn't give it to her then," Corlan said, his voice gentle. *Too* gentle. But that could only mean...Straid shook his head. It couldn't be.

"He gave her the knife roughly a year ago."

Straid slid sideways, his feet buckling from underneath him, and Carra was not fast enough to catch him. He did not care that he was slumped on the floor; his dignity had left him, along with his entire sense of the world.

Lyenna had died. Straid had visited her grave. He had held her as the illness had progressed. He had felt the bonds between them weaken with her life essence, and then snap violently the moment she had succumbed.

She.

Was.

Dead.

And yet...he had never seen the body. The grave had been dug, and inhabited, and filled with dirt all before he had managed to make it back.

But no. It could not be.

"Lyenna is dead."

Through blurred vision, Straid could see Corlan shake his head. "Fell has seen her threads where they shouldn't be, where they *couldn't* be. In Kexxia's house, and on your wound. A thin one tied to Carra, and a few around town that were stronger than they should have been. And the ones that lit up around Umber when Fell mentioned that you'd lost one of your staff. Lyenna's threads, in all these impossible places. She said it was *bright*, Straid. Not the thread of a mortal who died half her life-span ago."

Blood rushed in his ears. He couldn't do this. He couldn't—

His breathing came fast and heavy as the wound in his side burned. Around him, the world went dark.

CHAPTER THIRTY-ONE

Straid was unconscious.

In all the weeks she'd cared for him, including the night he had been stabbed, she had never seen him lose consciousness like this. Sleep, sure, but not…this.

Her vision tunneled, and her heart pounded hard enough she feared it would beat through her chest. "Is he going to be okay?"

"I…I don't know, actually." Corlan was pale, and his voice trembled.

Fuck.

Hastily, Carra dropped to her knees beside Straid and pulled up the edge of his shirt, revealing the bandage. It was mostly there as a precaution at this point; the wound had scabbed over, and she only changed it daily as a perfunctory matter of hygiene.

But now, the bandage bloomed red with a rapidly growing stain.

"Go to the kitchen and get me a bowl of water," she demanded. "Hot water," she added, realizing that Straid wouldn't be able to heat it with his magic this time. "And a clean cloth. Brey should be able to tell you where to find one."

He followed her directions with no hesitation, which only made her panic rise. She forced herself to take two deep breaths before slipping Straid's shirt off and gently peeling the bandage from his skin, making sure not to touch the wound.

The scab had split open, but the only color she could see was red. There was no white or black, no green or yellow. No signs of infection or necrosis. She breathed a sigh of relief.

She used Straid's shirt to wipe the beads of sweat from his brow, then shoved it underneath his back in a futile attempt to keep the carpet from staining with his blood.

Corlan rushed into the room, his arms laden with everything she had asked for, plus a second bowl of hot water and a small disc of soap. She washed her hands, and soaked the cloth in the scalding water, wincing as the heat stung her hands.

"You're going to be okay," she told Straid. "You have a ball to take me to."

"The Ousilie's ball?" Corlan asked.

She expected a further comment from Corlan, but he sat in silence with his jaw clenched as he watched her wipe the blood from his unconscious friend's side. She worked quickly, grateful that the blood slowed after mere minutes.

By the time she had a clean bandage on him, Straid was stirring.

"What happened?" she murmured, brushing a hand against his forehead. It was cool and dry; no sign of the fever that had plagued him in the aftermath of the stabbing.

He winced. "The wound burned. The pain overwhelmed me." Straid's mouth twisted, and his eyes fluttered closed. "A cursed blade. The curse prevented me from healing as I should have, and clearly learning of Lyenna's lies triggered another stage of the curse. Had you not nursed me back to health so thoroughly it likely would have been enough to end my life."

"It knocked you out when you were mostly healed. Imagine if the wound had still been infected," Corlan agreed with a shudder.

"How do you feel now?" she asked.

He didn't respond; only smiled ruefully, and Carra's stomach clenched.

"Come on, let's get you to bed." He complied without complaint, and they made it to his room before she remembered Corlan, still in the study.

"Do you want me to bring Corlan here or send him home?" she asked as she helped him into bed. Straid winced, they lay back, his eyes falling shut.

"Bring him."

She found Corlan at the top of the stairs, the bowl of bloody water in his hands, and her stomach lurched at the sight. "He wants you to come to his room."

"Of course. Let me just…" He lifted the bowl with a jerk of his head toward the stairs behind him.

"Of course," she echoed. "Come to his room when you're done?"

Corlan stayed just inside the doorway once he arrived, propped against the wall with his arms folded across his chest.

"So," Corlan said, his voice darker than Carra had ever heard it. Gone was any trace of humor, or fun, or hope. Instead, there was pure, unbridled fury. "She's back. And she's fallen in with Umber."

"That seems to be the case. I do not understand how it is possible, or why…why she would not have come back to me." Straid gripped her hand so tightly it went numb, and Carra squeezed back gently.

"Maybe Umber got there, in her final moments," Corlan suggested. "Right before she died, he could have stopped time and figured out a way to save her."

"He refused. I *begged* him, and he refused. Then I felt the bonds between us break." His voice wavered. "Every last one, simultaneously. We were free with our bonds; there were many that ended the moment of her passing. She died. I can tell you that with absolute certainty. Lyenna died." His voice broke on the final word, and Carra's heart along with it.

"Well, then something brought her back to life."

"Why would she want to kill you?" Carra asked, wincing as Corlan's gaze shifted to her.

"I think that's the question on all of our minds," Corlan agreed. "Fifty years ago, when she died, Lyenna was madly in love with Straid. So, what changed? Why does she want to kill you now? And did she come back with the sole purpose of doing it?"

"I do not know. She loved me. If not, she was a better actor than anyone could have guessed. The bigger question is *how* she came back. Necromancy is a delicate and dangerous art. Few succeed, and the results are paltry at best—a mere shade for an hour or two would be considered a great success. Even that requires the magic inherent in the soul of the deceased fae; there is no form of necromancy that works on mortals. Believe me, I looked. Alongside my search to keep her alive, I searched for ways to bring her back. This is not possible."

"Clearly it is." There was no fight in Corlan's voice, no bite to his words, just a tired resignation. Beside her, Straid deflated.

"So someone found a way to resurrect her. And maybe the price for coming back was killing you?" Carra struggled with the very idea of it all. Death was the one foe you couldn't beat; the one journey you could never return from. Even for the fae, there was no cheating death, as Straid himself had just confirmed.

"Does Fell know who did it? Who found a way to bring her back?" Straid asked, desperation in his voice. Corlan shook his head.

"It might be time to call in that boon."

Straid stilled beside her at Corlan's words. His fingers were rigid between her own, but she could not bring herself to ask when he meant, not with the tension so palpable between Corlan and Straid. The two fae stared each other down for long seconds, during which Carra's anxiety climbed steadily ever higher until finally, Straid closed his eyes in clear surrender.

"It is time," he admitted grudgingly. "If Umber is involved…"

"Unless he did this because she collected on a boon, his duty to you will override his duty to her. He will be compelled to answer. It's the only way. You know it is."

Straid sighed, scrubbing a hand across his face. "I dislike this but cannot deny that you are right. I will contact my brother and call in the boon."

CHAPTER THIRTY-TWO

Straid had hoped to hold the boon over his brother for much longer, to hold Umber's desperation over him for centuries to come. He never could have imagined that he would have to use it to discover how his dead love had managed to make an attempt on his life nearly fifty years after her death.

He could not call in the favor so soon after Fell had met with Umber—he would not expose his sister's sleuthing, not after she had risked so much to get him the information—but the Ousilie's Ball would provide the perfect opportunity. He would leave Carra with Fell, or Corlan, and speak to his brother in private for a few minutes, and he would call in the boon.

In the meantime, he planned exactly what he would say. Exactly how to word the boon to ensure there would be no loopholes, no way for his brother to provide anything less than every bit of information Straid sought.

While his brain worked on the Umber problem, his hands worked to make Carra's dress for the ball. He had wanted to begin sooner, but with the injury he had not had the time or the energy. Now, with the night of the comet's appearance approaching rapidly, he dedicated himself to drafting the dress whenever he found a moment alone, often falling asleep over the material with the needle still in his hand.

Sewing was the first hobby his mother had allowed him to indulge in. All his other interests had been deemed too messy, or below their station—but then he had grown fascinated with the royal silk spiders. He had spent his days in the spider gardens, watching as the spider-keepers cared for the creatures and harvested their silk. Weaving it into cloth had centered his mind, even as a child, and his looms had quickly become his most prized possessions, the things he turned to when he was upset, or happy, or simply needed to think.

By the time he met Lyenna, he had two personal clutters of silk spiders and clothes crafted by his hands had become one of the most coveted gifts in the Quarters. In fact, the last time he had seen his mother she had worn a dress spun by his spiders and stitched by his hand. An acknowledgement, perhaps, that she still valued her son even as she pushed him away.

When Straid moved to the townhome, he brought the spiders with him, lovingly installing them in a corner of the garden left untended for their benefit. In his grief, he had abandoned his love of silk, his love of sewing—and the spiders had been left to roam the gardens unsupervised.

But the spiders had passed stories of him down to their children, and when he visited them after so many years away, he found that he was left with more silk than he needed to make Carra's dress for the ball.

Fifty years ago, he had planned to make Lyenna's dress for the occasion. He had wondered how he would have to adjust his approach to clothe her aging body. She would have been nearing the end of the life just as he came into the prime of his own, but he hand longed to share the moment with her.

Perhaps he had been foolish to love her. Trusting her had certainly been a grave miscalculation. He wracked his memories for some indication that she wished him harm, but there were none. She had loved him—or she had been a damned good actress.

The betrayal was almost enough to make him turn from love entirely.

But every time he thought to, he caught a glimpse of honeyed eyes, or the echo of laughter in the halls, and his heart refused to harden.

He dyed the silk a pale green, the perfect shade for the woman who had spent so many hours carefully planting every shade imaginable in the observatory until it resembled something more akin to a greenhouse.

Carra still redressed his wound every evening, but he had begun taking meals in the dining room once again, only slightly surprised to find Niana and Brey at the table his first morning. Brey had stood, embarrassed, but he waved her back into her seat. She had not hesitated to join them since. The routine felt nice, and comforting, and for those few minutes three times a day he could almost convince himself that life continued as normal.

"This sauce is incredible." Carra speared an asparagus on her fork one night as they dined. Brey and Niana had taken leave to prepare for their own Ousilie's festivities and, much as he had grown to enjoy their company, he found himself glad for the time alone with his wife. He watched her eat—watched her lips close around the stalk and her throat bob as she swallowed. He could not drag his eyes away.

He did not so much as try.

"The sauce was made for you." His voice dropped low, and she smiled almost bashfully under his gaze. "I asked Brey to create a sauce that mirrored both your fiery temper and the sweetness that lies beneath." The words felt clumsy on his tongue; it had been years since he had been so direct with his admiration of a woman. But he forced himself to say the words. How else would she know how he felt?

"That's...wow. I honestly don't know what to say."

"Your appreciation is enough." He returned to his food with a deliberate focus, and when he caught her looking at him a few moments later he could feel his blood thrumming beneath his skin.

"It means a lot that you would ask her—that you see me that way." The words she so clearly wanted to say shone in her eyes. *Thank you.* He nodded in a silent acknowledgement, his own unspoken, *You are welcome.*

"Tell me more about the ball," Carra urged toward the end of the meal. "At least tell me about this dress you're ordering for me."

Her eyes caught his, and he allowed himself to savor her gaze until she glanced away, a blush blooming high on her copper skin.

"It, too, is being made with you in mind." He said nothing to disabuse her of the notion that her dress was being ordered, bought from a shop. If she never discovered that it had been crafted by his hands, he would not mind; Carra having the perfect dress was the only thing that mattered.

"I must attend to plans for the ball," he told her reluctantly as he finished his meal. He had eaten slowly, savoring every bite and had made sure he did not finish before her. "May I escort you to your room? Or the observatory?"

Carra shook her head. "Actually, I'm meeting with a client soon."

"Here?" His heart raced as she shook her head. He had not left the house since the night he had been wounded. She had not, either. "Jesson will be escorting you, then."

"Of course. I figured it would be better for me to go to him, since...the house is still recovering. I've noticed it seems to struggle a bit with visitors right now: the lights get dimmer every time Corlan or Fell come, and the hallway gets a bit narrower. I don't think I should bring anyone else here until you have fully recovered."

"That is thoughtful of you." The house had slowly regained

its strength as he had: rooms returned to their regular size, and two that had disappeared entirely had returned, though one of them still flickered in and out of existence. He could not fault her logic in keeping unnecessary visitors out of the home, though he wondered—hoped—a part of her worried how bringing her clients here might affect *him*, as well. "Keep Jesson close. He walks you to the door. If he must leave while you work, do not step outside until he has returned." He almost said please; he had to hold the word back as it fought to escape his mouth.

"Of course. I—I can stay if you want me to."

He shook his head. "You will be safe with Jesson. I have kept you from your work too long already."

"You didn't keep me from anything. I had three appointments at the house, before I realized the toll it was taking. It was my choice not to continue."

"You met with clients?" He had worried that caring for him had taken her away from her own life. That he was impeding her ability to work, and that she would resent him for it. The fact that she had found time to meet with her clients eased a bit of the guilt of the past few weeks.

"I did. Is that a problem?"

"It will never be a problem." He held her gaze as he delivered the words. "As long as you would like to continue this work, I will support it, no matter what else happens. I would never, under any circumstance, presume to tell you to stop."

He walked her to the door and dipped his head to her as she linked her arm through Jesson's before stepping beyond the wards.

The moment he was certain she was gone he returned to his room to put the finishing touches on the dress, muttering to himself about his brother all the while. With only two days until the ball, he needed to make sure everything would be perfect.

CHAPTER THIRTY-THREE

The night of the Ousilie's ball, Carra stepped out of Straid's arms and into the biting chill of winter. The air was colder than she'd expected, and the dress he'd ordered for her, though absolutely stunning, did little to protect her from the wind.

She'd been nervous when Niana finally allowed her to see herself this evening: after hours of bathing, dressing, hairstyling, and makeup application, Carra had begun to wonder if Niana's careful attention would be worth it, but she had gasped at the sight of the woman in the mirror.

The pale green dress clung to her figure, emphasizing the swell of her breasts, her round stomach, and the curve of her thighs. The silk looked as gorgeous as it felt: soft and luxurious against her skin. Her curls cascaded down one shoulder, studded with tiny flowers and lights that slowly blinked in and out, a soft, muted yellow against her dark brown hair. Fireflies, she'd realized as she leaned in for a closer look. Or some similar fae creature, winter's equivalent to the springtime insects in the mortal world.

Niana had tucked tiny pins into her hair that matched her

necklace perfectly, seamlessly tying the memento of her prior life into her new world.

Her face was equally stunning: Niana had somehow managed to both soften and emphasize her features. She looked herself, but not. She looked radiant. Ethereal.

Fae.

Straid's eyes had widened at the sight of her as she swept down the staircase, and her heart had risen in her throat. He'd said nothing, simply watched her as she approached, but the look in his eyes had said everything—more than words ever could.

And then he'd whisked her away, stepping into nothingness for one brief, uncomfortable moment before arriving…wherever they were.

"Welcome to the Ousilie's Ball," Straid murmured against her ear. She shivered at his nearness, and he dropped her hand, leaving her aching for any contact with his body.

She glanced around herself, eager to see this ball he had talked so much about, but there was nothing here, only trees and darkness. She'd expected hundreds of fae—or thousands. She'd expected music and dancing, food and drink, revelry unmatched in the human world. Instead, there was nothing but an empty forest in the dark of night.

She tried to tamp down her disappointment. Straid had been looking forward to this, after all. And if he was the only one to see her looking this good, well, he was the only one whose reaction really mattered, after all. And his speechlessness when she'd appeared at the top of the stairs had been enough.

"Carra."

She turned at the sound of her name, and the look on Straid's face, like she was the most beautiful thing in all the world, made her gasp. He looked at her with shining eyes and held out his hand. "Let me show you."

She took a step closer and put her hand in his, her breath hitching at the contact. Straid led her through the forest, and with each step a bit of the chill fell away, until finally they stepped out of the trees into a meadow—and though it was still the heart of winter, the air was richly warm.

The first thing she noticed, aside from the warmth, was the noise. None of the sound had made it through the trees—some kind of fae barrier, perhaps—but here, suddenly, music filled the air, and snatches of conversation drifted around her. Straid wound through the crowd, keeping a firm yet gentle hand on her lower back, and she was aware of hundreds of pairs of eyes falling on her. Conversations fell silent as they approached, and she could hear the murmurs begin again behind her.

She turned into him slightly, and he dropped his mouth to her ear as they walked.

"A mortal at the Ousilie's Ball is rare," he said, answering her unasked question, "though not entirely disallowed. As my wife you have every right to be here. Although the mere fact of you being my wife is yet another reason for people to stare. Here we are," he said, coming to a stop in front of a gorgeous fae woman with skin like morning dew and fiery curls that spilled from underneath her crown—the woman from the portrait in the library. When she'd asked Straid about the portrait, he had replied simply with "The fae queen." She radiated royalty in the portrait but here, in person, the effect was much stronger, and Carra found herself cowed in her presence.

Straid bowed before her, and Carra dropped into a curtsy at his side.

"You may rise," the queen said. They did so, and a moment later, Straid stepped forward and wrapped the woman in a stiff hug.

"Mother."

"My darling. Welcome to your first Ousilie's Ball. I only wish you'd attended with the family."

"I regret that I could not. However—"

"You have deemed other things more important. I understand." Her mouth twisted in displeasure. "Introduce me to this wife of yours."

The fae queen turned her gaze to Carra, who stood frozen to the spot.

Mother.

Straid had called the fae queen Mother.

Which would mean…

"Mother, this is Carra. Carra, my mother, Queen Zialania." Straid took her hand, and she gripped it hard.

"It's a pleasure to meet you," Carra said, dropping into another curtsy.

"Sweetheart, you're family. The one curtsy will suffice. I must say, it came as quite a surprise to all of us when we heard my son had married. And in his own backyard, no less, eschewing the traditional royal wedding traditions. You must be someone very special to put him in such a hurry to wed." The queen's words were soft and sweet, but underneath them ran a current of steel that made the hairs on the back on Carra's neck rise.

"I learned after the last time that life is too short to wait," Straid said, his voice steady beside Carra. There was no mention of the guard who had caught her. No mention of the fact that he'd married her to save her life, not out of love.

"Yes. Loving a mortal can be so hard. Their lives are so incredibly fleeting. Cherish her while she lasts," Queen Zialania said with a smile that was just a touch too cruel to be genuine. "Come find me later, I'm sure the three of us have much to discuss."

"You didn't tell me you were royalty," Carra hissed as Straid drew her away from the crowd. "You should have prepared me."

"I have spent much of my life attempting to leave that world behind. I did not want to claim it for myself, and I did not want it to color how you saw me."

"So you just let me come into this with no warning."

"I see now how that was, perhaps, not the correct approach."

Carra laughed, despite herself. "Oh, just apologize, you ass."

"I am sorry. Truly." He held her gaze while he said it, and her chest warmed as his words settled between them.

She gasped. "Oh. I didn't—"

"You were owed an apology. I gave it freely, because you were correct. I will do what I can to make it up to you," he promised, his voice softening. "Tonight, after the ball, I—"

"There you are!" Corlan swaggered over to them, and Carra found herself wishing she could order him to leave. Straid's eyes lingered on hers, full of promise, and Carra found herself smiling, even as she ached to hear what he had meant to say.

"Carra, I need you to dance with me. It's imperative." Corlan held out an expectant hand and winked, and she could smell honey and the sharp tang of alcohol on his breath. His easy grin was infectious, and she laughed as she shook her head.

"I'd like to dance with Straid first. If that's okay?" she asked, turning to her husband. "I don't know about fae custom, but it seems like I should probably reserve the first dance for my husband."

"Yes, you should." Straid spoke quietly, and the fire in his eyes threatened to set her aflame—she could feel a blush rising in her cheeks as she took his hand and allowed him to lead her to the dance floor in the middle of the meadow.

Beautiful music floated in the air around them, but Carra couldn't tell where it was coming from. There was no band, no instruments on display; the music simply existed all around them.

"One of the many mysteries of my mother's events," Straid murmured, pulling her close. "The music is simply there. Even I do not know how she manages it."

"It's beautiful." She leaned her face against his chest, mindful of the hundreds of fae watching them. She and Straid weren't the only ones on the dance floor, but they were the most notable: a human dancing with the *prince*. She forced herself to take a deep breath, and to keep her body pliant in his arms. She could do this. Her job hinged on her ability to act, after all; it had prepared her well for this moment.

Straid pressed a kiss to the top of her head and tightened his arms around her. "I am glad you are here to accompany me to my first Ousilie's Ball," he murmured against her hair. "I likely would have looked for an excuse to skip it, in my grief, if you had not entered my life. I am grateful, every day, that you did. You have brought me back to life in ways I never could have expected."

She glowed under the praise of his words and allowed herself to get lost in them. In him.

All too soon, the song ended, but Straid held her close.

"One more dance?" he asked, and she was powerless to say no. He had never held her quite like this, like she was precious and he couldn't bear to let her go. It felt as though the past few weeks had been building to now, to this moment that felt larger than the two of them, but also as though it belonged only to them.

She pulled back just enough to look at him and regretted it instantly. He was close. Too close. All she could think of was eliminating that small distance and pressing her lips to his. But he had been clear that he didn't want that—or, rather, that he would not allow it even though he did.

She quickly turned her head and pressed it back against his chest, and they danced in silence for the duration of the next song, his heart thundering against her own—until Corlan cut in smoothly, and Carra watched from Corlan's arms as Straid walked away across the dance floor.

CHAPTER THIRTY-FOUR

"*S*traid! Welcome to your first Ousilie's Ball." Fell threw her arms around him as he reached one of the many refreshment tables, and he made a show of grimacing at her overly enthusiastic welcome. To bystanders, he was still the prince who had locked himself in his home for fifty years after losing the human he had loved; they would not expect him to have softened toward Fell's effusiveness in recent weeks.

"Fell." He picked up a flute of honeywine, feigning disinterest in his sister.

"Come say hi to everyone," she said, dragging him to the table where their siblings sat. He stiffened, and anyone watching would believe that his acquiescence was reluctant.

Ash arched a brow at him as they reached the table, and he gave her one single, sharp nod in response. She was Fell's opposite in every way, and the one of his siblings he would have been most likely to get along with during his period of self-imposed exile. She had not attempted to contact him a single time in all those years—yet further proof of their compatibility.

"Wondered if we'd see you," Rowan said from Ash's side. The middle child of the royal family offered Straid a tight smile. His eyes searched Straid's, as though looking for proof that his youngest brother truly was here, alive, and as well as could be expected.

"I wouldn't miss my first Ousilie's Ball," Straid said, meaning every word. Even if he had lost his enthusiasm for the ball in the years leading up to it, he never would have dared to miss it. He had told Carra he would have looked for an excuse to do so, but he knew he would not have found one; he would have attended, miserable, and slunk away at the earliest possibility.

"Straid." Umber's eyes held no warmth, but neither did they hold any malice. There was no indication that his brother had aided in an attempt on his life.

Straid kept his face blank and his voice even as he responded. "Umber."

"Sit, and tell us what you've been up to. Maybe they'll have an easier time getting it out of you than I have." Fell directed him to a chair, which he obligingly occupied.

"You've seen him?" Ash asked.

"A few times. I finally got him to let me into the townhome. It took Corlan's help, and there was a *lot* of scowling on Straid's part. But he won't tell me anything about what he's been doing in the fifty years since he locked himself in that house," Fell pouted.

"There was nothing to tell."

"Nothing?" Rowan questioned.

"Nothing of import."

"You literally *got married*, Straid." Fell raised her brows at him.

"Ah, yes. Nothing *else* of import."

"Another human, Straid? Really?" Ash wrinkled her nose, a habit their mother had tried, and failed, to train out of the heir to the throne. "Why must you always fall for humans?"

"It is beneath you," Umber added, his voice low and dangerous as it always was.

"Carra is anything but beneath me." The words took on a double meaning in his mind, but he brushed it aside—this was not the time for fantasy. "I love her, just as I loved Lyenna. The fact they are both human is a mere coincidence. Given time, I am sure I will someday love a fae, as well. I understand that I will outlive Carra and did not want to waste time in wedding her as I did with Lyenna. I wish to cherish every moment I have with her."

"How did you meet?" Rowan asked.

"Oh, I know this! One of the rare times Straid left his house, he happened to meet her on the street. It was love at first sight, isn't that right, Straid?" Fell turned to him with a wide grin. He scowled in return.

"I was intrigued, nothing more. But as we became better acquainted, yes, I did fall in love." He had meant to say that he had grown attached, the "confession" merely a part of the story he wove for his siblings, but the gravity of the words that had slipped from his lips instead twisted in his chest.

The conversation turned to other matters, and he realized with a start that he had missed the rare times his siblings had all been together. Mere minutes later, Umber made his excuses and stepped away from the table.

"I have a private matter I wish to discuss with Umber, and then I must find my wife," Straid uttered, following his brother.

He followed Umber from a respectable distance, electing not to call after him. Umber stopped at the edge of the trees and turned toward Straid. "Yes?" he asked impatiently.

"I need to call in the boon."

"Now?" Umber stiffened, almost imperceptibly, but Straid could read the tension in the lines of his body.

"It cannot wait. I was attacked with a cursed blade, and the wound nearly took my life. I need you to discover who carried out the attack, and why, and tell me everything you know—any detail, no matter how small, that may be linked to the attack."

Umber's eyes narrowed. "Why me? Why not Fell?"

"Fell would be the obvious choice, yes," Straid conceded. "But employing her help would require me to give her more access to my life than I would like. I have aged these fifty years. I am no longer the carefree child I was when you knew me, and from her first visit, Fell exhausted me." She had, though he had come to enjoy his sister's presence once more. "Additionally, Carra seems to rather like having her around, and Fell's attempts to uncover threads would likely become social engagements. You know what Fell is like; imagine her constantly in my home when I am accustomed to solitude. Even having a wife could not thoroughly prepare me for that."

"Why not ask our mother?"

Straid leveled an unamused glare at his brother. He would not dignify such an asinine question with a response.

Umber nodded. "I am the best option you have. I see that."

"You owe me a boon. I am not requesting your help; I am informing you that the time for collection has come. I trust that you will work quickly and discreetly, and that you will be thorough in your investigation."

"You don't have to *trust* anything," Umber said with a sneer. "The boon will take care of that."

"It will. But were it not for the boon, I would trust your discretion still." For all his brother's faults, Straid had never questioned his discretion—it was perhaps the only area in which Straid trusted him now.

"Very well. I will do it."

"Find out everything you can and report back to me in one week. I will need you to follow every lead you find, and to divulge every piece of information, no matter how small or tangentially related. Anything regarding the blade, the person who wielded it, or anybody involved, no matter how distantly. Human or fae, alive or dead; if there was an involvement, I need to know. The debt of the boon will be settled once I possess all the information I seek."

"It is done." Umber strode away, and Straid took a moment to collect himself. He feared he might have tipped his hand too much, but his wording had been ironclad, without divulging his knowledge of Lyenna's involvement.

Long moments later, Straid returned to the dance floor, his eyes roving the throng of fae in search of the human in the pale green dress.

Finally, he found her, standing on the edge of the dance floor. Hundreds of fae crowded the space between them, and he ignored them as he wove his way toward her, stepping lightly between the dancing pairs. His wife stood between Fell and Corlan, and her gaze bounced between them as they talked, a gentle smile on her face. He found that he wanted nothing more than to dance with her, to hold her close.

Fell smiled at Straid as he neared, then excused herself and disappeared into the mass of fae crowding the ever-filling meadow, tugging Corlan along with.

"Dance with me," he murmured against Carra's ear, gritting his teeth as she arched into him. It seemed everything he did tonight inspired a reaction: shivers at his nearness, sighs at his innocent touch.

He swept her onto the dance floor, uncaring of the fae that watched. In this moment, nothing mattered but her.

Tonight, once the comet had passed, he would tell her every-thing: how drawn he was to her, how lucky he considered himself for having her in his life, no matter the circumstances that had brought her into it. He would tell her he loved her, in simple words that left no room for misunderstanding, and ask if she would have him.

Carra slid her hands around his neck, and he stiffened at her touch. The gentle press of her fingers against his nape made his heart race, and he wanted to whisk her away from here. He wanted to worship her, to feed her and unpin her hair at the end of the night. He wanted to hold her close and whisper sweet, dangerous things in her ear. It was not just sex he craved with her; it was everything. A lifetime, however brief hers might be.

"Thank you," Carra said with a blinding smile he found even

more captivating than the flare of cold that accompanied her words.

"For what?"

"For bringing me here tonight. For saving my life. For letting me in. For everything."

He brushed a wayward curl from her face. "Thank you for allowing me to do so."

Slowly, he became aware of the couple beside them, who had ceased their dancing and now watched them with wide eyes. Carra glared at them, and they whirled away, though they hovered nearby and whispered words that spread like wildfire: *The prince* thanked *his human wife, over something trivial.* As though it mattered, as though he would not do it a thousand times over. How easily, how gladly, he would incur a debt that would take a millennia to pay. Those months of avoiding new bonds between them seemed so far away, so juvenile, now. She could ask anything of him, and he would give it willingly.

He needed to be alone with her, needed to tell him how much she had come to mean to him. He could not wait another moment to tell her he loved her.

"Come, let us find a place away from the crowds," he murmured against her curls. "I find I would like to be alone with my wife."

CHAPTER THIRTY-FIVE

She followed Straid to the trees that lined the meadow but hesitated as they left the crowd behind.

"Don't you have…princely duties?"

"No. As I have not yet experienced the comet my powers are still in their infancy; I have nothing of value to contribute to the festivities this year. My siblings each have roles to play, but I am free to enjoy the night with you. I would like to find some privacy…unless you would prefer to stay with the others?"

A part of her did want to stay—the same part of her that wondering if she detected disappointment in his offer. She was worried that if she found herself alone with Straid tonight, she would do something foolish.

She had wondered at certain points tonight if Straid wanted her to be foolish.

He had turned her down the last time she had asked, but it seemed like maybe…

She shook the thought from her mind and reclaimed his hand in hers. "Lead the way."

A short walk through the trees led them to a smaller clearing at the top of a nearby hill. It must have been within the bounds of whatever magical barrier surrounded the ball; strains of music drifted up to them, with bits of laughter threaded through it. Straid settled into the grass, offering a hand to Carra as she marveled at the sight of him so devoid of pretense.

She hesitated. "I don't want to ruin this dress."

"You will not."

"It's silk. The grass, and the dirt—"

"I do not create garments so delicate they must be shielded from the elements."

"You—" She must have misheard him. Perhaps he'd said he didn't *commission* delicate garments. Because he could not have made this, the most beautiful dress she had ever laid her eyes on… "You made this?"

"I did." His eyes burned in the darkness, and tears sprang to hers. For a moment, she forgot how to breathe.

"You made it for me."

"Yes."

"Why?"

"You deserve the best. And…I simply wanted to."

She took his hand, and he gently pulled her down beside him. He brushed a thumb across her cheek, wiping a tear she hadn't realized had fallen.

"You are crying."

"I am honored."

Straid smiled at her as she settled in. It was wide, unrestrained, unlike every other ghost of a smile she had ever seen from him. She had come to love the tiny quirk of just one corner of his mouth, but the way his face transformed now had her melting under his gaze.

"Tell me about the comet," she asked, her breath catching as her eyes lingered on his lips.

He told her. Straid, normally so reserved, wove a story of a comet that returned every hundred years and bestowed strength on the fae. He spoke of power and beauty and the magic that connected all fae. He spoke of his family, and the stories they had shared of their own first times. The awe and longing he had felt as a child.

"I still can't believe you haven't reached your full power yet," she murmured, closing her eyes against the warmth he had wrapped her in the moment she'd begun to shiver.

"My power is a mere whisper of what it will be."

"But it's strong enough to kill someone. You pulled back that night, but you could have." The thought no longer scared her. She knew him well enough to know he would never do so—that even without his vows, she would always be safe with him.

He lowered his head slightly in acknowledgement. "I am royalty, so my powers are stronger than most. Rowan was born at dusk moments before Ousilie's comet passed overhead. His powers are suspected to be the strongest any fae has ever known."

"What's his gift?"

"He will not divulge it. Many believe he is simply moderately gifted in all the ways of the fae."

"Do you think they're right?"

"I have not spent much time wondering. When he is ready to divulge it, he will. But I do not want to speak of my brother now."

"What do you want to…speak of?" His eyes had caught hers, and she felt trapped, unable to tear her gaze from his, though no part of her even wanted to do so. Silence stretched between them, and she wanted to lean forward, to capture his lips with her own. Instead, she asked, "When will the comet be visible?"

"Mere minutes, now," he said, his voice impossibly soft. His pupils widened, his silver eyes turning nearly black. Her breath hitched at the sight, and his breathing grew ragged, his brow furrowing as though the moment pained him.

For the span of seven heartbeats, they stayed like that, their gazes locked.

She didn't know who moved first; she just knew that seconds later, his lips were on hers. Gentle, at first, a sweet kiss that felt precious, entirely their own. He brushed his mouth against hers and shivers ran through her body. He groaned and slid an arm around her, drawing her in closer until she was settled in his lap.

She moaned into the kiss, releasing her hold on all of her desire, her hope, her fears, everything he had made her feel since she had met him: she poured it all into the kiss, and gasped as he gave it all back.

He pulled back with a shudder, his breathing ragged, his chest heaving in the dark beside her. She leaned toward him, desperate for another taste, but he turned his face to the sky without another word. There was no dismissal in the action, but a reverence, and she turned to follow his gaze. Moments later, a brilliant white light streaked across the sky.

Carra was mortal, a human; this comet had no greater significance to her than any other. Yet it was one of the most beautiful things she had ever seen. Even the air shifted around her, as if the world itself agreed.

Beside her, Straid stood, as if in a trance, angling his body toward the source of his fae power. She felt his absence at her side, even more so as he took a step toward the comet, then another. It moved impossibly slowly across the sky, as if it were lingering over the fae, taking its time bestowing its centennial gift on Straid's people.

The light faded incrementally, and still Straid stood, his face turned to the sky. All tension had drained from his body, as though the walls he had built around himself had crumbled, dismantled by the celestial body overhead. She couldn't pull her eyes from him; he was as riveting, as beautiful, as the comet itself.

Nothing could ruin this moment; nothing could detract from its perfection. There was nothing in the world but her and Straid and the comet, nothing but power and magic and…love.

He had kissed her. He had kissed her and looked at her as

though he wanted more. And for one brief, shining moment, she allowed herself to hope, allowed herself to feel the depth of the emotion she had worked so hard to ignore these past weeks.

For one brief moment, everything was perfect.

Until a hand pressed against her mouth, large and calloused, and the world went dark around her.

CHAPTER THIRTY-SIX

Carra awoke on the floor of a dark room, with something sharp digging into her hip. She groaned and rolled onto her back, taking a moment to try to make sense of her surroundings, but it was pitch black. Aside from a quiet drip of water and the tiniest echo, there was no sound—save for a quiet ragged whisper she feared might be breathing. She closed her eyes against the thought, though it made no difference in the darkness.

She scrambled backward at the sound of an echoing cough, crying out as her elbow hit the hard stone wall behind her.

"You're awake," a voice said from somewhere to her right.

"Where am I?"

"Dunno. We were hoping you might be able to tell us."

"We?"

"There are six of us, now you're here. Would be seven, but they took one away."

Her whole body ached, and she wondered how long she had lain on the stone floor. If the throbbing in her hip was any indication, she'd been here for a long time. She cursed softly, flinching at the humorless laugh that echoed through the chamber.

"That's about how all of us responded when we first arrived."

She had hoped, at first, that she'd misremembered the hand, coated with an acrid oil, that had caught her by surprise—but the resignation in the other woman's voice disabused her of the notion. It had happened, and whoever had attacked her had brought her to some sort of dungeon. And she wasn't the only one.

"How long have you been here?" Carra asked, fear slithering up her spine.

"Atria was the first. She's been here since spring. What day is it out there?"

Carra shook her head, knowing the person speaking wouldn't be able to see her. "It's winter. Ousilie's Ball," she said. "How long have you been here? What's your name?"

"Elesina. I've been here—"

"Since summer." Since shortly after Carra had arrived in the Quarters. And in all that time, with people searching, nobody had found her.

Despair tugged at her, but Carra fought it with everything she had. She would not give up. She *could* not give up, if she wanted to make it out of here alive.

"Yes," Elesina said, clearly surprised. "You know me?"

"I'm Carra. We hired you to work in our kitchen right before you disappeared. Straid looked for you, but we couldn't find you anywhere."

"I have been here, in this dungeon. Straid looked for me? Himself?" Elesina's voice filled with awe.

Because Straid was the prince. Carra had married fae royalty.

And now she was trapped in a dungeon, kidnapped mere steps away from him, his title and his precautions not enough to keep her safe after all.

"He did. He was helping a friend look for someone else who went missing, and when you disappeared, they realized there might be a connection between the two of you. And others, as well. Straid and Corlan spent months looking for you both, and I helped once they told me. There are people looking for you, still. For—for *us*."

"Did you say Corlan?" another voice asked, pitched lower than the first, and located somewhere beyond Elesina. This voice was raw, ragged, as if the woman speaking had spent hours screaming and now talked through a shredded throat. "Was—was he looking for Kexxia?"

"He was. Is that you?"

"Yes."

She had found her. Not intentionally. Not in a way any of them would have hoped, but she had found Kexxia, and Elesina—and three of the others on their list of the missing. But she had no way of telling Straid.

"Who took you—*us*?" Carra asked, her voice louder than intended. She cringed, softening her voice, though that did nothing to hide the fear laced through it. "And why?"

"None of us knows," Elesina murmured. "They feed us regularly—almost enough. They don't torture us, but they won't tell us why we're here, either. They took Scher two days ago and never brought her back, but she's the only one they've taken away. They refused to tell us where she went."

"Who is they? Guards?"

"Guards, and the humans who bring us food. The humans occasionally stay and talk. They've answered our questions, but…they're mortal. They can lie. We assume that's why they were chosen."

"What do you all have in common?" Carra thought back to Straid's notes, to the meetings she, Straid, and Corlan had had, ensconced in Straid's study. They had failed to find a connection, but surely the women who had been taken had found one, in the months of their captivity.

"Nothing," Kexxia rasped. "Scher, the one they took away, was human, as is Lessem."

"You make the third human out of the seven," Elesina added.

"The rest of us are fae. We have tried to find connections between us, but there is nothing that ties us all together."

"Wrong." A clear, cold voice rang through the darkness and Carra froze, her heart thundering. "You are all here because I need you. You each serve a unique purpose, and together you are more valuable than you could ever imagine."

Silence descended, broken only by a quiet dripping of water. Whoever had spoken was clearly not one of the captives, and a chilling certainty settling around Carra's shoulders. Still, she asked the question she knew the answer to, hoping beyond hope that she was wrong. "Who are you?"

"Your husband didn't tell you about me?" The voice twisted in displeasure. "The love of men, whether human or fae, is clearly fickle."

"Lyenna."

Somewhere in the darkness, Kexxia gasped.

"Well done," Lyenna crooned.

"You really did come back to kill Straid." She was going to be sick.

"Oh, dear sweet girl. I have no interest in killing Straid. I had no interest while he remained loyal, anyway. Now he means nothing to me; if he would like to get himself killed at the end of my blade, that is his prerogative, but I am certainly not going out of my way to waste any amount of time on him."

"Then why are you doing this? Why did you come back?"

"Because I died!" Lyenna yelled. Her voice reverberated in the small, damp room, and Carra flinched despite herself. "I knew there must be a way for me to become fae, to survive the pathetic trappings of my mortal body, and he failed me, and I *died*. I found a way to do the impossible, and you have reduced my quest to nothing more than revenge against a mediocre man."

"There is nothing mediocre about Straid."

"He allowed you to be taken right from his side. Either he is mediocre, or he does not love you as much as you think he does," Lyenna gloated.

"He doesn't love me at all, actually, but that's beside the point." She forced herself to stay detached, to sound as apathetic as possible. Inside, her heart cracked at the truth she had just uttered; but she had known from the beginning what this was. She hadn't *wanted* his love. Not at first, anyway. Even if she'd begun to wonder tonight if she might have it, she knew one kiss, no matter how exquisite, didn't mean he loved her.

"What do you mean he doesn't love you?" Lyenna's voice sharpened, and Carra involuntarily shivered in response. "He must love you. He married you."

"He did," Carra agreed. "But not all marriages are built on a foundation of love. If you were hoping to hurt him by kidnapping the love of his life, I'm sorry to disappoint you, but you've failed. The love of his life died fifty years ago, and I can assure you, I have not replaced...you." She stumbled over the last word as it sank in that the woman Straid had mourned for so long really was here—and behind the disappearances.

"No." Carra could hear the panic creeping into Lyenna's voice. Panic that would not be there if this were simply about revenge.

"I was not wrong about you," Lyenna spat. "Not twice."

"Twice?" Carra's question was met with silence, so she asked it again, more forcefully.

"First Lord Astrea, and now Straid. One of them must have loved you; I cannot have been wrong on both counts."

"Lord Astrea?" Despite herself, Carra laughed at the absurdity of it. "Lord Astrea is a client. A friend, if that. And Straid is someone who happened to find me on the worst night of my life and offered me a solution that would keep me safe. I'm his damsel in distress, not the love of his life."

It rankled to refer to herself that way, but it had been true that first night, even if their relationship had evolved since then.

"He must have fallen in love with you in that time."

Carra scoffed. "Have you met Straid? He doesn't love easily."

"Actually, I found that he fell much faster than anyone I have ever met. I suppose he just needed the right…inspiration." Lyenna's sneer bled through her voice, and Carra sucked in a breath. It hurt, despite the fact she knew it shouldn't.

"The way he talked about you, it does sound like he fell fast, and hard. Maybe he was just young; maybe you were his soulmate. Whatever the reason, he loved you deeply. Probably right up until the moment he discovered you'd tried to kill him. But he doesn't love me, and I doubt he ever will. And I'm okay with that." The lie sat heavy on her tongue. "Why does it matter so much to you?"

"Each of you here serves a purpose. But if you are not loved by a powerful fae you are useless to me. I will need to begin my search again thanks to your deception."

Deception. As though Carra had intentionally misled Lyenna. As though Lyenna had been a consideration in *any* of her actions. "So that's what everyone here has in common? They're loved by a powerful fae?"

Lyenna laughed, sharp and cruel. "Oh, my gods, no. That was your purpose. The others have their own."

"What are they?"

Lyenna sighed heavily. "I suppose it won't hurt to tell you now; you'll be dead soon, anyway."

Carra swallowed the bile that rose at Lyenna's words.

"I needed one who shared my blood to begin the sacrifices. One who is the last of a third; one loved by someone with ultimate power; one with the power to bestow a gift; one who is innocent by choice; one who has taken more lives than their age; and finally, another who shares my blood."

"So you plan to sacrifice us."

A gasp echoed from somewhere in the dungeon, followed by the sound of retching.

"The others are. You are apparently of no use to me, so the

manner of your death really doesn't seem to matter, does it? Not a sacrifice, just…dead."

"I'd argue my death is the one you should be most worried about."

"Oh? And why is that?" Lyenna sneered.

"Straid might not love me, but he did marry me. I'd think a fae prince would be willing to go pretty far to get his wife returned to him in good health—and even farther to avenge her death. He will find you, and he will kill you, and if I'm already dead there is no amount of begging that will grant you mercy."

"He can't find me. I am protected by someone he cannot control and would never suspect."

"Oh, you mean his brother?" Carra retorted. "The one who owes him a boon, and is compelled to tell Straid absolutely everything he knows about you and your plan—and who is bound to never acknowledge the boon to anyone but Straid? I'm sure he'll provide great protection from Straid. But, by all means, kill me if you want. Kill us all. I'm sure Straid will be generous and let you live." Sarcasm dripped from her words, and she reveled in the ensuing silence. For the first time since waking in the dungeon she felt powerful. Hopeful.

"So, Lyenna? What will it be? Let us all go, or die very slowly and painfully once my *husband* finds you?"

CHAPTER THIRTY-SEVEN

The hold of the comet lessened as its light faded from the sky. It had drained the tension from his body, had replaced it with a thrall he was powerless to fight. He did not know how long he stood under the comet, how long he reveled in the feeling of the power slowly building beneath his skin.

As the comet's tail faded from the sky, one final burst of power surged through Straid, unlike anything he had ever felt before. His body thrummed. He could feel every particle of air around him. Every particle of air *inside* him.

No stories of the comet had done this feeling justice; it was beyond anything he had imagined in his seventy years.

The power and the beauty of it overwhelmed him and he took another moment for himself—to learn the feel of this new power coursing within him, to marvel at the change. Slowly, delighting in his every movement, he turned toward Carra, ready to press his lips against hers once more and finally utter the words he had spent long nights practicing saying to her.

The field was empty; she was gone.

The grass where she had sat was bare, no trace of the woman who had sat beside him. Panic flared, but he set it aside, reasoning with himself. He could not say how long he had been held in the comet's thrall. Perhaps she had grown thirsty and gone to fetch a refreshment. He forced his feet to slow as he retraced their steps to the crowd below. He would not cause a scene simply because his human wife had grown bored waiting for him.

In the meadow, the party had grown wilder, the surge of power thrumming amongst the fae in attendance.

There was no sign of Carra.

No dark curls with fireflies threaded through them; no pale green dress he had labored over. His desperation grew as he searched, his footsteps growing harried, frantic.

"Have you seen Carra?" He grabbed Corlan in the center of the dance floor. His grip was too tight, yet he couldn't make his fingers lighten their hold.

Immediately, his friend's levity disappeared. "No. She was supposed to be with you."

"She was. She slipped away while I was under the comet's thrall. I had hoped she had found you, but it appears she is missing. Perhaps she found Fell."

"She isn't with Fell, either." Corlan inclined his head subtly toward Straid's sister, who was wrapped around a fae woman he did not recognize. Straid ripped her from the woman's arms, uncaring of the stranger's protests.

"Carra is missing. Find her. Find the threads."

"Carra's threads," Fell mumbled, her words heavy and her breath smelling of honeywine. She frowned, her glassy eyes flitting over the crowd. "There are so many people, and the wine… the threads are overwhelming. They shine too bright the night of the comet; it's hard to tell them apart, even if I were sober. But I'll look. I'll find her for you, Straid." Fell stepped into the crowd, her head swinging every direction as she sought the threads that only she could see.

The party continued long into morning, and Fell stayed behind until every last guest had disappeared, searching. She had scoured the dance floor, the refreshment tables, the hillside to which Straid and Carra had retreated—to no avail.

Carra had simply disappeared.

He returned home after searching the hillside, in case she had somehow found her way back, but the house was empty, utterly still. He had broken the wards to her bedroom, had charged inside knowing he would find nothing, and yet the confirmation that she was not there had threatened to cleave him in two.

The sun rose, and still she was not home.

Fell pounded at the front door as the scent of cooking reached him, and he reluctantly let her in. She swept into the foyer followed by Corlan and Jesson and led the way to the dining table. Brey bustled in from the kitchen, a question on her face, but she stopped short at the sight of them.

"Carra is missing," Fell informed her. Behind him, someone gasped. "She disappeared from the ball. I couldn't find any threads to lead me to her."

"We'll find her. If—if she is alive." Niana had entered, at some point, the dining room full. More people than he would have chosen to inform, had it been up to him. Right now, he did not care. The only thing that matter was finding Carra and bringing her home.

"She is. Her threads are bright in here; they haven't started fading yet. She's still alive, Straid."

"Then we must find her." He did not recognize the desperation in his voice, had not felt any like it since Lyenna's final days. He growled at the thought—and at the certainty that Lyenna was involved.

"Her, and Kexxia, and Elesina, and anyone else Lyenna may have taken," Corlan agreed.

Straid no longer cared about the others; only Carra.

They planned late into the night, and Straid sent a missive to Umber: he would find Carra, and he would find her alive, or the Quarters would burn.

Umber arrived once the sun was high in the sky, and

everyone save for Corlan had left. Umber dropped into a chair, his expression bored—annoyed, at having been summoned so soon. Fury rose within Straid at the sight.

"Perhaps you'll learn your lesson about humans after this," his brother drawled. "Falling for them has only led to trouble."

The temperature in the room plummeted. The sweat on Straid's brow crystallized, frozen. Corlan winced, but Umber held Straid's gaze, utterly ignoring the ice that clung to his own face.

"I have no control over who I fall in love with, and I will make no apologies for it, nor will I ever regret a single moment."

"So you do love her, then. Is it their weakness that makes you love the humans?"

"The fact she is human has nothing to do with why I love her."

"You've loved twice, and both have been mortal. The evidence would suggest otherwise, brother."

"I did not love Lyenna because of her humanity; I loved her in spite of it."

"You say that, so you must believe it to be true, but how you fall for your own deception confounds me, Straid. Her humanity fascinated you. I have never seen you so intrigued by anything, to this day. It was *sickening*, the way you allowed it to infect you —to infect the whole home."

"Lyenna's humanity fascinated me, yes. Intrigued me, as you say. But her humanity was her biggest flaw—perhaps the only one I was capable of seeing."

"And yet you were willing to throw your life away for it."

"For *her*. She was allowed one flaw. I have many more."

"One flaw you have once again allowed to ruin your life— Carra shares that particular flaw of Lyenna's, in case you had forgotten."

Straid glowered. "She is different."

"She is human."

"Yes. But her humanity is nothing like Lyenna's. Carra is

clever where Lyenna was cunning; kind where Lyenna was nice. Everything about Carra is softer, but in a way that belies her strength. I loved Lyenna despite her humanity, but I love Carra without qualifiers. Not in spite of her humanity or because of it; her humanity is simply a part of who she is, and I love her."

He closed his eyes against his fear, and vowed to the universe, out loud, that he would not rest until he found her.

EPILOGUE

She ran down cobblestoned streets, her chest burning with every breath. Her bare feet had long gone numb: a welcome respite from the bite of frost, but the sensation was uncomfortable nonetheless. She knew this area, had strolled these streets with Straid countless times, but that felt like a lifetime ago.

A shout rose from behind her, followed by quick, heavy footsteps, and she forced her feet to move faster, even as her vision spotted.

Straid. She had to reach Straid and then everything would be okay.

"Carra! Stop!"

Faster and faster she ran, until her foot landed on a patch of ice and she careened backward, landing with a heavy thud that stole the breath from her lungs. Her pursuer drew nearer but she couldn't rise, couldn't run; she was spent, unable to gather an ounce of energy to save her own life. She pressed her eyes closed against certain death and whimpered, holding her breath.

Maybe her pursuer would be quick, merciful as he meted out her punishment.

"I'm taking you to Straid." Gentle arms slid guided her

upright, and she trembled at the touch. "I'll Travel you there; it will be faster." She recognized the voice. Last time she'd heard it had been at a ball, detailing all the ways she wasn't good enough for his brother. Wasn't good enough to be a part of the royal family. She'd slipped away, had found Straid and done her best to put the conversation from her mind. She hadn't chosen him for his title; she loved him, pure and simple.

"Umber?" Her voice sounded strange in her ears, as though it belonged to someone else. Someone who had not spent the night running for her life from a horror just beyond her memory's grasp.

"I will take you to him now." Umber lifted her from the ground and the world went dark around her.

She awoke sometime later with silk against her skin and slumber clinging to her stubbornly. She attempted to open her eyes, to speak, but found herself too weak.

"Umber found her." Straid's voice settled around her. Calming. Safe.

"Umber? And he didn't demand anything in return for bringing her to you?"

"He is bound by the boon; he had no other choice."

Silence fell, during which she struggled against the bounds of sleep. She wanted to take Straid's hand, to throw her arms around him, to kiss him until she forgot the horrors of her night.

"We will retrieve Kexxia," Straid murmured. "When Carra awakes, she will tell us what she knows."

That name again. Carra—perhaps someone who had witnessed her earlier plight, who could explain what had happened?

She stirred—and this time, her body listened.

"Carra." Straid's voice was strained, but tender, and his fingers threaded through hers. She squeezed, with what little strength she had left, and he returned the gesture. "I feared—but you have returned. You are safe. You are safe," he repeated, his voice breaking.

"I'm safe," she murmured, knowing it to be true; she was always safe when he was around.

"Yes. You are safe." It was a litany on his lips, and she smiled. But there was something… "Who—"

"Corlan and Fell are here, as well. Umber departed shortly after he delivered you."

She shook her head, the motion sending pain rattling through her skull. "No. Who is Carra?"

His grip on her hand tightened, and he cursed softly—something she had rarely heard him do in all their time together.

"Fell, bring the mirror beside you, and the perfume, as well. They aided her memory last time." Moments later the bed shifted beside her, and his finger traced fragrant oil along her wrist. "Open your eyes, and look."

She did so, her eyes protesting against the soft light of the room, but her gaze landed on Straid, and she almost wept in relief. He looked older than she remembered, as though the events of tonight had aged him fifty years—though fifty years was not so much, for a fae.

"Look at yourself," he commanded gently, and her gaze fell to the mirror in his hand, to the woman who stared at her from its center. A woman with skin a shade darker than her own and honey-colored eyes set in a face that was softer than hers had ever been.

A stranger, in her reflection.

"That's not me," she gasped, fear clawing at her throat.

"You do not remember," Straid murmured. "It has happened again. Rest assured I will do everything in my power to help you remember who you are."

"I know who I am." She meant the words to bite, but she was exhausted. So exhausted. "You know who I am, too, Straid."

"Carra. My wife."

Her blood ran cold, and slowly, she shook her head.

"No. No. Lyenna. Your fiancée."

ACKNOWLEDGMENTS

This book has been a labor of love, and I could not have done it without my incredible writing community. I want to thank the members of The Creative Cottage, The Grove, The Writerverse, and my coven for all of your support throughout this process. I am forever grateful to have found you all.

I came to the Bi+ Book Gang and The Binding Lines later, but I want to thank everyone in those groups for your support, as well.

Molly, Adi, Amy, Jenna, and Kristin: thank you for being such amazing beta readers and for all the brainstorming help. Your feedback fixed so many problems and kept me going when things got hard. And an extra thanks to Amy for holding my hand through the design process.

Andee, of course, for always supporting me and for talking some sense into me when it comes to deadlines and work-life balance.

And to Scar: thank you for everything.

Now onto the business side of things. I had two absolutely incredible editors for this book, both of whom fixed way more errors than I would care to admit. Karis Rogerson and Leslie Fannon, I cannot thank you enough for all the work you put until Mortal Memories. This book would be a mess without the two of you.

And finally, I want to thank my sister, Aisha, for always encouraging me to chase my dreams, no matter how weird or hard or (initially) secret they may be.

ABOUT THE AUTHOR

F. A. Eden was born out of a desire to write the kinds of books I love reading—while having some level of distance from my real name, because I work with children in my day job. My writing is informed by my own queerness and disability, which is ever-present in my writing.

You can find me at my website: https://www.faedenbook s.com or through email at faedenbooks@gmail.com. I am also on most social media platforms under the username faedenbooks.

9 781964 846019